PRESERVATION

Also by S.L. Stoner
in the
Sage Adair Historical Mystery Series
of the Pacific Northwest

Timber Beasts
Land Sharks
Dry Rot
Black Drop
Dead Line
The Mangle
Slow Burn
Bitter Cry
Unseen

PRESERVATION

A Sage Adair Historical Mystery
of the Pacific Northwest

S. L. Stoner

Yamhill Press
www.yamhillpress.net

This Book is Dedicated To

George R. Slanina

And

Librarians Everywhere
Extraordinary Treasures One and All

ONE

THE MURDER RISES, SUMMONED INTO the twilight sky by the day's slip behind the western ridge. Midnight wings flap as the birds converge on the central city, their harsh caws cutting the chill air. Sunlight's last gleam glistens on feathers high above the spreading blackness below where human dramas are spinning out. The crows neither care nor notice, fixated as they are on reaching their roosts before the light dies.

A lagging bird's wing beat stutters when sharp cries fly skyward from beneath the house roof. There, dimly lit by an oil lamp, a haggard woman hunches, a blanket-wrapped bundle clutched to her breast. Kind hands stroke her back, consoling words try to soothe. "Now, now, there's nothing more to be done. He's gone." The woman feels only black despair, hears only rushing blood in her ears. Her arms tighten around the lifeless body, as she rocks and chants: "It's my fault. My fault."

He paces as the dying fire lets the night chill seep in. He doesn't notice. Instead, entwined fears send his thoughts careening down city streets before tossing them back into the barn outside. Production is off. There's not enough alfalfa and clover to carry the cows through winter. That worry spirals downward until it hits bottom and catapults his thoughts back onto the city streets. Where is the boy? He's hours late. Weary hands swipe across his face, leaving tears wet upon his fingers. He orders himself to bed. Before daybreak, there'll be cows to milk. After that will come the search for his missing son.

"Damn them!" Lifting her eyes from the microscope, the chemist picks up a pen to note the number. Straightening, she rubs the small of her aching back and ponders what to do next. Dusk has left the single electric bulb too weak for counting creatures. Raucous caws draw her eyes to the window as the flock glides in to settle onto roosts outside her window. A weary headshake and she lifts both test tube and dropper. Chemical reactions don't need bright light. Minutes later, quiet curses fill the laboratory.

"It's a terrible idea." She didn't beg. That wasn't her way whenever stubbornness set him charging down a ruinous road. "I warned them," he replies. Breaking the shotgun open, he loads the shells. More cartridges drop into the pockets of his scruffy overcoat. A caress of her face, a quick hug of her shoulders, and he's out the door. Determination gives length and speed to his stride into the darkening night. Thirty minutes later, shotgun blasts scare dosing crows skyward, their outraged caws making a dreadful din that echoes between the buildings.

TWO

He wove between the empty tables, heading toward the restaurant's kitchen doors, his thoughts lingering on the vision of sunlight bright in dray horse's chestnut coat. Fall was a spirit-lifting season in Portland, all crystalline skies and brilliant colors until the rains.

I'm content. Happy even, Sage realized. Life is settled for a change. St. Alban hasn't sent us on a mission in a while. He must be busy organizing that one big industrial union he's always talked about. Ahead stretched days of peace, savoring of friendships, and lazy hours with his lady.

Those feelings persisted only until he stepped inside the kitchen to find Sergeant Hanke sitting at the small table.

The policeman often visited Mozart's kitchen, always happy to partake of Ida's leftovers. It was the lack of a cheery greeting and the lines scoring the man's youngish face that made Sage pause. More worrisome, was the plate of food sitting untouched before a man who could clean his plate faster than "a cow's tail twitch" as Sage's mother once observed. Not today.

"Sergeant, whatever's the matter? As Mrs. Clemens says, "You look like 'you've been drug through a knothole backward.'"

The man's unseeing watery blue eyes rested on Sage before sharpening, entreaty in his look. Sage dropped onto the empty chair and said, "What's happened? Did someone die? You look like you've suffered a shock."

Hanke shook his head. "No one has died, I hope." He cleared his throat and began, "I have a friend. As kids, we ran Chicago's streets together. His name's Eli Yoder. He has a small dairy farm out Canyon

Road near Cedar Mill. It's just him and his son running the place. Eli's wife passed a year or so ago during childbirth. She and the baby didn't make it.

"Fact is, Eli's the reason I'm here in Oregon. He kept writing, saying I'd find life easier here. Promised he'd help me make a start. And, he did. Him and Arabela treated me like family."

The big policeman's glum expression made Sage wonder whether Hanke might be reevaluating that move.

Ida approached and silently set two mugs of coffee on the table. Her sweet, round face creased with worry as she cast a questioning glance at the policeman. Sage waited for the rest of the story.

Hanke slurped and then continued, "Every day, Eli hauls his milk into town. The Purity Creamery buys it from him. Last couple months, on Saturdays, he's trusted his fourteen-year-old son, Noah, to bring the milk to the creamery. I promised Eli I'd keep an eye out for the boy. Usually, I've been near the creamery about the time Noah's wagon rolled in.

"Five days ago, that's what happened. I saw and spoke to young Noah like always. He'd already dropped off his milk and was hefting the empty cans into the wagon bed. He told me he'd be visiting the new kinetoscope parlor before heading back to the farm. Said his pa'd okayed it. I added a few nickels to his stash. He planned to leave the horse and wagon ring-hitched in front of the creamery, visit the parlor, and return to drive the wagon home. He said he'd only be gone an hour. Last I saw him, he was heading down the street to the parlor, all swinging arms and light of foot, like all excited lads."

Hanke fell silent until Sage pushed a bit, "And, what happened? Is the boy alright?"

Hanke passed his big hand over his face before answering in a voice heavy with defeat, "That's what I don't know. Near as I figure, I was the last person to see him. I've searched everywhere these past five days. At first, the whole police force looked for him. After two days, though, the Chief called a halt. He says it's pointless to keep looking—he thinks Noah's long gone, run away, shanghaied, or somewhere dead.

"I've been doing my job days and hunting for Noah at night. So far, I've found no trace of him. He's vanished."

"Did the wagon and horse go missing?"

An exasperated sigh accompanied Hanke's doleful headshake. "Nope. The next morning, when Eli brought the milk into town, he found horse, wagon, and empty cans still parked outside the creamery, where I last saw them. The horse needed watering and feed so I figure Noah never returned that day. He's not the kind of boy who'd let an animal suffer.

"Anyway, Eli's been running himself ragged, taking care of his cows, hauling the milk into town, spending all day and half the night, searching for Noah. We've found neither hide nor hair of the boy."

Tears glistened in the tough policeman's eyes. Sage looked away, giving him a moment to recover before asking, "I suppose you've gone around to the hospitals and such?"

"I did. He's not there. The folks at the kinetoscope parlor say he never came in that day. Somewhere between the Purity Creamery and the parlor, Noah vanished. I'm near wit's end trying to figure out what happened to him."

Hanke set his mug down carefully and leaned forward, an imploring look on his face. "So, I'm here hoping you folks will help me look for Noah. I know it's a lot to ask, but you're able to search in ways I can't."

Sage didn't need to ponder Hanke's meaning. Despite the policeman's misgivings, he'd aided a number of their wild missions. Thus far, most had ended well. Because they needed to keep secret, their roles as undercover labor union operatives, they always made Hanke take the credit for bringing malefactors to justice. They did so over the policeman's objections. He often declared he owed his sergeant stripes to that deception.

Sage held a more nuanced perspective on the relationship. He believed they owed the big policeman as well. His contributions had enabled the success of more than one mission. Bottom line, when Sage and his friends fought on the side of angels, the stoic Hanke often stood right beside them—despite knowing failure would jeopardize his career.

After briefly regretting the loss of his anticipated contentment, Sage said, "Of course, we'll help, Sergeant. It sounds like we better enlist the aid of Fong, Solomon, and Eich."

Hanke nodded eagerly. That proposal evidently matched his hopes. All three men were uniquely positioned to search for a missing boy. Fong's fraternal tong brethren kept a keen eye on shanghaiers and other miscreants. Angus Solomon, among his many endeavors, operated the New Era hotel for the railroad's black porters. More than once, the porters had provided key information about people riding the trains passing through Portland. And, they needed Herman Eich who knew the city like no one else. Every day, the ragpicker poet trod between the city's rubbish bins and the back doors of its homes, peddling his salvaged items to various household servants. Those people proved to know vital information. The three men were a thorough and an unbeatable team when it came to discovering the city's secrets.

And, there were secrets aplenty, Sage mused. Straddling the Willamette River, the city was growing in importance and size. Houses dotted the western ridge and were starting to fill the rolling land eastward, even beyond Mt. Tabor. Already, it was a bustling city in a state less than 50 years old. That was the Chamber of Commerce's spiel.

What the Chamber didn't advertise was Portland's reputation for being the West Coast's shanghai capitol and home to over 500 whorehouses. Despite its veneer of staid respectability, corruption riddled Portland just as it did every other American city.

His musings were interrupted when the kitchen doors whapped open and Mae Clemens entered, her face grim. Spotting Hanke she halted. Narrowing her deep-blue eyes that were just like her son's, she demanded, "What's wrong? You both look lower than a milk cow's udder." Her hands-on-hips stance forestalled any evasion.

As always, Sage had to admire the swiftness of her perception. She claimed second sight ran in her blood. It could be true. She picked up on situations faster than most—like now.

Gesturing, he said, "Ma, you best pull up that chair. This will take a bit." He didn't hide their relationship from the police sergeant because Hanke knew their secret: Mae Clemens, the restaurant's manager, was also Sage's mother.

Once she learned about the missing Noah and their plan to ask Fong, Solomon, and Eich to help, she nodded. "Herman will be here soon so maybe you better come up with a good description of the boy."

That she knew the ragpicker poet's schedule was no surprise. Something had transpired between the two of them while they'd been trapped and facing a fiery death together. Nowadays, they were "keeping company" as his mother primly put it.

He understood why Herman Eich was smitten. While not beautiful, Mae Clemens had a noble face. It reminded him of a ship figurehead. Her dark blue eyes penetrated while her silvered black hair, knotted in a bun, added to her regal look. Her figure was rangy; telegraphing that here was a strong woman, honed by hard work. Her hands, large and scarred, confirmed that perception. Her's was a commanding presence. And, her intelligence matched her appearance. Despite being schooled only through the sixth grade, she was one of the smartest people he'd ever known, possessing a mind both incisive and practical, able to condense abstract thoughts into a few simple words.

Likewise, he understood her attraction to the neatly bearded Herman Eich. Morally incorruptible, the highly-educated ragpicker poet chose a life of deliberate scarcity. He earned his money collecting, repairing, and selling people's castoffs. His home was a tidy lean-to perched on the edge of a Portland ravine. There he did his repairs of porcelain and other items, read voraciously, crafted poetry, and philosophized.

He abandoned that train of thought once Hanke began describing Noah as being about 5 feet, 5 inches tall and dark-haired. Most interesting was Hanke saying, "But, the most noticeable thing about Noah is that he has double cowlicks. One is in the front. His hair swoops up from his forehead like he's facing a stiff wind. The other is on top of his head, just like someone reached down and twisted a hunk of hair. It pokes straight up unless he pomades it down. Looks like a crow feather about to fly off."

Description done, Hanke sighed, scooted back from the table, and said, "I best return to the station. I can't thank you enough. Noah and Eli are family to me. I don't know how Eli will react if we don't find his son. He took his wife and baby's deaths hard. Noah is all that keeps him going."

In the pause that followed this declaration, tears washed across the Sergeant's eyes. He bent to quickly retrieve the beehive helmet at his feet. Wordlessly he stood, donned the helmet, nodded, and exited out the alley door leaving Sage and Mae staring at his untouched plate of food.

Mae straightened and took a deep breath. "Well, that's a first for him." With a rueful headshake she said, "Apparently we've got a new task. Too bad it's not the only one."

Sage groaned, remembering her grim face upon entering the kitchen. "What else has gone wrong?"

She pulled two papers from her apron pocket and tossed them onto the table. "Before your fanny left the bed, these letters came from last night's customers. It seems each fellow spent a wild night in his privy. Both say they got sick from eating here. This is the second time this month someone's said Mozart's poisoned them."

"Where did they sit? What did they eat?" As with any restaurant, Mozart's reputation affected its success. Food poisoning was their greatest fear.

She huffed in frustration and answered, "That's the ding-dang problem. They dined in two different parties, at two different times, and ate different meals."

"Damn. We better find the source quickly." He weighed their two tasks and made his decision. "Finding Noah is our priority. You tell Herman about Noah as soon as he appears. Meanwhile, you and Ida can check for bad food in the kitchen. I'll go visit Fong at his provision store then head to the Portland Hotel and talk to Angus. I need to catch him before the hotel dining room opens. Damn. It's never just one problem at a time, is it?"

They exchanged dismayed looks and Sage said, "You realize that Fong out searching and Matthew studying for his test will leave Mozart's short-handed? It'll be just you, me, and Homer."

Her lips quirked and she shrugged. "Won't be the first time. Bet you'll be haring off somewheres too."

THREE

As always, the pungent odors hit first. Sage couldn't guess their source. The Fongs' shop sold a myriad of exotic spices, fungi, and herbs that filled the air with a powerful scent. Once his eyes adjusted to the dimness, he spotted tiny Kum Ho Fong standing behind the counter, fountain pen in hand, a ledger open before her.

"Ah, Mister Adair. Much nice to see you!" she chirped. She was a pretty woman, always pleasant and fiercely proud of her husband. Her loyalty was justified. After meeting her, Fong had mounted a raid to free her from slavery inside San Francisco's Chinatown. Although Fong related the story just once, Sage never forgot. Sometimes, when he encountered this dignified woman, he wished he'd never heard it.

"Good morning, Mrs. Fong. It is very nice to see you also. I wonder if I might find your husband here. I know it's a bit early for him to be awake." Fong worked most days and nights at Mozart's Table, in addition to helping his wife in the provision store.

Initially, Kam Tong Fong worked at Mozart's only to learn the restaurant business. He'd intended to open a high-class Chinese eatery. He abandoned that plan the night he rescued Sage from a brutal attack. Instead, he became the first member of their undercover crew and Sage's martial arts teacher. Fong had other talents; his mediation skills kept peace among the Chinese tongs and his flute playing was admired by his fellow Chinese—though that particular talent sounded painfully off-key to Sage's Western ears.

"Husband taking morning tea." Kum Ho said, gesturing toward the ornately carved wooden door that opened into their small living quarters. "Please to go in. No need knock."

Sage opened the door and paused before stepping into their parlor. Its spare beauty always affected him. A low ebony table, fronted by two carved ebony chairs, sat on a red, oriental carpet. The precious flute lay on the small black cabinet standing against the far wall. Above that cabinet hung a scroll, its calligraphy bordered by water-colored birds.

"What does that scroll say?" he asked.

Fong was drinking tea from a tiny cup and reading the impenetrable squiggles of the Chinese news daily. He ignored Sage's question, instead declaring, "Ah! The most honorable John Sagacity Adair honors me!" Placing both cup and paper on the table he rose to his feet and bowed low in gentle mockery.

"Cut it out, Mr. Fong," Sage said without heat.

"You here for snake and crane lesson?" queried his teacher. That question was also mocking because those lessons always took place in Mozart's attic—another place benefitting from Fong's decorative sensibilities—a white-washed haven of skylighted illumination, polished fir floor, solitary wall scroll, and nothing else. Fong insisted the space's minimalism helped focus Sage's "jumpy" mind.

"I'll have you know that I practiced for two hours this morning." Sage said, hoping to stave off another of Fong's jabs and get down to business. "When I came downstairs, I found Hanke sitting in the kitchen. He wasn't eating the food Ida served him."

Fong's eyebrows rose over his near-black eyes. "Oh boy, that bad sign."

"The worst," Sage agreed. "He's searching for a friend's son and needs our help."

"Friendship is strong tie. Brings much joy and sometimes heartache." Fong leaned over and filled a second small cup with tea. Handing it to Sage, he said, "Tell how I can help."

Sage related the Noah story. At its finish, he broached the idea of Fong, Eich, and Solomon using their contacts to learn of the boy's whereabouts.

Fong nodded and said, "No problem. I will ask if anyone see cowlicks boy." His face saddened. "I also ask if ship look for cabin boy. He is perfect age."

"I thought the shanghaiers avoided snatching local boys. That they're afraid it will cause too much of a stink."

Fong nodded. "Stink true most times. Sometime they still take if local man sells boy. Maybe someone need boy gone for reason."

"I can't imagine why a farm boy would need to vanish," Sage said as he rose and started toward the door before pausing to ask again, "So, what does that scroll say?"

Fong's answering smile was enigmatic. "Like I tell you many times, when you ready, I translate."

"At least tell me if it's one of the Lao guy's sayings."

Fong shook his head in mock disgust. "Many times I tell you, Lao Tzu, not 'Lao guy.'"

Sage waved a dismissive hand and again headed for the door. Fong's voice stopped him. "Today, I give you other Lao Tzu words."

Sage looked back at his friend and teacher, knowing it was a gift being offered. Fong's Chinese sage quotes often resonated and informed when they didn't just confuse him.

"Lao guy say in *I Ching* book, 'Seek union with others. Proceed firmly, with caution.'" Fong raised an admonishing finger as he finished the quote, "Only by paying careful attention to each step does one arrive unharmed."

A chill skittered up Sage's back. He bowed and exited.

Minutes later, as Sage strolled up the Portland Hotel's semi-circle drive, he pondered Fong's words. "Who could a fourteen-year-old boy threaten?" The best outcome of their search would be that one of Solomon's porters saw Noah on a train. It would mean the boy simply skedaddled with the family's milk money. That was the least dire explanation for his absence. The other alternatives were so much worse.

He smiled, remembering Fong's ancient wisdom quote. Seeking unity with Angus accorded with old Lao Tzu's advice. As for avoiding danger by attending to the steps, he'd try. Of course, first, he needed to discover those steps.

As expected, Angus's maitre d' podium stood unmanned in the hotel's empty dining room. Lunch didn't begin for another hour. Clashing pots and laughter sounded from the kitchen. Its doors swung open and a waiter entered the dining room carrying a tall stack of clean plates. The smile on his lips faded when he saw Sage. Setting the plates on a table, he advanced to say politely, in a soft Southern drawl, "I'm sorry, sir. The dining room is closed until eleven o'clock."

Sage didn't recognize the young man. "Yes, I know that. I'm not here to eat. I hoped to speak with Mr. Solomon before lunch started."

The waiter dithered a moment, wanting to avoid embroiling his boss in trouble with this unknown, well-dressed, white man. Such situations required caution.

Sage spoke to reassure him. "You are new, I think. I'm John Adair, a friend of Mr. Solomon's. I am certain he'll wish to see me."

Tension eased from the young man's face. "'John Adair', you say? I will go and inquire of my uncle." He turned on his heel and reentered the kitchen, leaving Sage to ponder the fact that the nephew also spoke with the same precise, elevated diction that his uncle used. He concluded both must come from an interesting family back there in the Carolinas.

Immediately, the kitchen door opened and a tall Angus Solomon strode out, a broad smile on his burnished mahogany face. He had high cheekbones he attributed to a Chickasaw ancestor and dark sloe eyes. His competent warmth made him popular with most of the hotel's white, high-class clientele, thereby affirming the hotel owner's gamble that a well-trained black wait staff gave the dining room class.

Angus gripped Sage's outstretched hand with both of his own. "It is wonderful to see you, Sage. It has been too long." Solomon was one of the few Portlanders who knew to call him, 'Sage'. Ordinarily he was known as "John" by those in the "outside" world. His and Solomon's relation-ship had evolved far beyond that of being mere acquaintances—they'd worked together on too many missions.

"I had to go out of town for a bit. There was trouble to the south of here on an Indian reservation," Sage said by way of explanation.

Solomon gestured toward a far table while signaling that the waiter should bring coffee.

"Yet another nephew?" Sage asked with a nod at the young man.

Solomon laughed. "Yes, indeed. They just keep coming. Not sure when it will stop. I have a passel of nephews waiting in the wings. While it's not perfect here, my brothers and sisters are most eager to send their sons away from the South. These days, old Jim Crow is starting to flap his wings a bit too vigorously."

Sage responded with a commiserating grunt and shake of the head, though he knew he'd never entirely comprehend just how difficult it was to be black in America, especially in the South. Or, depending on the location, Chinese, Indian, or Hispanic. He only knew that life proved much harder if one didn't spring from white European stock.

Once the coffee was before them, Angus sent him a questioning look and Sage quickly launched into the story of Noah's disappearance.

Anticipating Sage's request, Solomon offered to query the railway porters, though he cautioned, "Some time may elapse before we are able ask everyone. Some runs, such as those to Chicago or Los Angeles, take five days. I will ensure, however, that all are queried when they check into the New Era."

He brushed away Sage's heartfelt thanks. "I owe Sergeant Hanke. He helped resolve the Cooper boy's little dust-up with that white boy. His respect and integrity meant a lot to the Coopers. Unlike many police officers, the Sergeant is a fair man. Besides, a youngster is missing. I cannot imagine the terror his father must be feeling."

They discussed the situation. Unfortunately, Angus and Fong shared similar opinions about the fate of Eli Yoder's missing son. "Noah sounds like a good boy and not the type to steal his father's money and take off for parts unknown. I fear that someone has kidnapped or killed him," Solomon said.

Sage soon left to return to Mozart's, Like Angus, he too had lunch hour meet-and-greet duties. "Kidnapped, killed" each word kept time with his steps. But, for God's sake, why and where? And, who could do such a thing?

FOUR

Fong was unlocking the door and flipping the sign to "open," as Sage arrived. After graciously stepping aside to let waiting customers go first, Sage also entered and tossed his overcoat onto the rack. His mother stood at the mahogany buffet, setting dishes and cutlery out for easy access. Homer, their frog-faced waiter, welcomed the incoming customers, seated them, and distributed menus. Finished at the buffet, Mae glanced in Sage's direction. He cocked an inquiring eyebrow. She shook her head, exasperation in her face.

The restaurant got busy. When Sage wasn't escorting customers to tables, he was refilling coffee cups, milk, and sugar. The full dining room was heartening. It meant word hadn't gotten out that Mozart's poisoned customers. If, and when, that nasty fact went public, there'd no longer be a Mozart's Table. Unease kept him observant. Thus far, he saw no indication of any illness.

Losing money wasn't the issue. His Klondike gold, judiciously invested, provided more than enough financial security. The restaurant closing, however, meant they'd lose their cover. Sage's in particular. To Portland's elite, John Adair was the attractively shallow proprietor of an exclusive restaurant—almost one of their class though not quite. Their misperception relaxed them, easing them away from their customary discretion.

More than once, over jovial offerings of good food, Sage and his crew learned of shady doings. Sage's social status also enabled him to meet and mingle in folks' homes, clubs, and other places where they felt "safe". Basically, Mozart's created opportunities he didn't want to lose.

Once the dinner service was over and teatime two hours away, a weary Mae sat down and told Sage, "We checked every scrap of food. Anything older than two days, we tossed it." She caught his surprise, "Yes, I know, that's costly. But, losing the restaurant would be more costly. I even scooted out to buy fresh milk and cream—just in case."

She sighed, worry weighing heavy on her. "Sage, this is seriously bad for us. We found not a single morsel of spoiled food."

"Did we change vendors anytime in the last few months?" Sage asked.

Mae nodded, her expression glum. "We did. We switched to the Quality Emporium for our dairy. But, the milk, cream, and butter are all fresh, like new. Actually, the milk seems to be of better quality. Ida says it's thicker and stays fresh a good while longer than what we used to buy. Still, we threw it out and I fetched more from the Emporium.

"I swear, we're like chicks lost in high weeds. There's no figuring why those folks took sick. Can't be a coincidence."

Sage couldn't think of any more they could do. His mother and Ida covered all the bases and he told her that.

Mae slapped her hands on the table and stood. "That's right. We did all we could do. Anyways, I sent Ida up to take a short nap. I need a snooze myself. All that pulling, sniffing, throwing, and storing tuckered us out."

She paused, shooting him a pointed look. "You best go bring Miss Lucinda into our hunt for that boy, Noah."

Sage's brow wrinkled. How could his lady friend, the madam of the city's high-class parlor house, help hunt for Noah?

Lips tightened by irritation, Mae just glared at him until he caught her point. Besides being a runaway, shanghaied, or dead, there was that other possible fate for the missing fourteen-year-old boy. "Damn, I hate to think that's what happened to him. I thought we closed the last house."

His mother raised a disbelieving eyebrow. "Really? You thought that'd be the end of it?" She shook her head in mock disbelief before adding, "As long as there are indecent folks out there, they'll be trying to make a buck any way they can. They rise to the top like scum in a cesspool. I don't know where the new house might be but I'm darn sure there is one. Our Lucinda has the best chance of locating it."

He felt a frisson of warmth at those two words, "Our Lucinda." He'd been surprised and gratified when he realized that his mother felt affection for the woman he'd come to love. And taken aback when she'd tartly informed him there'd been more than one prostitute in his own family. She went on to admonish that he best not "get above" himself just because he had money in his pockets.

Heading out as instructed, his thoughts were still on Lucinda when he reached the park blocks and turned south beneath the trees. He admired the foresight of the town's early citizens who'd preserved this strip of parkland. The blocks-long green space was fronted by elegant two-story houses and brick apartment buildings. He always smiled at the audacity of Lucinda's chosen location.

Ah, Lucinda. He remained conflicted over that honey-haired woman with her cornflower blue eyes. Despite her repeated rejections of his marriage offer, they'd grown ever closer. Even though she no longer serviced clients, he wanted her out of the business. He fantasized about her in their kitchen with their children at her feet. Sometimes, a haunted look in her eyes made him think she dreamt of that too.

Still, the reasons she gave for her refusal created a stalemate because they were logical. She was right; he couldn't carry on his undercover work among the city's wealthy if he violated their social norms and married the city's most notorious madam. Certainly, no eyebrows rose at her employees entertaining the city's prominent men—nor did Sage's exclusive patronage of the house's owner create a problem. But, in their hypocritical world, marriage to Lucinda would make him a social pariah.

They'd discussed marrying and moving to another town. That option meant abandoning Mozart's and Portland and everything they'd built— the most important being their productive alliances with Fong, Solomon, Eich, Hanke, and a host of others.

Besides, his mother might refuse to move yet again. There was her relationship with Eich, for one thing. And, they'd both come to cherish the city's progressives—folks like Harry Lane, the poor people's doctor, Fred Merrill, its bicycle king and pesky councilmember, David Campbell, the fearless fire chief, and all the women spearheading the city's social progress.

Climbing the granite steps to the mansion's black lacquered door, he again vowed to be content with the status quo. Besides, the future had a way of creating itself independent of his will.

One fall of the brass knocker and the door swung open. Elmira stood there, a smile bright in her dark face. Putting a finger to her lips, she gestured him inside, and pointed down the narrow hallway that led to the kitchen. Her eyes gleamed impishly.

He knew the why of her amusement. The city's most elegant madam hated for Sage to see her wearing the faded calico she always donned when doing housework.

The kitchen door stood ajar. His finger pushed it further open and he stepped inside. The cook, Mrs. Miller, saw his signal for silence and flashed him a smile before turning back to the sink.

He snuck up behind Lucinda. She stood vigorously blackening and polishing the iron cook stove—her whole body engaged in the effort. He'd never understand her desire to make that stove glisten.

Throwing his arms around her waist, he pulled her against him.

She stiffened, then relaxed. "You rascal! One of these days you'll do that and get a snoot full of stove black. Mr. Fong has been teaching me some tricks."

"How'd you know it was me?"

She laughed, turning about in the circle of his arms, and said, "I'll never tell. It's one of my many secrets."

Truthfully, he teased, "I always love seeing you in gingham with that dusting of sooty beeswax on your face.

She feinted a sooty slap at him before going to wash at the sink. That done, she gestured for him to follow her. Once they were seated at a small table in the back parlor, she asked, "So, Sage, why are you here interrupting my housework?"

"I don't know why you persist in doing it," he evaded. "With all the women living here, at least one of them must be capable of keeping house."

She gazed at him silently, making him wonder whether he'd hurt her feelings. She seemed to read his mind because she smiled easily. "I see your point. I guess I find housework satisfying. It's real. Doing it makes me feel like a normal woman instead of a businesswoman responsible for everything and everyone here."

She flapped a dismissive hand at the luxurious surroundings she'd created for her elite clientele. "Maybe one day. . . ." Her words trailed off. He knew what she'd been about to say; that maybe one day she'd be a normal housewife with this life far behind her.

Today, however, she discarded that thought. Straightening, she brushed a dangling lock of hair from her forehead and said brightly, "Enough of my blather. You are here for a reason. What is it you need?"

"Ouch, you wound me," he said. "Mayhap, I only needed to rest my eyes on your lovely countenance."

She just folded her arms across her chest, eyed him, and waited.

He huffed before flashing a sheepish smile and saying. "Okay. So, maybe this is one time when you're right."

Elmira came in carrying a tray of tea and treats. "Here's something to sweeten things up," she said before shooting them a cheeky smile and departing.

The tea pouring over, he told her about Noah going missing. When he finished, she looked away, her eyes gazing into the middle distance. He visualized cogs whirling around in that golden head

With a faint smile, she again met his eyes. "You need me to find out if a house has acquired a fourteen-year-old boy in the last month or so." Fortunately, her tone was gentle. She'd not been offended by his unspoken request.

He nodded.

Chin in hand, she thought a bit before saying, "Since we shut down those two houses, I've not heard of a new one starting up." Her lips twisted and she said, "Of course, there has to be one since those accursed customers remain."

She straightened in her chair. "Alright. I'll give it a try. It means visiting with some of the other madams. I'm sure they'll be willing to help."

He knew what she meant. Lucinda only associated with women she considered ethical—which meant no forced prostitution, no addictions, and, above all, never children. In the past, those women proved helpful in similar situations. Lucinda once explained why. Like her, many had experienced horrific childhoods in similar houses. They wanted those houses stomped out.

Minutes later, Sage was on his way back to Mozart's Table, his thoughts on terrorized children. During two of their prior missions, they'd rescued drugged and abused children from those houses. The idea that young Noah might be trapped in a similar situation made him want to hit someone. Catching the avidly curious looks of those he passed, he realized his angry stride was making him noticeable. He slowed, breathed deeply, and held that breath for a few beats before releasing it in a forceful huff. As promised, Fong's martial technique delivered calm.

That calm ended when he opened Mozart's door. His mother, Fong, Ida, and their waiter, Homer, were awaiting him in glum silence. "Oh, crap. Noah's dead?" he asked.

All four shook their heads. He breathed a sigh of relief and guessed again. "Another bout of food poisoning?"

The three others looked at Mae who answered, "Yup. This time the squirts hit the fellow an hour after he lunched here today. He swears he's going to report us to the food inspector."

"Crap," Sage said, taking an empty chair. "If the inspector finds a problem, it'll turn up in the newspapers sure as heck."

"Yup," she said.

FIVE

Sage swiped his coat sleeve across the fogged window. The view beyond was rain-drenched and dreary. He was riding the morning train because Hanke asked him to meet and speak directly with his friend, Eli Yoder. That's why they'd undertaken this trip, despite the unrelenting downpour.

Minutes later the first part of their trip was ending at the Beaverton interurban station. From here, they'd head north toward Cedar Mill. Eli Yoder's farm sat somewhere close by. Sage hoped it wouldn't be a long slog through heavy rain.

Hanke seemed to read his mind because he chuckled. "Hey, now. A little rain never hurt anyone," he said. "Don't worry, you won't get totally wet. Not with that fine rubber coat and those boot covers." He eyed Sage's hat. "Though, I suspect your headgear won't be much help."

"That shows what you know. This hat is made of the best nutria fur, guaranteed to keep my head dry," Sage bantered back, his good humor restored.

Hanke reached over and tapped the rigid brim where it dipped. "This here little spout is perfect for dripping water down your neck," he observed.

The train halted beside the station platform and both men stood, eager to abandon the hard seats and unheated car. Once inside the station and warming themselves before the potbellied stove, Sage asked, "So, we've got to walk how far?"

Hanke snorted. "Walk? In this rain? Why it's at least four miles to Eli's farm. I don't think we'll want to walk that far in this downpour."

"Don't tell me we're going on horseback. You know I don't like riding horses." Except for one particular horse, he silently reminded himself. Sage still chortled at the memory of that horse dropping down onto its haunches and refusing to carry a murderer away.

The big policeman raised a hand. "You wait right here. I'll go arrange things."

Sage harrumphed but nodded his agreement. Pulling off his gloves, he stretched cold hands toward the station's crackling stove and hoped that Hanke would rent an enclosed, two-seater carriage. The absence of cabs in the countryside left only three choices: driving a buggy, riding a horse, or walking it.

When the big policeman returned, Sage peered past him. No carriage waited outside the station's double doors. Damnation, he thought, Hanke's rented horses. He tensed at the prospect of riding a frisky horse through slippery mud. Most likely, he'd end up walking and leading the horse by the reins. It wouldn't be the first time.

"It's all fixed." Hanke approached grinning but puzzled Sage by saying, "It'll be a bit breezy and damp but no horses. Leastways, not ones you'll dislike."

Once they exited out the double doors, Hanke headed toward the station's freight dock. There a steam engine rhythmically puffed into the rain. Four big-wheeled, trailers were daisy-chained to its rear end. Three of them were empty. Four men were rapidly moving the fourth trailer's load of railroad ties onto a nearby rail flatcar.

Hanke pointed at the metal ladder attached to the engine. "Let's get on up there out of the rain. The engineer agreed to take both of us to Cedar Mill for twenty cents apiece. I figure that'll be way better than walking, even though the engine moves mighty slow.

Sage thought the steam engine a fine solution. A roof completely covered the engineer's platform which was big enough to hold all three of them. The smokestack jutting skyward would keep the smoke from hitting their faces. He gave Hanke's shoulder a grateful pat before hauling himself up the steps.

A short time later, a rotund fellow wearing denim overalls, a flannel shirt, heavy work boots, and a fleece-lined duck coat exited the station and joined them. The engineer was almost as short as he was wide, the top of his head level with the center hubs of engine's iron-clad wheels.

He reminded Sage of a penguin he'd once seen at New York's Central Park Zoo.

Once aboard, the engineer gave the freight loaders a cheery wave and began turning dials and cranks. Slowly, the gigantic wheels rotated, edging the engine away from the dock, its empty trailers rattling behind.

They crawled along, mud caking the big wheels with every rotation. A few minutes later, they mounted a sawdust-covered plank road heading north. Once atop the planks, the engine picked up speed though it still seemed to inch along. Hanke was right. It'd take some time to reach Cedar Mill. They'd get there sooner if they walked. Still, for Sage, time was a secondary concern since the roof overhead was sheltering them from the now pounding rain.

Hanke tugged on Sage's sleeve. "Don't get too cozy with that firebox," he cautioned. "Those rubber coats melt fast as cheese on a stove top."

Sage stepped back and the engine inched forward over the planks. The three of them stayed dry except when a wind gust blew the rain sideways. And the firebox, though now a bit more distant than Sage liked, kept the platform a few degrees warmer.

The ride was not silent. The engine puffed and hissed and the engineer liked to talk. While steering the wheels, twisting the dials, and feeding the firebox coal, the engineer began by instructing, "You boys call me Smoke." He then proceeded to educate them about the marvel on which they rode. He said it was a "brand new 1904, Russell, 50 horsepower, traction steam engine. Her name is "Clementine," he advised and leaned forward to affectionately pat the engine cowling.

Their slow advance toward Cedar Mill gave Sage plenty of time to admire the rolling, patchwork of fields and wooded land. They eventually approached the Cornell crossroads with its cluster of houses and other buildings. Encircling it, in every direction, lay the fenced, fallow, and stubble fields of fall, long ago cleared by men wielding primitive axes and shovels.

Eventually, Clementine reached the crossroads and they descended her ladder, thanked Smoke, and set off east toward the Yoder dairy farm. Miraculously, it no longer rained. The fresh air, heavy with moisture, carried the sound of a nearby rushing creek. The mud-churned road wasn't walkable so, they trod along its grassy verge. The drenched grass, slick underfoot and pocked with puddles, needed mindful stepping.

Less than half a mile later, Hanke turned up a narrow track that was just two wheel ruts flanking a weedy median strip. A small, one-story farmhouse stood at its end, smoke whisping out the tin pipe anchored to its side. Sage began anticipating a hot drink beside a warm stove.

Hanke mounted the covered porch to knock on the front door. While they waited, Sage surveyed the farm. A barn, four times the size of the house, stood close by. From it came the sounds of shifting, munching, milk cows. He liked that Yoder cared enough to bring the cows in out of the rain.

Sage expected Noah's father to be tall like Hanke. He wasn't. Instead, Eli Yoder was compact, standing at least three inches shorter than Sage's six-foot height. His hefty shoulders and arms bespoke of heavy labor. His hair was light, like Hanke's. According to Hanke, Yoder was Swiss-German, a descendant of Mennonites who fled Switzerland, hoping to find religious freedom in Chicago.

His face showed pleasure at seeing them but once that faded, the dark beneath his eyes and the trembling of his lips said he was struggling to hold on. Yoder reached both hands toward Hanke and the men shook, tears sparkling in Yoder's eyes as he said, "Thank you, thank you, for coming, my friend."

"Sorry I didn't get here sooner," the big policeman responded. "I didn't receive the telephone message until late last night when I returned to the station after searching for Noah."

Hope sparked in the other man's face until doused by Hanke's doleful headshake. Yoder sighed and looked at Sage. Sticking out a hand he said, "Eli Yoder, father of Noah. You must be Mr. Adair. Norm told me that you are helping to find my son."

Sage drew off his glove to shake a hand warmer than his own.

Yoder gestured them inside. "Come in, come in. You're chilled. You need a hot drink. We've both tea and coffee already made. Heaven knows, there's lots of fresh cream to soften its bite." He nodded at the barn.

Hanke and Sage exchanged a look. Yoder lived alone with his boy Noah. So, who was the "we" waiting inside? The answer came once they'd cleared the small vestibule and stepped into the warm parlor. There sat several people, many of them women. Curious eyes turned toward the newcomers.

An awkward pause followed while Eli hung their coats on hallway pegs. Appearing beside them he explained, "I apologize, I didn't know when you'd arrive. Our Grange meeting was scheduled for this morning. We always meet right after milking."

To the group, he said, "This is my friend, Sergeant Norm Hanke of the Portland Police and Mr. John Adair. They're helping search for Noah."

Approving mutters and smiles greeted the newcomers. As one, the seven folks rose and filed out, each giving Yoder a heartfelt hug or handshake in passing. Soon the three of them were alone.

"We didn't mean to scare off your guests," Hanke said. "I figured given the rainstorm, a message telephoned to the general store couldn't reach you before we did."

"Absolutely no problem. We'd already finished our meeting so your timing is perfect."

Sage knew little about the Grange organization. He'd been surprised to see so many women present. "They looked to be a fine group of people," he told Yoder.

A fond smile lit the other man's face. "They're the best. They've been searching too, every time one of them goes to town they stay to search." The silence felt leaden as each contemplated the failure of all those searches.

Yoder's thoughts returned to the present. "Come into the kitchen. I'll bet you're hungry and boy howdy, there's food enough for an entire army."

Sage saw what Yoder meant when they entered the tiny kitchen. Loaves of bread, baskets of produce, and casseroles covered the wooden table and single counter. The sight reminded Sage of the condolence food that always appeared after a death in the family. Not a good thought.

Since they'd jumped aboard the train before breakfast, Hanke and Sage diligently consumed the neighborly offerings. Yoder kept urging them on, saying there was more food than he could eat before it spoiled.

As they munched, Sage asked about Yoder's Grange. Pride straightened Yoder's shoulders as he explained he was the group's 'master', adding, "Of course, we're small in number so pretty much all of us will take a turn at the office sooner or later."

"Even the women?" Sage wondered aloud.

If anything, Yoder turned prouder as he said. "Ever since the Grange was established in 1867, it's endorsed women's suffrage and equality. Why, right today, there's an Oregon Grange with a woman master. We're farmers. We know how crucial a woman is to a farm's success ..." His voice dropped, trailing off. Undoubtedly, the memory of his dead wife had overtaken his thoughts. Hanke's big hand gave the man's shoulder a sympathetic squeeze.

Yoder stirred and continued his explanation. "Today, we were discussing moving our meetings to the new Woodman's Hall instead of holding them at our farms. Also, we're sending a delegation to Salem to lobby the politicians. We needed to plan for that. And, we had other business as well." He stood up, snatched the coffee pot off the cook stove, and refilled their cups.

Sitting down again, he changed the subject. "Can we talk about Noah? I am out of my mind with worry. Purity Creamery is accepting delivery of my milk twice a day just so I can also search at night. The Purity folks are doing their best to help. Have you learned anything about what happened to my son?"

Sage and Hanke exchanged a look. Sage cleared his throat to relate that, so far, no porter reported seeing Noah on a train. "It's still early days. Not every porter has returned to town. Some are still out. And, like you, a number of us have been out talking to folks. No one remembers seeing Noah after he left the creamery. The good news is that, so far, there's no evidence that anyone shanghaied Noah onto a ship."

He said nothing about Lucinda's inquiry into pedophilia houses. If Yoder hadn't considered that possibility, Sage wasn't going to put that idea into his head. He moved on, saying, "We want to talk to Noah's teacher and schoolmates. Maybe he told one of them about his plans."

"Noah is not a runaway!" Yoder's palms slapped the table with angry emphasis.

Hanke's tone was gentling as he said, "Eli, we don't think he is a runaway. Please understand, though, that every single avenue needs exploring. Maybe he planned to do something that took him near danger. You know young kids; sometimes they will tell their friends things they'd never tell their parents. We need to discover whether Noah planned to do something he didn't tell you about."

Eli Yoder sighed and stood. Going to the cupboard he fetched both pen and paper. "I better write a note to the school teacher, giving her my permission to cooperate with you every way she can," he said.

SIX

THEY WALKED BACK TOWARD THE crossroads through a gentle mist. Sage liked Eli Yoder. That made him even more determined to find the man's son. Just before the settlement, Hanke veered off the road toward the area's public school. It was a weathered, unpainted, single-story, clapboard building. The wall facing the road had a single door opening onto a wooden stoop. Along one side, three evenly spaced windows let light inside. A well-trod path curved around the building, heading toward two privies.

Hanke mounted the wooden steps and entered with Sage close behind. They found themselves in a cloakroom where a variety of coats hung from wooden pegs. Hanke crossed to the threshold of the interior door. Beyond him, the classroom was a large, single room with a chalkboard on its farthest wall. An animated teacher stood before sixteen children sitting at shared desks. Seeing the two men, she ceased lecturing and advanced, smiling.

Hanke stepped back into the cloakroom in an effort to talk out of the children's earshot. "I am sorry to disturb your class, Miss Ellison. I am Sergeant Hanke of the Portland Police and this is John Adair. We're helping Eli Yoder search for his missing son, Noah. He's given written permission for you to talk to us." He handed her Yoder's note.

"Oh dear," she said after scanning Eli's words. "I am so distressed that Noah is missing. He's a good boy and a good student and well-liked. We all miss him. Thank goodness someone is helping Mr. Yoder look for him."

"We want to know if Noah said something to you or to his classmates that might help us find him," Hanke said.

She frowned and shook her head. "He said nothing to me. I've spent hours wracking my brain, trying to figure out where that child might be. It makes no sense. I can't recall him saying that he planned to do anything out of the ordinary or risky."

Grabbing the bull by the horns, Sage asked the question he knew Hanke would not ask. "What do you know about Noah's home life? Was he treated well?" He sensed Hanke's start of surprise and caught his disapproving look.

She again paused before replying, "I know what you are asking. And, with some of these children, well, I wonder whether they are hit or not fed properly. I've never for a second wondered whether Noah was in a bad situation. He's always been a cheerful child, not gloomy like those I worry about. And his Karo Syrup lunch tin is always full. He's a kind child. I've seen him share his food with some of the others. So, I'm positive that he's well-treated, even more so since he lost his mother. It can't be easy for his father. But, from everything I've seen, he's doing an admirable job raising that boy."

Hanke cleared his throat, switching the teacher's attention back to him. "Will you permit us to address the children as a group?"

She nodded briskly. "This is a good time. I intended to send them out for recess now that the rain is stopping. Hopefully, there's half an hour or so before it returns."

She led the two men to the front of the class and said they were searching for Noah. When she nodded, Hanke stepped forward. "Children, we are here to ask whether you might know anything that will help us find Noah. We know he went to Portland ten days ago, on Saturday. Did he say anything about his plans for that day?"

The children sat in rows, in stair-step fashion, with the smallest in the front and the oldest children in the back. A hand shot up in the back row.

The teacher acknowledged the boy, "Yes, Joseph. Please stand and speak clearly."

Joseph clambered to his feet and said. "Noah told me that his pa gave him permission to go to one of them kinetoscope parlors and see a moving picture. Even gave him a few nickels so's he could."

Miss Ellison seized the teaching opportunity. "Go to one of the, not them, kinetoscope parlors, Joseph."

The poor kid flushed and shuffled his feet before thumping back down onto his bench.

During the ensuing silence no other child raised a hand. Sage noticed a girl about Noah's age sitting in that back row. Her wispy dark hair fluttered above big brown eyes. In the gray light from the window, he thought he saw a tear. When her finger shot up and appeared to flick it away, he was certain. He stared at her. Her eyes widened but she made no move to speak.

Hanke thanked the teacher and the children before heading toward the door with Sage trailing behind. As he passed the last row, Sage nodded at the girl. She responded with a glare.

Once outside, Hanke started toward the road until Sage caught his elbow. "Sergeant, I am sorry about that question. I believe that Eli treats his son well. Still, you and I both know that sometimes bad things happen to children behind closed doors. We needed to know for certain."

Hanke gave one of his big sighs followed by an easy smile. "I know. I didn't like it but I'm glad you asked it." As he again turned toward the road, Sage said, "Wait. I think a girl in there has something to say. The kids are coming out for recess. I want to try talking to her."

They waited near the steps. From inside came the sounds of benches scraping and heavy boots clomping on the wooden floor. Soon the cloakroom filled with childish chatter until the door flew open and the children poured out. They quickly organized their play, the smallest racing around in a game of tag, the older ones setting out with jumping rope, bat and baseball. The girl Sage noticed exited last. She shot Sage a look before slipping around the building's corner as if heading toward the privy.

Hanke intercepted the look and nodded for Sage to follow. Uncertain whether the girl went to visit the outhouse or wanted to talk, he rounded the corner. She waited there, shifting her booted feet, a determined look on her face. "Do you know something that might help us find Noah?" he asked her, keeping his tone gentle.

She gave an emphatic shake of her head before saying, in a soft voice, "Me and Noah are good friends." The scarlet flooding her cheeks suggested the two were something more. He let that pass, saying instead, "Friends sometimes share secrets."

She nodded as she said, "We shared secrets. He told me nothing about why he disappeared." She scowled up at him as she spoke in a rush, "Mister, I heard what you asked Miss Ellison in the cloakroom. You need to know that Noah loved his father more than anything. He was proud of him. He talked about how good a dairyman he was and about how he was master of the Grange hereabouts. His show-and-tell in class was about the time when Mr. Yoder traveled all the way to Salem to talk to the Governor himself. Noah would never, ever, run away from his dad. He just wouldn't!" Her eyes filled with tears and before Sage found words in reply, she dashed off, disappearing into the outhouse labeled "Girls," its door banging shut behind her.

Sage headed back to the front of the school. When Hanke shot him a questioning look, Sage responded with a head shake. Still, they'd learned that Noah was a good student, likable, happy, well-fed, and proud of his father. All of which made him a most unlikely runaway.

As it happened, they had a fairly comfortable return to the railway station. Heading west, they soon crossed the plank road and reached a general store. There a roof jutting from the store's western-style false front sheltered a high porch.

Inside, shelves covered every wall from floor to ceiling, each one stuffed with tinned goods, bins, or bags. Standing tables displayed a variety of bigger items; hats, tin ware, dishes, and farm gear, all vied for attention. Full cotton seed bags were piled high atop a corner platform. A large potbellied stove warmed the room, fire flickering behind its mica window. The mismatched chairs and benches pulled up around the stove's chrome foot rail declared this to be a community gathering spot.

Hanke approached the sole man sitting by the stove, feet on the rail, hands stretched toward the heat, and asked, "Is that your delivery van out front?" When the man replied that it was, Hanke requested a ride. The man agreed, telling them he'd soon be driving to Beaverton as he was nearly warm.

Once they were outside again, Sage was happy to see the man climb aboard an enclosed van. While Hanke sat beside the driver, Sage rode in the back. It was a rough ride but he was dry as they rolled down the plank road much faster than Clementine.

A wait for the train delayed their return so it wasn't until after the noon dinner hour that Sage opened Mozart's door. On their return trip, he and Hanke agreed that they needed to discard the idea of Noah running away. Sure, they'd wait to hear what the railway porters might say but felt certain that was a dead end. Likewise, Eli Yoder was adamant that no one hated him enough to harm his son. Sage silently wondered how long they should continue searching if they turned up no new leads.

A welcome sight greeted him when he stepped inside the restaurant. His mother and Lucinda sat at a table with teapot and treats between them. "Ah, you're back. I promised Lucinda you'd soon turn up. Many thanks for not making me a liar," his mother declared.

He squeezed his mother's shoulder as he said, "You know I always try to make you look good."

She swatted his hand away. Lucinda smirked, obviously enjoying their banter. He gave her a quick kiss, again grateful that Mae Clemens liked his lady friend and approved of affectionate displays. Even so, she started in surprise when he also kissed her on the forehead. She gave him a bright smile and said, "My goodness, aren't you in a good mood. Was your trip west a success?"

"Well, no horse riding was involved. To me, that alone made it a success," he said. Sitting down, he poured hot tea into an empty cup, "We learned but two things. The first is that Eli Yoder dearly loves his son and that love is reciprocated. We also learned the boy is smart, well-liked, and generally, a happy kid. In sum, Hanke and I doubt the boy voluntarily abandoned his father. Unfortunately, that's all we learned." He looked at Lucinda and teased, "Oh, though I did have the pleasure of making the acquaintance of a delightful and unique lady named Clementine."

Lucinda's twinkling eye said she wasn't threatened. "And, you tell us about this Clementine, why?" she asked.

He laughed and told them about his pokey ride atop the steam engine. "At least her 50 horses didn't buck us off. And, we stayed dry until our tramp to the Yoder farm."

Lucinda shifted on her chair, eager to share her information. She related it succinctly. "The bad news is that another house has already started up. The good news is that it does not have a fourteen-year-old boy on offer."

"Sounds like a job for Millie Trumbull and her crusaders," he said.

The two women looked at each other and laughed. His mother said, "That is exactly what we were saying as you came in the door."

Millie Trumbull was a respectable matron they'd met during a previous mission. She was determined that every child be given a decent life. To that end, she and her coterie of picketing crusaders had already closed down two lucrative child sex operations with a subsequent fire sending one of them into permanent oblivion. The police never caught the arsonist. Hanke reported they'd made little effort to find the Chinese man seen running from the fire.

"A little dash of Fong might also be good," observed Lucinda, triggering laughter from all three of them.

"Speaking of Fong," Mae said, "he's up in the attic waiting for you."

Sage climbed the steep steps to an attic warmed by the building's rising heat. A clean skylight let in daylight to gleam the fir floors and brighten the whitewashed walls. By way of greeting, Fong slowly raised his hands—in the first of the gentle sequences comprising the martial art he called "the snake and crane."

Sage slipped off his shoes, took a position behind Fong, and copied the movements. Despite being desperate to know if Fong heard of any boy recently getting shanghaied, he also knew not to interrupt the exercise. For the next half hour, they moved through 108 different movements.

At the exercise's end, they stood in silence until Fong looked at Sage. "Go ahead. Ask question. You not concentrate until question answered."

"Did you learn anything about Noah?"

Fong's face saddened and he shook his head. "No story in town of stolen boy. Cousins pretty sure." Raising a finger to halt Sage's dismayed response, he said, "But, other cousin go to Astoria today. He plan to work in cannery. Now is fall salmon run. He carry pigeon and question. Maybe we get lucky. Pigeon due very soon."

Both of them looked up toward Fong's rooftop pigeon coop. The homing pigeons supplied fertilizer for Sage's garden boxes up there. More important, the pigeons provided a way to send messages privately—much more than did a telegram read by the operators and others.

"I go look for bird now." Fong mounted the ladder, raised the trap door, and disappeared through the opening. Sage waited, trying to recapture the calm that the exercise had given him.

Despite that effort, hope surged at the sight of Fong's feet on ladder's top rung. After what seemed like forever, his teacher reached the floor. Fong's brow was lowered in thought. He triumphantly waved a nub of rolled paper in the air. Sage waited as the paper was spread out to reveal tiny Chinese squiggles.

"Maybe something," Fong said. "He write people saw man row youngster out to whaling ship. Boy look asleep. They think him drugged. Ship sail yesterday night on going out tide."

"God, not a whaling ship!" The whaling life was brutal and often deadly. This late in the season, whalers often disappeared beneath the Bering Strait's icy waters.

"Cousin say ship stop in Victoria before sail to whale grounds."

"We better rescue that boy. No matter who he is. He won't survive, otherwise."

Fong's lips compressed. "Yes. Best I go," he said.

"No, not you. That's too dangerous. You'd have to sneak into Canada and sneak back into the U.S. Immigration inspectors refuse to let Chinese enter either country. It's far too risky for you to try crossing either border."

Fong nodded. "Yes. That true. But, you cannot go. Maybe it not Noah boy on whaler. Also, there is restaurant problem. You best to fix it."

Sage started to protest, to insist he go to Victoria until he realized Fong had it right. They couldn't be sure Noah was the shanghaied boy. Portland remained the best place to discover whatever happened to him. And, as Fong noted, there was still the food poisoning problem.

SEVEN

James Laidlaw stood at the counter in easy conversation with a scruffy-looking sailor. Sage stepped inside, closing the door on a sun rising into a cloudless azure sky, its distant fire warming the early morning nip.

The British consular's office occupied a small storefront near the harbor. From there, Consular Laidlaw protected British subjects and promoted British trade. Neither task was easy given Portland's reputation for shanghaiing.

Sage knew Laidlaw from a few years back when he'd been trying to find a shanghaied union organizer. The British consul was a fierce opponent of the practice. He, along with the city's other foreign consuls, were trying to stop it.

Thus far, their efforts met only failure because the city's wealthy merchants opposed any restriction on the practice. This was because sailors reaching the West Coast often jumped ship, stranding their ships. A sailor shortage raised freight costs and kept ships from sailing into Portland. The merchants wanted shanghaiing to continue because kidnapped labor kept ships arriving and freight costs low.

Laidlaw sent Sage a warm smile and ended his conversation. He opened the counter gate and gestured Sage through. As they shook hands he said, "It's been some time since you darkened my door. It's good to see you."

"I know. You haven't been coming into the restaurant like before. I take it that you are no longer a fan of Ida's cooking?"

Laidlaw's face scrunched in disgust. "Ah, no! Far from it. The wife says I'm bulging a bit here and there." He patted his rounded belly. "So, no more delicious noontime meals for me. Instead, she sends me to work with my rabbit lunch in a bucket, like some school child."

Instructing his clerk to "mind the counter," Laidlaw led Sage into his tiny corner office. Closing the door, he sat and said, "Take a seat, Adair. Tell me what you need."

As always, Sage appreciated the man's forthrightness. Their initial collaboration had quickly blossomed into a battle-forged friendship that made social chitchat unnecessary.

"Since it's been a while since we spoken, I'm a bit ashamed to admit that I am here to ask for your help. But I will," he said. "My problem is that Fong has to enter Canada. He's going to try to sneak in but, if caught, they'll return him to China. Doubtless, he'd make his way back here from Shanghai. But, we don't want to take that chance. Returning would be a months-long journey and we can't spare him."

Laidlaw frowned. "You're right to be worried. My Canadian brethren are just as prejudiced as the U.S. when it comes to the Chinese. They recently levied a $500 head tax on Chinese immigrants. That effectively means none are being admitted. But, won't Fong find it just as dangerous to re-enter the U.S.? I assume he has no passport."

"Yup, no passport. He came in through Mexico years ago. He seems to think his Chinese contacts up north can smuggle him into both countries. Evidently, quite a few of them work in the San Juan Island canneries or fish those waters."

When Sage related the reason behind Fong's journey to Canada, Laidlaw understood the dire situation. "An abducted cabin boy on a whaling ship this late in the season? There's no worse fate." He leaned forward. "I will help. Tell me what I need to do."

"I was hoping you'd create a written document. One that might provide Fong with safe passage should the Canadians intercept him."

"I'd be glad to. That's a good idea. I'll write that he's my emissary on a mission to find the missing boy, though I'll need to say the boy's a British citizen. I'll slap some official seals on it. That might help with the Canadians." He raised a cautionary finger. "But, that letter won't help if he's caught while reentering the U.S. He'll be on his own there. Additionally, he has the added challenge of sneaking the boy back in. I cannot imagine how he'll accomplish that."

With no further discussion, Laidlaw took a sheet of consular stationary from his desk drawer and picked up his fountain pen.

Mid-morning, Sage, Fong, and Eli Yoder met in Mozart's empty dining room. The evening before, via the Cedar Mill store, Sage telephoned a message asking Yoder to stop by Mozart's following his next day's milk delivery.

Yoder was waiting when Sage returned after seeing Laidlaw. So was Fong. Wearing his finest suit, he looked like a prosperous Chinese businessman. Sage told Yoder that Fong would sneak into Canada to rescue the boy aboard the whaler and then smuggle them both back into the United States.

Tears welled in Yoder's eyes. "Mr. Fong, I can't believe you are willing to undertake something so dangerous to help us," he said.

Fong gave him a steady look and said, "Not good your son taken. But, Mister Yoder, best you keep hopes low. Boy maybe not your son."

"I know, but he's somebody's son." Yoder reached into his pocket and withdrew a worn leather wallet. "I'll give you all the money I have on me right now and I'll bring more this evening."

Sage laid a staying hand on Yoder's arm. "No, Ira. Put your money back. Money is not a concern. That's taken care of."

Their plan was simple. Fong would ride the train all the way to Anacortes, some distance north of Seattle. After that, he'd take a steamer to Orcas Island where numerous Chinese lived, either working in fish canneries or crewing fishing boats.

Once there, he'd find and pay a Chinese boat captain to smuggle him onto Vancouver Island. Upon reaching the island, he'd make his way to Victoria's port and be waiting there when *The Freeman* whaler docked. Somehow, he'd snatch the cabin boy, whoever he might be, rendezvous with the fishing boat, slip onto Orcas Island, get from there to the mainland, and, finally, they'd take the train to Portland.

Having explained their plan, Sage leaned forward to say, "What we need from you, Eli, is a letter to Noah, telling him to trust Fong absolutely and do everything Fong tells him to do,"

At Yoder's eager agreement, Sage nudged a fountain pen and blank paper toward him. The farmer quickly scratched out a message.

"What happens if it isn't Noah on that whaler?" he asked as he handed the note to Fong who tucked it into an inside coat pocket.

"That's why we'll keep searching for him here. Until we know whether that boy on the whaler is Noah, it's better to assume that he's not," Sage said.

Fong held no illusions about the trip's dangers. Already people waiting in Union Station's marble departure lobby were casting a mix of curious and chill looks at him. There'd been a minor set-to over the class of ticket Sage wanted to buy. Sage insisted on first class but Fong rejected that idea. "You buy first class, I still ride second," he said, settling the argument.

Sage understood Fong's reasoning. First-class passengers would be hostile to a Chinese man in their midst. Fong's presence in second class was less likely to stir up trouble.

The train chugged into the station. Once aboard, Fong chose a rear seat in the corner and raised a newspaper before his face. The paper served two purposes: Improving his English and making his Asiatic self less noticeable.

Still, he couldn't use the paper as a shield the entire trip. Eventually, the train's rocking and the fact he'd risen before dawn overtook him. He slipped into slumber, the paper dropping onto his lap.

Sometime later, a hand shaking his shoulder jerked him awake. His training took over instantly and sent the conductor sprawling across the adjacent seat, his arm caught in Fong's painful grip.

Fong released the man, apologizing profusely. Unfortunately, others in the car noticed, especially the two coarse-looking men sitting a few rows ahead.

The conductor was gracious. "I apologize for touching you, Sir. You didn't hear me when I came to tell you that you must switch trains in Tacoma. This one doesn't join up with the Anacortes train. That transfer's coming up in about ten minutes."

Fong stood to grab his small satchel from the overhead rack. A glance told him that the two men who'd noticed him were drinking from a liquor flask. One of them stared at Fong, a frown on his face. Since he didn't want to be cornered while between the seats, Fong made his way to the rear platform, as if preparing to deboard. He sensed that both men were focused on him, their stares drilling into his back.

Out of the corner of his eye he saw them stand, their voices now loud and slurring—as if ginning up courage to act.

Fong sighed, set his satchel down on the vibrating metal floor, and made ready, his feet apart. The men advanced down the aisle and stood before him, crowding closer than necessary.

One of them smirked as he asked, "Where you going, Chink?"

"I go north of Seattle," Fong answered quietly.

The second man said, "That's a real nice watch chain decorating your little chest. Looks like it's gold. How about you sell it to me? I'll give you ten cents."

"No, thank you. I not wish to sell watch." Fong kept his tone mild even as he moved one foot back and bent his knees slightly, assuming the traditional bow stance, ready to fight.

"Ah, come on. I'm betting you don't even know how to tell American time. Sell me that watch." This time it was a demand, not a request. Doubtless, the man counted on the fact that he and his friend stood a foot taller than their prey.

Again, Fong responded with a mild, "No, thank you."

The first man said, "Well, if you won't sell, I guess we'll just be taking it," and reached for the chain. Seconds later, he was yelping, down on his knees, his hand bent backward at a severe angle. As the other man started forward, another voice sounded.

"Here, here. What the tarnation is going on?" It was the conductor who'd returned to man the exit door. Fong released the wrist he held.

The man scrambled up from his knees, shook his finger in Fong's face, and whirled to push past the conductor, heading back to his seat. The second man snarled, "You got lucky, you little yellow bastard!'

The conductor, who'd already felt Fong's steely grip, shook his head. "Somebody just got lucky but I'm thinking it be them, not you." His smile held a touch of delight.

As instructed, Fong switched trains in Tacoma. His attackers remained aboard, their train heading east. As the north-moving railcar clacked along, Fong stared out the window at meadows, settlements, and forests. What lay ahead wasn't going to be easy. The toughest part would come after he landed on Vancouver Island and tried to find the boy. Breathing slow and deep, he let his thoughts release into the centeredness of his dantien. Meditation would yield the sharp focus he needed for the challenges ahead.

Many hours later, frigid water soaked the top of his naked thighs as Fong slipped overboard to wade ashore. He carried his simple drawstring trousers stuffed into the bag tied around his neck, keeping company with his dry coat, tunic, shoes, and stockings. His better clothes remained on Orcas, inside the satchel he'd shoved into a rock crevice near the ferry landing.

Shivering, he reached land and dressed beneath a fir tree's concealing limbs. The most difficult part lay ahead. He was five miles from the city's inner harbor. Somehow he needed to cross the city without drawing attention to himself. The sole fact in his favor was that most Chinese traveled in the opposite direction—fleeing Canada for the United States. Once near the harbor, he could adopt the guise of a foreign sailor briefly ashore.

There were few people about in these hours before sunrise. Closer in, those he saw strode purposely, seemingly unaware of him. He reached the bustling inner harbor sooner than he'd expected. He looked around for his own kind and spotted a small sloop being loaded by a Chinese man. Sidling forward, he hoisted a burlap bag onto his shoulder and mounted the ramp onto the sloop.

A furious Cantonese hiss sounded at his back. "You there! Stop! Loading this vessel is my job! What are you doing?"

Fong dropped the bag on deck, turned, and replied in the same dialect. "I am just helping you, my friend. I do not want money. I just need some information. That is all."

"What information?" The man's anger dissipated.

"I am looking for a whaling ship called *The Freeman*. Has it docked?"

The man's answer eased Fong's worry. "No, you are just in time. That ship is expected to arrive on tomorrow morning's high tide."

Fong helped the man finish loading before bowing and sauntering away down the dock. Time to find something to eat and a hiding place as well.

EIGHT

Sage found his mother bustling between Mozart's dining room and kitchen when he returned from the train station. Searching her face, he saw nothing worrisome.

"Any more missives from people we've poisoned?' he asked, keeping his tone light though his gut churned in anticipation of her answer.

She flashed him a smile. "Nope. Not a word about it so far."

Perplexed, Sage said. "I don't understand. You and Ida figured out the cause?"

She shook her head. "Still mystified, we are. Though, you and Herman asked me the same question."

"What question was that?"

"Whether we'd bought anything from a new supplier. I got to thinking. Our single change this month was ordering milk, cream, cheese, and butter from the Quality Emporium. So, yesterday morning, Ida tossed out everything we'd bought from them and we switched back to buying dairy products from the Purity Creamery. So far today, no complaints."

"Hmm. Purity Creamery is where Eli Yoder sells his milk. If the neatness of his farm is any indication, Purity's dairy products ought to be good."

She shrugged. "I expect it's too soon to know if that's what made folks sick. I'm just holding my breath. It's been just one day since we switched back and it's not even noon yet. So, it's too early to celebrate. Best keep a lid on your hopes."

❀   ❀   ❀

During that night's supper service, a nearby diner exclaimed, quite loudly, "That Harry Lane! He's crazy I tell you!"

Sage paused beside the man. "Why do you say that, Mr. Kenner? What antics did Doc Lane get up to this time?" he asked while refilling the man's coffee cup. At the man's invitation, Sage took the empty seat at the table, knowing Kenner and his love of gossip. He'd proved a reliable source of information in the past.

Sage was always interested in Harry Lane. He considered the doctor a friend as well as one of the city's finest citizens. Lane descended from one of Oregon's most prominent pioneer families.

In Sage's opinion, however, the man's real worth came from his doctoring of the city's poor. He also persisted in goading the powerful into taking actions beneficial to his patients. The story was that, some years ago, politics cost Lane his post as director of the State Insane Asylum. Just recently, he was appointed to the State Board of Health. More than likely, some politician thought that was a way to sideline the good doctor. The tactic had already proved a failure.

Kenner chuckled aloud, his delighted expression showing that he relished the chance to tell the story. "Well, lately, he's been raising a ruckus over the Chinamen's gardens."

While Sage was very familiar with the terraced gardens west of the central city and knew that they fed many, he'd never heard of Lane's concern.

Noting Sage's puzzlement, the man explained, "Well, you know, Lane is adamant about stomping out typhoid, diphtheria, and other contagions."

Sage nodded, still waiting for an explanation of the man's initial remark.

Kenner wrinkled his nose. "You happen to know just how those Orientals fertilize their vegetables?" he asked.

After a moment, Sage recalled the big clay jars arranged beside the garden plots. "City night soil?" he guessed.

"Yup. They haul their handcarts from privy to privy, cleaning them out and trucking the stuff back to their gardens where they store it in those big clay pots. After a bit, they spread it around the gardens." Kenner sipped his coffee and continued, "Anyway, there's been a bee in Harry's bonnet about that practice ever since he got on the State health board. He says using night soil as fertilizer spreads disease. Wants the Chinese to use cow dung instead."

"Does night soil spread disease?"

The man shrugged. "Who knows? Most folks wash their vegetables so I'd think not. But, word is, Lane asked that Hampton woman to test some of the garden's fruits and vegetables. He didn't like what she found."

"Hampton woman?" Sage vaguely recollected the name.

"Oh, you've assuredly heard of her. She's one of those lady doctors. She's also a chemist. Her name, Victoria Hampton, was recently in news articles about the Homestead murder trial. Most folks think her testimony about the blood is what hung that Williams fellow. Anyway, Lane didn't like what the tests of that produce showed."

"Okay, you're right. That trial's where I heard her name. It sounds reasonable though—both the testing and Lane's reaction to the results."

Kenner laughed. "Maybe. Still, the Chinese kept ignoring Lane, so you know what our esteemed doctor did?"

Sage shook his head.

"Well, it seems that Doc Lane took his shotgun up to the gardens a few days back and blasted every single one of those clay pots to smithereens!"

"Good Lord!" Sage exclaimed. "Are they sure Dr. Lane's the one who blasted them?"

"Well, no one saw him do it but he's acting pretty coy. He just smiles whenever anyone asks and changes the subject. But, you know, a few folks claim they saw him out and about the night it happened."

Kenner leaned forward to continue in a conspiratorial whisper, "They say he was carrying his shotgun."

Sitting back in his chair Kenner added in a more normal voice, "It's no leap across the pond to conclude that Lane's the one who done the deed. Can't help but think that since he's been raising such a fuss about the Chinamen's night soil pots. You ask me, Lane levitated a bit above himself if he did that—broke the law you know."

Sage shook his head at hearing of Lane's bold action. Inwardly, he was delighted. It sounded like the doctor's concerns were legitimate. Whatever made food safer was okay by him. So, bravo for Lane, if he's the one who shot up the night soil jars. Especially, since Mozart's sometimes bought that garden's produce.

For a moment he wondered if that's why Mozart's customers recently took sick. But, no, that couldn't be the cause. They'd complained of sudden, virulent attacks, not diseases that came on slower, like typhoid, diphtheria, or the other such contagions.

Sage admired and liked Harry Lane. He'd heard a rumor that Lane might seek the mayor's job. If that happened, Sage planned to make a significant contribution to his campaign. Lane's unrelenting advocacy for the poor, downtrodden, and ignored earned him the animosity of Portland's wealthy. And, it was exactly why the rest of the city's people revered him.

By supper hour's end, he'd heard at least five different people regale others with the tale of the night soil jars being blasted to smithereens. He smiled inwardly at every repetition.

Around nine, as the last customer exited, a messenger boy popped in through the front door, a telegram clutched in his hand. Mae Clemens took it, tipped the boy, and looked for Sage. Spotting his worried look, she said, "Nope. Not a report of someone taking sick after eating here. That's two days straight with no complaints."

She waved the telegram. "This is from Fong. He sent it from Anacortes. It says he's on his way to Orcas Island. He ends with, 'Will split bamboo tonight.' What's that mean?"

Sage grinned. "It's great that he made it that far. The bamboo bit means he's going to find a fisherman willing to help out. He always says tackling problems is like splitting bamboo. The first successful cut makes the rest easier. If all goes well, our Mr. Fong will be on Canadian soil tonight. He thinks that's the hardest part. Next, we need to hope he's in time to intercept *The Freeman* and rescue the shanghaied boy.

An hour later, Sage hailed Angus Solomon just as the last customer exited the Portland Hotel dining room.

"Greetings, my friend. I was about to send you a message," Solomon said. He gestured to a table and the two sat, the nephew instantly setting cups of hot coffee at their elbows.

"That nephew of yours is quite diligent," Sage observed.

Solomon smiled. "He lives in fear that I'm going to send him back to his mama. He does not want to return to the Carolinas. He tells me that, while it is not perfect here, he is not as fearful walking the streets. In his off hours, he helps out in the Rutherford brothers' businesses. He hopes to learn both haberdashery and barbering. He is still a bit short on sense but very long on ambition. I hope time grants him sense before ambition trips him into trouble."

Sage chuckled. "You sound just like a doting uncle."

"I suppose that is what I am," Solomon agreed. "But, it is late and you look tired, my friend. Mozart's was busy tonight?"

"Yes, thank God."

His fervent response wrinkled the other man's normally serene brow. Sage told him about Mozart's sick customers. Solomon commiserated, agreeing that food poisoning rumors were the death blow to a restaurant.

"But, we've gone two days now, with no complaints. So, maybe the dairy sickened them, though I can't figure out how—milk is milk. And, Mom and Ida both say it smelled fine and stayed fresher longer than our previous supplies. Still, since they switched back to our original supplier, no illness has been reported." He waved a dismissive hand. "But, forget all that. Did any porter see Noah Yoder aboard a train?"

"Well, I intended to message you with the information that no porter recalls seeing a white boy like Noah. Of course, there is always the possibility he hopped a freight train."

Given what they learned about Noah, Solomon's information simply confirmed their conclusion that the boy hadn't run away, "Everyone says he is a smart, likable, good-hearted, and untroubled kid who loves his dad."

"Certainly, not the type to run away," Solomon agreed.

Sage's lips twisted ruefully, "Nope, which leaves us with worse scenarios to consider. Your comment about hopping the freights indicates what my next step needs to be."

Solomon studied him, his eyes alight with realization. "Time for John Miner to visit his old haunts?"

Sage pushed back from the table and slapped his fedora on his head. "Yup, and I better get cracking if I hope to sleep tonight."

The scruffy man shuffling up to the wind-flicked fire, deep within the alder grove, didn't need to pretend exhaustion. The night felt endless. He'd made the rounds of skid road saloons, sipping just enough watery beer to fit in. John Miner was a familiar sight, known for buying folks beers and sometimes helping them out with a coin or two. What he'd learned this night was that no one had seen a fourteen-year-old, cow-licked kid hanging around or asking about freight-hopping.

This hobo camp was his last stop. Here was where the serious hobos hung out—the itinerants looking for work and hoping for a better life. If Noah Yoder hitched a box car ride, these hobos might have seen him. They'd also be the ones who'd know if Noah tangled with a railroad bull or low-life boxcar robber.

"Wahl, lookee here. It be that John Miner ain't it?" The voice was chipper and welcoming. Sitting his butt on a stump, Sage accepted the tin can of hot coffee thrust into his hands.

"Howdy, Rusty. How you been doing?"

"Oh, bit down now and again. Still, mostly I been keeping fine." Rusty Baker was a regular in this hobo camp. Sage knew the man roomed nearby. He was here because he liked the company he found here. Like most of the men frequenting this camp, Rusty seldom drank. The nearby saloons held little allure. Usually, these men bought a single beer for the free bread and sausage that came with it. It was tales of the road, both somber and funny, that bonded the men around this particular campfire.

"I have a friend, . . ." Sage began.

"Wahl, Mr. Miner, I'd say you've gathered up a passel of friends," Rusty interrupted as he sent a quelling look at the five other men around the campfire. They were strangers and didn't know John Miner or his reputation.

"Why thank you Rusty. I hope you're one of them," Sage said, smiling at Rusty's emphatic nod. "I mean to impose on that friendship by asking two questions."

First, Sage described Noah. None had seen him. Next he queried, "Would you be willing to ask traveling folks if they've seen him? His pa is frightful worried. I'll check back with you in a few days if we still haven't found him."

There was a murmur of assent and as soon as polite, Sage rose and bid them goodnight. He left a small cloth bag containing tobacco, coffee, bread, and a jar of sweet honey on a nearby stump. One of the men began to rise and call after the departing figure. Rusty's hand on his arm stopped him. "No. Never you mind. That's how John Miner does things. He never likes to hear thanks. Irritates him, it does."

NINE

Sage found Hanke sitting at the small kitchen table when he made it downstairs late the next morning. While he ate the eggs and toast Ida set before him, Sage related that none of Solomon's porters saw Noah on a train and neither had the hobos.

"Hell, I knew he'd never steal his pop's money and run away. Fact is, I told you that, right off the bat," Hanke groused.

Sage refrained from noting that Hanke's feelings hadn't been facts. Instead, he imparted other good news. "Lucinda reports that Noah is not being held in any sex house."

Relief lightened Hanke's morose face and Sage followed up by telling the Sergeant they were already following another lead. He cautioned, "I don't want your hopes getting too high because what I'm about to tell you is improbable." Despite that preamble, Hanke leaned forward, his face eager.

Sage took a deep breath before saying, "Fong discovered that a young boy was shanghaied onto a whaler out of Astoria. The timing works if it was Noah and they kept him locked up for a few days and transported him downriver to Astoria. Though it eludes me why anyone would do that."

Sage saw excitement rising in the other man. "Sergeant, you know that it's a stretch to think anyone would transport Noah all the way to Astoria--that's a hundred miles. If they intended to shanghai him onto a ship, Portland is the easiest place for it. Still, Fong's off tracking down that ship. He intends to rescue the kid, whoever he is."

The hope on Hanke's face faded. A moment later, realization struck. "A whaler? This late in the season? You're saying Fong's heading for Alaska? He'll never be able to find that ship up there. Good Lord, man. He'll be too late."

Sage understood the Sergeant's alarm. Sailing this late in the season usually meant the captain was financially desperate and his ship ill-equipped. The prior autumn, Portland's newspapers had stories about two whaling ships that vanished with all hands aboard.

"Thankfully, Fong needn't go all the way to Alaska. The ship is off-loading cargo in Victoria, B.C. That's where he is now, I hope. He's resourceful. If it is Noah, the boy will be home before we know it."

"What if it isn't Noah on that ship? Where else can we look? I fear the boy's dead. That someone's threw his body into the river and it's halfway out to the sea."

The silence between them thickened under the weight of that depressing idea. Sage shook it off. He refused to accept it. "Sergeant, I'm convinced that we've missed something," he said. "Think, man. How often is a local kid murdered or abducted? Hardly ever. The only time I remember is that newsboy a while back. And, from every account, Noah's a smart boy—not one to go into a dangerous situation, unless . . . ." Sage fell silent, pursuing the wisp of an idea that just streaked through his thoughts.

"Unless, what?"

Sage swallowed the last of his coffee and stood. "I don't know—I lost the thought. No point in trying to chase it down. It'll resurface if it has merit. In the meantime, let's walk the route Noah took from the Purity Creamery to the kinetoscope parlor. See if something along the way could have snagged his attention."

Once outside, Hanke led them east, toward the river. The day was clear, crisp, and downright nippy whenever they passed into the shade beneath awnings. Front Street was filled with deafening sounds, the jangle of the electric trolley, delivery van wheels rattling, men shouting while loading and unloading freight, and the iron shoes of horses thudding atop street bricks. Fortunately, the cold air muted the horse manure's stink.

Hanke paused before the Purity Creamery, pointing at an iron hitching ring bolted to the cement curb. "This is where his horse was tied up and where he and I spoke. Last I saw him, he was going that way," he said, pointing south.

"So, we head in that direction. How do we know which parlor he planned to visit?"

Hanke smiled, "He told me. He was so excited. He blurted out everything in his head. He planned to visit the kinetoscope parlor on Salmon between Fourth and Fifth Avenues.

Four blocks later they rounded a corner to head west. Soon they passed the Quality Emporium. Seeing it, Sage decided to tell Hanke about Mozart's bout with food poisoning because the problem seemed to be solved. Besides, the Sergeant was completely trustworthy when it came to keeping secrets.

After telling of the complaints, Sage ended, "It's the darnedest thing. Mrs. Clemens switched back to our previous dairy supplier, Purity Creamery. Since that switch, we've received no complaints. So maybe it was the milk, cream, butter, or cheese. That's strange because she and Ida swear that the Emporium's dairy products were fresher.

"Huh." Hanke came to a dead stop, forcing the pedestrians behind them to step around his formidable figure.

"Huh?" Sage echoed, hoping something had jarred Hanke's memory.

Realizing he was impeding foot traffic, Hanke stepped sideways to stand before a storefront. "You know, about every two weeks I meet up with Eli and Noah for lunch," he began tentatively, seeming to search his memory.

"And, you remember something?"

"I do. I remember that, a few weeks back, Eli told me he squabbled with the owner of the Emporium. A fellow named Block."

"What about?"

"Block wanted to buy Eli's milk. Eli refused to sell to him. He's loyal to Purity," Hanke said, adding, "And it's justified. Purity's owner has his employees looking for Noah. From what Eli says, they're doing it willingly, even on their off hours. They all liked the kid. He's been riding in with his Pa since he was a tyke." Hanke's chin trembled.

After a moment, Sage nudged the man into a safer channel of thought. "According to Eli, there was no other conflict with the Emporium's owner—one that might cause Block to kidnap Noah?"

"Well, I'm not sure. Maybe I'm forgetting something because Eli was pretty het up over the exchange. Seems like it was more than a simple disagreement."

"Tell me about the owner of Quality Emporium? Do you know him?"

Hanke's face showed distaste. "Well, I know of him. His name is Aldus Block. Folks tell me that he's ambitious, greedy, and a bully. He's trying to force his competition out of business. And, he's unfair with his employees."

Sage decided the time had come to clutch at straws. "Their disagreement sounds minor. Still, we better get the full story. How about you send word to Eli? Tell him to come talk to us tomorrow after he makes his morning delivery. Let's meet in your office."

"When I'm back at the station I'll send word through the Cedar Mill general store. Eli says his neighbors are good about bringing him messages. Just to be sure, I'll tell the folks at Purity Creamery. They'll tell him too."

They started walking again and soon reached the kinetoscope parlor. It filled a narrow storefront with tall machines lining both side walls. Several men and boys were bending over the machines, their necks craned down as they peered through the eyepieces. Here and there short boys on tall stools did the same. The parlor owner came bustling up. "Sergeant Hanke, have you found that missing boy?"

"Afraid not, Mr. Reddin. How about you? Any word on the street that might tell us what happened to him?"

The man gave a doleful headshake, saying, "I've asked every customer, and none remember seeing him in here or on the street."

They departed when a boy came up to request change for the machines. Once outside, they strolled in silence until shaking hands outside Mozart's. Hanke headed for Purity and Sage entered the restaurant.

Lucinda came through Mozart's unlocked front door a few minutes after Sage and Hanke left to retrace Noah's steps. She was speaking as she stepped inside. "I am so sorry I'm late. A little upset at the house delayed me and—Oh!" she exclaimed, having just noticed Mae Clemens was not alone. A moment later a smile lit her face and she stepped forward eagerly, her hand outstretched. "Mrs. Trumbull! It's been some time since last I saw you."

The woman rose from the table where she and Mae Clemens sat, smiling in return. "Miss Collins, it is nice to see you again," she said, reaching to shake hands. Millie Trumbull was what the polite call, "a robust lady" and neither beautiful nor pretty. Even handsome might be a stretch. Yet there was strength of character in her firm chin, intelligence in her wide brow, and most of all, compassion in her large brown eyes. The warmth of her greeting was genuine. Theirs was an unusual relationship—the respectable matron and the beautiful brothel house madam. Yet, they had bonded over a mutual hatred of child prostitution.

"It's Lucinda to you!"

Mrs. Trumbull smiled. "Only if you call me, Millie." The women shared a laugh as Mae Clemens smiled with relief. Even though the two women worked together before, Mae had felt somewhat nervous about Trumbull's reaction. Mae loved Lucinda like a daughter and would tolerate no unkindness towards her.

They soon got down to business. Millie Trumbull spoke first. "Well, I received your letter, Mae." She turned to Lucinda, "Mae wrote that we have you to thank for finding the address of the city's newest despicable house." Lucinda nodded so Millie continued, "I checked at city hall and once again, the owner of that building is hiding behind a corporate name. I am hoping that you can discover his identity as well."

Trumbull's jaw set and she said, "It looks like the ladies will be making another fuss. I've called a meeting. I'll let you know when we decide to act. Maybe Mr. Adair will interest that Oregon Journal reporter in our protest, like he did last time."

She paused. sipped tea, patted her lips with a napkin, and changed the subject. "As for the matter of the boy, Noah Yoder, I talked to the director of the Boys and Girls Society Shelter Home. There is no fourteen-year-old boy fitting Noah's description in their custody."

She saw their faces fall and rushed to add, "But, I decided to question some of their recent arrivals. Just on the chance that one of them saw something of Noah while they were living on the streets."

The other two women leaned forward. Millie didn't keep them hanging. "One youngster said he saw something 'funny' around the time Noah disappeared. The boy was sleeping under cardboard against a building. It was early morning. He saw a man with a hand truck wheeling a large wooden crate down the sidewalk and loading it into a closed van."

Mae and Lucinda exchanged disappointed looks. Wooden crates were a common sight on Portland's streets. Millie intercepted their exchange, raised a staying hand and continued, "Maybe I misspoke. It wasn't what he saw that made him think it was peculiar. It was what he heard. Something was alive in the crate because it was banging the sides, making a racket. He heard it as the hand truck rolled past his bit of cardboard shelter and he poked his head out to take a look."

"Where? Where was the poor child sleeping?" Mae asked.

"On Salmon Street, between First and Second."

"Did he see where the hand truck came from?"

Millie shook her head. "I asked. He didn't know. He'd been asleep. It wasn't until the crate rattled past making thumping sounds that he looked out."

The kitchen doors burst open and Ida bustled in, her face flushed and apologetic. A tall, bulky man followed close on her heels. "Mrs. Clemens, I am so sorry to interrupt. This is Mr. Block. He came to the kitchen door and insists on speaking with you. I tried to tell . . . "

Mae cut her off. "It's fine Ida. I will speak to Mr. Block." Mae rose to her feet, chin high, "Hello Mr. Block," she said, not offering her hand.

A smarmy smile lifted the corners of Block's lips while his eyes stayed pebble hard. Mae didn't smile in return.

"Mrs. Clemens, my clerk tells me that you came in and canceled Mozart's standing order. I want to know why. Your first order from us was just a month ago. If we delivered spoiled products I will replace them immediately. Just let me know."

Mae eyed him, seeing the big hands bunched into fists, the puce flush of his face, his bull neck stretched forward, everything telegraphing angry and stubborn. She decided not to tell the man about the food poisoning. He was just the type to spread the story.

"Your product was fine, Mr. Block. We just decided we wanted to continue dealing with Purity Creamery. I make no criticism of your products and will speak of none."

Her reassurance failed to slow the fury gathering in his body. "That dolt at Purity charges more for his dairy than I do!" he exclaimed.

"Yes, I know that," Mae spoke calmly, glancing toward the two women avidly following the exchange.

"I'll not hear you malign my products!" His words came loud and angry.

"As I said, I am not and, I will not, say anything negative about your dairy products," she repeated.

"I can't believe the owner of this establishment agrees with your decision. It makes no financial sense at all. Where is he?"

"He is absent at present. But, he does know of and agrees with my decision."

"I don't believe you! I think you lied to him,"

A look of cunning flashed across the man's countenance. "I know what; Purity's giving you a kickback. That's it!" He grinned at the two women watching the scene as if expecting them to agree with his accusation. Instead, his grin was met by two stony faces staring back at him.

For the first time, Mae Clemens felt her anger rise. She bit it back. No way was this bully was going to drag her down to his level.

The smarmy smile was back, the voice now low and insinuating. "Tell you what, Mrs. Clemens. I'll double whatever Purity is giving you and lower the price of the product by a few cents. You just tell your boss I lowered the price for you. You and I and these ladies here will keep our sweetening arrangement private."

Mae kept her voice level. "Mr. Block, I'll thank you not to malign my integrity. You need to take yourself off, right now. There is nothing more to discuss. At this point, I wouldn't buy from you if you were the last dairy creamery in town." Mae gestured toward the front door.

Block moved toward her but halted when Lucinda jumped up to stand beside Mae, a bread knife in her hand.

He shook a fist in Mae's face. "You'll be sorry. You don't know the man you are dealing with!"

"I didn't, but I certainly do now. Get your fanny out of Mozart's and don't ever return! We exterminate rodents here!" she shot back.

He swiveled on his heel, strode to the front door, and flung it open. The front windows rattled in their frames when he slammed the door shut behind him.

Mae and Lucinda retook their seats. The three women looked at each other, shocked at what they'd just witnessed. Lucinda was the first to speak, "Well, I must say, Mae, I couldn't have handled that as well as you did."

Millie added her emphatic murmur of agreement, saying, "What a dreadful man."

Mae shrugged but noticed her hand shook when she reached for her teacup.

TEN

"You just missed Eli," Hanke said when Sage appeared at his office door.

"Missed him? I thought I was early." Sage was dismayed. Didn't the man want to find his son?

Hanke seemed to read his thoughts. "He was upset that he couldn't stay. He needs to meet folks at the Armory Annex. He's on the committee that's organizing the Grange Convention that's coming to Portland in a few weeks. The committee is meeting at the convention location to finalize the arrangements. He was already late so he asked us to meet him at the Armory Annex."

They set off, deciding to walk the dozen or so blocks to the Annex instead of hiring a cab. Though the sky was leaden, the fat, gray clouds were holding onto their rain.

The Annex was the largest entertainment venue in the city. The wooden trusses supporting its roof made the building unique. Unlike every other venue in town, the trusses created a large open space free of sight-blocking pillars.

"Tell me Hanke, what was the reason for building the Armory? It doesn't seem like there'd be much need for one in the middle of the city."

"Happened in the late 1880s. They expected riots against the Chinese and violent worker strikes. They wanted a close-to-hand base for the National Guard. At the time, Oregon established armories in almost every town for the same reason. The first armory built here was too small for the First Regiment National Guard to drill inside, so they added the Annex."

"The Annex holds a lot of people. How many are expected to attend the Grange convention?"

Hanke brightened. "It's going to be big. We've already held meetings to discuss police protection. Three thousand Grangers are descending on Portland, plus their spouses. That will mean lots of overtime for our officers who, God knows, need the money."

Sage knew what Hanke meant. While the city grew considerably in recent years, neither the number of officers nor their pay rate kept pace. The situation made it hard to recruit and keep officers. It also created an opening for bribery and corruption to creep into the police force.

From a block away, the imposing Annex looked like an ancient fortress with its massive stone facade and two corner turrets crowned by crenellated parapets. Sage eyed the gun slots in the turrets. A shiver twitched up his back at the thought of soldiers shooting people from behind those slots.

They climbed the few steps leading into a semi-circular arcade and entered the building. Once inside, they spotted a mixed group of men and women. Eli Yoder stood among them. Seeing them, he hurried over. "I am so sorry about making you come here," he rushed to say while vigorously shaking Sage's hand.

"No problem. Since it's not raining, the walk was a good way to start the day," Sage reassured, noting the black smudges beneath Eli's eyes. Worry about his son was taking its toll.

Yoder's next words proved him right. "Have you heard anything about my son? About Noah? Was Mr. Fong able to find the ship?"

Sage stated his belief that Fong was already in Victoria but probably still waiting for *The Freeman* to dock. That reassurance given, he moved on to the reason for their meeting. "Eli, the Sergeant says you and the Quality Emporium owner got into a dispute. What was it about?"

"Surely that can't be the reason why Noah's missing."

"Probably not. To be honest with you, Eli, we're flat out of obvious leads. Now we need to follow every trail, no matter how faint. So, please, tell us. What was the argument with Block about?"

"Milk. He wants me to sell to him. I refused. I've been with Purity Creamery ever since my cows started producing. They've always been good to me. Besides, I like how Purity runs its operation."

"Did you tell Block that?"

"Yup. He didn't like it. Started yelling, threatening me and Purity."

"What kind of threats?"

"Said he was going to drive Purity out of business and that, once he did, I'd be without a place to sell my milk."

"Are those threats realistic?"

"Well, the Emporium is underselling Purity. I think Purity has lost customers because of it. As for me not being able to sell elsewhere, that's an empty threat. There are creameries all over. At least twenty are right around Portland, and two new condensed milk factories just started up in Hillsboro and Forest Grove. They'll need milk. So, I wasn't worried. I do worry about Purity, though, they're decent folks."

Sage thought it good that his mother switched their business back to Purity. She'd told him of Block's bullying intrusion of yesterday afternoon. He wanted to confront the man but she talked him out of it. Telling him they had "enough on their plate."

To Yoder, he said, "Why do you say Purity has a better operation?"

Yoder paused to reflect before saying, "Purity has long-term employees. Some of them started there before I've been bringing them my milk. They seem content, cheerful even. More important, the creamery is spotless."

Yoder's nose wrinkled with disgust as he continued, "At Block's initial request I was polite and asked to tour his operation. The workers looked sullen, downtrodden. And, his bottling and buttery area smelled bad and looked dirty."

Earnestly, he leaned forward to say, "Mr. Adair, I take great care to make sure my milk is pure and wholesome. Especially, after I attended a Woman's Club lecture where the two doctors on the City Health Board talked about dairy products. Since hearing them, I've doubled down on making sure our hands and the cow's udders are clean, that the milk is kept chilled, and that the cans are sterilized. Purity sterilizes the empty cans but once I get them home, I sterilize them again just to make sure. I even asked the state dairy inspector to come check my barn. He gave our dairy operation a good rating, though he said my barn's ventilation needs improving."

"I didn't realize the dairies were inspected." Sage said.

Yoder gave doleful headshake. "There's a desperate need for more inspections, yet we have just one inspector. I believe bad milk is killing people. It's long been an important issue for dairy farmers and the Grange. Fact is, if you are interested, the Woman's Club is offering another lecture on that topic late this afternoon. You might want to attend since you're in the restaurant business. I plan on being there."

A Granger approached. Reaching them he said, "I apologize for interrupting gentlemen." He turned to Yoder, "Eli, the Annex building superintendent has arrived to give us a tour and finalize our convention plans. Since you chair the planning committee, I think you're needed."

After again saying he'd be attending the afternoon lecture and telling them its location, Yoder made his apologies and re-joined his group.

Sage looked at Hanke. "I didn't realize milk was such a big deal."

"Me neither," Hanke responded.

Sage and his mother strolled up Washington Street to the Selling-Hirsch Hall. They'd been freed from the restaurant by Ida. She drafted her nephew, Matthew, to help with the late afternoon tea time. Their waiter, Homer, also agreed to come in early.

"Goodness," declared Mae when they reached the hall. "That is one fancy building."

They stood between 9th and 10th streets, across from the block-long, three-story, brick-and-stone building. Its pitched roof, ten ornately trimmed segments, and entrance cupola justified the word, "fancy." He studied the people gathered around its entrance and spotted Yoder and Hanke waiting as promised.

Once inside, they climbed stairs to the third floor. Sage was surprised to see the hall half-way full with about two hundred people, two-thirds of them women. Yoder waved a greeting at an already seated group that Sage recognized as the Grangers he'd seen at the Annex. Yoder kept moving toward the front of the hall, leading them to four seats along one side.

Three women and one man sat waiting on the small, raised stage. The crowd quieted when one of the women rose and approached the podium. She was an imposing, square-faced matron, with deep-set eyes and a determined jaw. Her unamplified voice was clear and loud enough to be heard by all.

"Good afternoon, ladies and gentlemen. My name is Sarah Evans. On behalf of the Portland Woman's Club, I welcome you to this lecture. We are honored to present three distinguished speakers today. Our topic is the need for pure food legislation. Our first speaker is Dr. Esther Pohl, a member of the City's Health Board. She will be followed by Dr. Victoria Hampton. She is the physician to that Board and her talk will be followed by Dr. Woods Hutchinson. He serves as Secretary to the State Board of Health.

Sage knew Dr. Pohl by sight. He'd seen her at various events and she occasionally dined at Mozart's. He'd liked her forthright, plain-speaking ways, and sense of humor.

Pohl took the podium and launched into her talk. "Greetings, I appreciate the opportunity to speak to you. It is always an honor to speak before this fine organization. I note that the Oregon Daily Journal recently reported the Club as being filled with "Earnest women who are operating the chief levers of civic progress." Her nod in Sarah Evan's direction elicited scattered titters from the group, the reason for the amusement flying over Sage's head.

Pohl continued, "I warn you, I am here to ask that you pull those levers with all your might. My first request is that you demand the city create the position of market inspector. My second request is that you demand that the city enact local pure food legislation."

She paused to survey her audience before saying, "Now, let me tell you why both are necessary. I will give you a brief overview. As for the specifics, I defer to the expertise of my esteemed colleagues here on the stage with me." She nodded toward Hampton and Hutchinson. Pohl kept her following words short and to the point.

"President Roosevelt's message this year emphasized the importance of pure foods, and indirectly underscored the importance of chemical laboratories for the detection of impurities, adulterations, and preservatives. At present Portland has more than enough work to employ both a bacteriologist and a chemist full-time.

"We have neither. We lack a chemist to identify food poisoned by additives. We lack a bacteriologist to discover the germs in our food. Nor is there a market inspector empowered to seize and send suspected foodstuffs to be tested. We desperately need a local ordinance creating these three positions as well as the funds to buy the necessary testing equipment and supplies."

Anger charged her next words as she leaned forward over the podium to say, "The State is unhelpful. The Food and Dairy Commissioner has proven hostile to the idea of a city ordinance governing these matters. He assures the public that our food is safe and that a local ordinance will hurt commercial interests. He is wrong. His opposition means, at this point, that for us to ask the State to guard our city's health is like asking a seller to guard his purchaser. It isn't going to happen until hell freezes over."

She paused, as if gathering her thoughts, then continued, "We need to find and condemn all diseased and unwholesome meats, dairy, vegetables, and fruits sold in our markets. The issuance of any license to sell prepared foods and milk in the city should depend on the conditions under which these foods are created, prepared and packaged. No milkman, merchant, or restaurateur maintaining unsanitary conditions should be licensed to do business in Portland."

Her voice was stern as she raised a cautionary finger and said, "In the meantime, do not trust the labels on your foods. Be extremely cautious about what your family eats. An example of the danger you face can be found in the farce of the so-called 'sanitary' milk bottle.

"Today, the label 'sanitary' guarantees nothing. While that bottle may have been sterilized before filling, it also may have stood at the bedside of a person with an infectious disease or been used as a drinking cup, collected, simply rinsed out, and passed along the line with a fresh "Sanitary" label attached."

She chuckled grimly at the gasps that followed that assertion before saying, "Now that I've scared the bejesus out of you, I turn this podium over to Dr. Victoria Hampton. She will do an even better job of scaring you than I have. By way of introduction, in addition to being a licensed physician serving the City Board of Health, Dr. Hampton is also a skilled chemist and one of the city's few forensic scientists." Pohl nodded at Hampton and retook her seat.

Sage snuck a glance at Yoder and was pleased to see him clapping as hard as the rest of the audience.

An unsmiling Hampton took her place before the podium. She was a pretty, whip-thin woman with a mass of dark hair and heavy-lidded eyes dominating an oval face. She looked to be almost two decades younger than Sarah Evans and near Dr. Pohl's age. Once she began speaking, all thoughts of her appearance vanished from Sage's mind to be replaced by rising alarm.

In the end, Hampton and Hutchinson's lectures lasted half an hour followed by another half-hour of questions and answers. Once the session concluded, Mae and Sage headed down the stairs and outside. Dr. Pohl called it right. The imparted information was so worrisome that only snippets of what Hampton and Hutchinson said stuck with Sage. Their focus had been on dairy products. Because anger had overwhelmed his thoughts, only their most startling assertions lodged in his memory.

The Secretary to the State Board, Hutchinson, was a sincere, forceful speaker. In appearance, he was a slender, big-eared man whose eyebrows, slanting up towards the middle of his forehead, gave him a look of perpetual astonishment. Like Pohl, he also urged funding of a market inspector, one with police powers. His focus was impure, dirty milk. To prove his point, he asked an usher to pass around bottles of milk. When one reached Sage, the brown sediment in the bottom of the bottle was unmistakable.

Hutchinson went on to report that out of the nine Portland milk samples he tested, three were pure, three contained foreign matter and sediment, and three contained pus cells indicating that the milk came from infected cow udders. The audience gasped at his assertion that Portland's impure milk tested at a level of over four million bacteria in one teaspoon. His concluding statement was that some of the city's milk contained more bacteria than he'd found when testing the city's sewage outflow.

Despite her dry, scientific delivery of facts, Dr. Hampton's comments were equally disturbing. She also focused on dairy but from the angle of adulteration. Her initial statements caused Sage and Mae to stiffen. She reported that her tests showed not a single city milk sample was fit to drink because she found preservatives or embalming fluids in them all.

She called the State Dairy Commissioner's claims of unadulterated milk grossly misleading since the State's chemists did not test for poisons like coal tar and other preservatives. Sage and Mae exchanged startled looks when Hampton noted that the milk, cream and butter adulterated with coal tar-based preservatives or embalming fluid thickened and never soured or spoiled."

Now that the lecture was over Sage and Mae were standing on the sidewalk in stunned silence when Yoder and Hanke joined them.

Yoder asked, "Well, what are your thoughts on the lecture?"

"I'm alarmed and angry by what those doctors told us," Sage responded.

Yoder nodded. "Yup, we need that ordinance Dr. Pohl wants. That's why we Grange folks are joining up with the Woman's Club. We're going to push for pure food legislation together at both the state and local level."

"The Grangers are active in that effort?" Sage was puzzled.

"Yup," Pride infused Yoder's words as he continued, "The National Grange was the first national organization to make pure food legislation one of its goals. We voted for it fifteen years ago, in 1889. The Oregon Grange adopted it soon after. We've lobbied for it ever since. So far, the big food processors are fighting us tooth and nail. We're more hopeful now that Roosevelt's in office and women are stepping up their involvement."

Mae spoke up for the first time. "Why are the Grangers so interested in it?"

"Self-respect and self-preservation, mostly." Yoder elaborated, "We feed the country. Most farmers are proud of that and work hard to produce quality food. The problem is that so many people are moving into the cities. That's given rise to large-scale industrial processing. The industrial processor is free to do whatever he wants to the food. As a consequence, the food quality and safety has gone way, way, down."

He took a deep breath and elaborated, "Used to be, a farmer would meet the consumers of his product in his local community. Seeing and knowing them, and how fast word spreads in communities, he daren't sell bad food. That's no longer the case. Nowadays, food travels clear across the country to reach your table. There is no way to know how or where it was grown or processed or what's been added to it."

For a moment, weariness sagged his face. "That's true even when the producing cows are just up the road. We farmers no longer sell our milk products direct to our neighbors. Now it's the creameries processing huge batches, using milk from god knows where. Believe me; I've seen some of those dairies. You wouldn't want to drink anything coming out of them. As Dr. Hutchinson said, some of them and their animals are filthy. And, Dr. Hampton is absolutely correct when she says additives are being put into dairy products."

Sage asked the question lurking in the back of his mind throughout the lectures. "What's the economic impact on the dairy farmers? I've been trying to puzzle that out."

"Well, if dirty milk keeps sickening people, they'll stop buying it altogether. Worse, adulteration's really costing us. If the milk, cream, and butter never spoil, they can be sold for a much longer time than any pure product. Adulteration creates a surplus that drives down the price paid to the farmer."

"You certainly seem well-versed about the problem," Sage commented.

Yoder laughed. "I recently was part of a delegation that visited Salem. We talked to the governor and the legislators. So, I learned our spiel backwards and forwards."

Yoder cleared his throat, his words becoming hesitant, "I know it's useless to ask again, but is there any word from up north since I last saw you? Anything at all from Mr. Fong?"

Sage told him "No" and watched despair wash across the man's face.

ELEVEN

Fong's belly was full. The night before, he found a decent noodle house. Tender noodles with fish balls made for a delicious, hearty breakfast. Even better, the owner rented him a cot in the restaurant's storeroom. Early this morning, he learned the location of *The Freeman's* expected moorage and stationed himself on a nearby stack of cut lumber. There he sat, the stiff sea breeze chilling his face. To keep warm, he thought of Kum Ho, her peach blossom eyes bright with humor and love. She was his greatest treasure.

As high tide reached its peak, a ship rounded the point. Nearing the inner harbor it was clear that it wallowed, burdened by age and sheets of copper. That was not a good sign. There was no telling how worm-eaten and rotten the hull was beneath that sheeting.

At least the helmsman proved competent because the docking ship gently nudged the wharf. Before anyone jumped to tie off, Fong was shipside, catching the thrown mooring lines and looping them around the bollards.

Seconds later, a gangplank spanned the gap between ship and wharf and the men of *The Freeman* quickly disembarked. "Thank you, Chinaman," said one sailor as he passed Fong who'd returned to his pile of lumber. There was no boy among the scruffy crew. Of course, anyone shanghaied wouldn't be allowed ashore. If the boy was on board, he'd be locked up.

A portly man strode onto the deck and spoke to two men remaining aboard. His confident stance and gestures indicated that he was the captain and issuing orders. Both men looked unhappy as they nodded their heads. The apparent captain gave one of them a friendly cuff on the shoulder and crossed to the wharf. After casting a sharp eye in Fong's direction, he stomped away toward town. The man had the red veins and puffy eyes of a daily drinker. More bad news for those sailing aboard *The Freeman*.

Once the captain rounded the distant warehouse corner and was out of sight, the two men on the ship also crossed the gangplank to the wharf. They stayed shipside, stumping up and down as if trying to lose their sea legs. After a few minutes, they advanced to stand before him, hands on their hips. He straightened and sent them a hesitant smile.

"What you doing here, Chinaman?" asked the man with gaps between and on both sides of two big front teeth. Fong thought he looked like a beaver.

"No talky English. Want load, unload, ship."

The two men exchanged a look with the beaver one saying, "No load, unload until tomorrow."

"You cook?" asked the other.

Fong made a show of wrinkling his brow. "Me cook? Sure. Cook good."

Beaver glanced at his companion. "Jack didn't the captain say we needed a ship's cook after that last mess you fried up."

"Hey, now. I never claimed I knew how to cook. I sure never signed on to be one."

"Yeah, well. There weren't much choice after Cookie jumped ship in Astoria."

"How about we try him out?" Jack said.

The men's attention returned to Fong. Beaver pointed a dirty finger at the ship and then jabbed it at Fong, saying, "Chinaman, you go cook?"

Fong gave a vehement head shake. "Me no sail ship."

Both men exchanged looks again and Beaver held up a finger as he said, "One time, only. No sail." He held out a coin.

Fong nodded and took the money. "I cook," he said and crossed the gangplank before they changed their minds.

They followed close behind, the one called Jack saying in a low voice, "If this Chink cooks decent, we'll keep him."

"Hell, yeah. 'No sail' my arse," agreed Beaver with a chortle.

Once on deck, Fong paused. He knew about sailing ships, having worked his passage from Canton to Mexico on one. *The Freeman* was barely seaworthy. Rot freckled the deck planks, frayed rigging dangled above, copper held the hull together, and the furled sails, lying against mast and boom, looked more patched than whole. The ship's condition was testimony to kerosene's negative impact on the whale oil business.

"When ship sail?" he asked.

"Tomorrow night, with the tide," Beaver responded.

Jack stepped around Fong and headed toward the rear of the ship, saying. "Come with me, I'll show you the galley."

As with most ships, the cooking area sat behind the main deckhouse. Fong saw with some approval that the rear deck housed chickens in cages and goats in pens. At least there'd be eggs and butter for the captain and his mate. If this was like most ships, the rest of the crew would eat watery, salt meat stew out of a common pot.

Weak light shone through a porthole, revealing a small, narrow galley. Overhead, unlit whale oil lanterns hung from hooks driven into the ceiling beam. Casks, barrels, and boxes filled the spaces beneath a wooden counter along one side while the walls supported shelves stacked with cans, bins, and bags. Tall woven baskets, filled with apples, potatoes, and other produce, crowded the aisle. At its end stood a small, iron cook stove. It sat in a box of sand atop a layer of bricks. Big open crates filled with coal stood on either side of the stove. Iron pots and pans hung from walls and beams. Every available space overflowed with unwashed dishes, even the floor held crusted pots, leaving just a narrow path open.

Jack looked embarrassed when Fong shot a questioning glance over his shoulder. "Umm, sorry for the mess," he muttered before backing out. Fong sighed and started to work. As the ship rocked gently, he scrubbed, tidied, and cooked. An hour later, he carried tin plates to the two men playing cards in the main cabin. They dug in eagerly, grinning at each other after the first bites.

As he was bringing in a steamed apple pudding for their dessert, he heard Jack say through a mouthful of stew and biscuit, "What say, we keep him?"

Fong smiled to himself.

Once they'd fed and burped, Beaver pointed at his plate, held up two fingers, and said, "Fix two more plates."

Fong nodded and hurried back to the galley hoping that the two extra plates meant two prisoners were aboard. When Jack stood, took the plates, and disappeared out the door onto the deck, Fong hurried back into the galley and slipped outside. He was in time to see Jack raise the forward hatch and give the plates to hands reaching up from the hold.

That sight gave Fong immense satisfaction. There was a folded paper baked into one of those biscuits. It said, "Get ready to run."

Fong was thoughtful as he cleaned the galley. He'd free the two prisoners once the sky darkened. At present, Jack and Beaver posed the only threat. Later, the others might return to their bunks. And tomorrow, there'd be cargo handling with the full crew aboard. Besides, Jack and Beaver might launch their shanghai attack at any time given their plan to "keep him."

Once the men left to walk the deck, Fong stole through the main room and into the captain's quarters. A low cupboard beneath the row of portholes sported a large padlock. Fong smiled, took a letter opener off the captain's desk, and soon the lock swung free. As he expected, whiskey bottles filled the cabinet. He took one, locked the cabinet, and headed back to the galley. There he filled two tin cups with the captain's brew before carrying them out to the two men. They took the cups, sniffed, and stared at each other.

"Where the heck did you find this hooch, little man?" Beaver asked.

Fong made his face look confused. So, Beaver rephrased, "Where you get?" he demanded, pointing at his cup.

"Galley have," Fong responded, feigning mystified innocence at the question.

Surprised, the men exchanged yet another look. Jack supplied an explanation. "Betcha it's Cookie's stash that he forgot to grab when he took off."

The men shrugged, grinned at each other, and downed the captain's whiskey. Minutes later, they took the precaution of checking on Fong. He lay curled into a ball on the galley floor, pretending to doze. Fifteen minutes later, he rose. Tiptoeing to look, he found them snoozing, their heads down on the table.

Fong again exited out the galley door and sped across the deck to the forward hatch. Heavy clouds darkened the night so he lit the lantern he'd carried from the galley, raised the hatch, and shone its light into the hold. Below two people stared up at him. One was a man with tufted hair, a narrow face, and squinting eyes. The other was a boy, his face fearful.

Fong whispered, "You find message?'

The two below nodded.

"Hurry up ladder. Come out quick." Fong lifted the lantern and backed away.

There was no need to say it twice because they instantly scrabbled up the wooden ladder to the deck.

Leaving the hatch open, Fong gestured at the gangplank. As they stepped in that direction, trouble appeared. Jack and Beaver apparently could hold their liquor better than he'd figured.

"Just what the hell do you think you're doing, Chinaman?" growled Beaver.

"I am escorting this man and boy to safety," Fong said, grinning when his improved English startled the two.

"Like hell you are!" Beaver started across the thirty feet between them. Fong sensed the man from the hold moving forward, intending to join the confrontation. Fong threw him a warning glance and said, "No. I handle. First chance, you get boy off ship. Run fast away. I catch up."

Taking a single step toward the sailors, Fong dropped into the bow stance and waited, knowing he looked both small and ineffectual. Beaver paused, his brow wrinkling until, with a roar, he charged forward, his fists raised, confident he'd make short work of the much smaller man standing between him and the two captives.

That didn't happen. Beaver's swinging fist gave Fong a fine opportunity. A quick grab and twist deflected the man to one side. He flew past to slam into the main mast. All was quiet.

Fong's focus stayed on Jack who stepped forward with his fists raised.

Out of the corner of his eye, Fong saw the two escapees standing frozen, their attention riveted on the fight. "You go now," he ordered, using the sharpness in his voice to break their trance and spur them into fleeing. They took to their heels, with Fong moving to shield them from Jack. Moments later thuds sounded as they ran away down the wharf.

"Damn, you! The captain's gonna have our hide!" Jack growled as he snatched a metal belaying pin from the bulwark and took a swing. Fong dropped and it swished harmlessly over his head.

Fong regretted that there wasn't time to play more gently with the two sailors. He couldn't lose track of the man and boy. This fight needed to finish quickly.

Jack swung again, this time aiming at Fong's gut.

Fong stepped forward, chopping the outside edge of his right palm into Jack's elbow as his left hand seized the man's forearm. That maneuver drove the pin downward until Fong twisted the man's striking arm up and over Jack's back. To escape the intense pain, Jack dropped the pin and bent over, allowing Fong's knee to thrust upward into his stomach. With an oomph, Jack dropped onto the deck and lay gasping.

Boots scraped as Beaver lunged from behind. Fong whirled, his right foot slicing in a high arc, delivering a hard kick alongside the man's head. Beaver collapsed, unconscious, the knife in his hand clattering to the deck.

Fong yanked Jack up by the back of his overalls and frog-marched him to the hold. Once there, Fong said, "Climb down ladder or I throw you." Jack's feet quickly found the topmost rung and he descended. Fong dropped the hatch cover.

Next, Fong drug the unconscious Beaver to the hold. Raising the hatch, he rolled the man over the edge, slammed the hatch down, and shot the bolts. Without pausing he raced away, a smile on his face. Good outcome, he congratulated himself.

Once across the gangplank, a look down the long wharf told him the man and boy had, indeed, fled. He couldn't see them anywhere. He took off running, hoping he'd be able to find them among the wren of warehouses.

It was an unnecessary worry. As he reached the end of the wharf, a hiss sounded from the deep gloom followed by a whispered, "We're over here." He slipped around a stack of wooden crates and sure enough, there waited the man and boy, both of them filthy, hollow-cheeked, and breathing heavily.

"Whoever you are mister, you just saved our lives. Thanks be to God for what you did. We couldn't run off until we saw that you escaped," He grabbed Fong's hand and shook it vigorously.

"You sound like Englishman," Fong responded.

"Ah, I am of sorts. A Scot by birth but London-raised. Name's Abner McBride."

"You been Victoria before?"

The man shook his head. "I rode trains from New York to Astoria where I was supposed to meet my cousin. He never showed. I ordered me a beer and next thing I know, I'm coming to, aboard that damn hell ship, locked up in the hold with this boy."

They both looked at the boy beside the man, his fearful face pale and his body shivering.

Though Fong thought he already knew the answer, he asked, "What is name, boy?"

With trembling lips the boy stuttered, "No . . . Noah Yoder, Sir."

Fong smiled, telling the Scot, "Follow me now. I show you British consul office. In morning, you go there."

He set off walking with the two trailing behind. He'd seen the office the day before. Like Laidlaw's, it sat close to the harbor. Once they stood before it, Fong told McBride, "Take this money. Find bath, place to sleep. Stay far from saloons and harbor."

The man stood dumbfounded until he cleared his throat to say, "I, I, I don't understand. First, you risk your life to free us and now you give us money?"

Fong gave him a toothy grin. "Today your lucky day. That money for you. I keep Noah. Take him to father."

The man looked alarmed and said, "I'm not sure I should just hand Noah over to you. I'm very grateful for the rescue but he's so young and we're in another country. I feel responsible for him."

"You a good man," Fong said and turned to the saucer-eyed boy. "This note for you, young Noah," he said, handing Yoder's letter to him. The boy stepped beneath a nearby streetlamp to read it.

When he looked up, he was grinning even as tears poured down his face. He waved the paper at the man, "It's okay, Mr. MacBride. This note is from my father, I recognize his handwriting. I am to go with Mr. Fong. He's going to take me home to my Pa!"

After heartfelt exchanges of goodbyes, MacBride set off. "I'll hole up in a decent rooming house until that damn hell ship sails," he declared as he strode resolutely away from the waterfront.

Once MacBride was out of sight around a corner, Noah asked. "How are we getting all the way home from Canada?"

Fong, his face sober, said, "That good question." After a beat, he cracked a smile and asked, "Can you swim, young Noah?"

TWELVE

Sage suppressed an exasperated huff upon seeing a glum Sergeant Hanke once again sitting at the kitchen table. Whatever the news, it couldn't be too bad since the plate before the Sergeant was empty. Nodding at the police officer he headed to the coffee urn. Back at the small table, he took his first sip of the day.

"Sergeant, you look as if your favorite goat just died. What's happened?"

"Before we talk about that, any word from Fong?

Sage shook his head. "It's too soon for him to telegraph. Things are pretty tough for the Chinese up in B.C. right now. He's not free to move around. He'll need to get word to us without drawing attention to himself. So, tell me what's happened. Why are you looking so upset?"

Hanke took a drink of his own coffee before saying, "Eli Yoder's in trouble. After the lecture yesterday, before heading home, he stopped by the Quality Emporium. Aldus Block was there and they tussled. A nearby officer got involved and called for me because he knew I was Eli's friend. We had no choice. We arrested Eli."

"Why? What do you think he did?"

"He took a swing at Block. Knocked him into a shelf holding glass jars of stuff that fell to the floor and broke, making a big mess. Eli didn't have the money to pay for the damage. Plus, he admits to being the first to hit."

"What charges does he face?"

"Right now, assault and disturbing the peace."

"He still in jail?"

"Yup. They'll set bail this morning."

"Did you find out what happened? Why Yoder slugged Block?"

"Conflicting stories. Block says Eli stormed in and started swinging."

"And Yoder? What's he say?"

"He says that he stopped in the store just to ask if anyone saw Noah the day he disappeared. Like us, he was retracing the boy's footsteps, stopping in every one of the stores along the route. When he entered the Emporium, he says Block got hostile. Told Eli that his son probably ran away because Eli was a shitty parent. Eli admits he snapped and hit Block. Says the goods got broken by accident. Didn't know his own strength." Hanke's smile was rueful as he added. "Must be all those hay bales he tosses."

"Well, I'll go the bail. What's the cost of the damage?"

"No more than five dollars."

Sage dug in his pocket and handed Hanke a twenty-dollar Double Eagle. "How about you pay Block for the damage plus extra on your way back to the station? Urge him not to press charges. If the bail is more than ten dollars let me know."

"Thanks! I'll give it a try." The big policeman stood, picked up his helmet, and turned it in his fingers. Sage rose to face him.

"Mr. Adair, I'm getting worried about Eli. He's acting hopeless. I don't know how much longer he'll hold on. And, if he loses it, . . ." Hanke's words trailed off, with the lingering silence finishing his thought. With a sigh, Hanke slapped the helmet on his head and stepped out the kitchen's back door into the rain.

By late afternoon, Sage's anxiety was up. Two days gone and still nothing from Fong. He hung on to the explanation he'd given Hanke—because Fong couldn't move freely in B.C., sending a telegram took some maneuvering and therefore some time. Still, worry was beginning to overtake his thoughts. A simple check of Fong's papers would land him, first in jail, and then on a slow boat to China.

Mozart's supper hour brought a welcome distraction. The doctors, Esther Pohl and Victoria Hampton came in, their umbrella's dripping water. He shook and potted the umbrellas before showing them to a table. After seating them and giving them menus, he said. "I much enjoyed, though "enjoyed" is not the proper term, your talks of yesterday afternoon."

Pleasure brightened their faces. "Oh, it is gratifying to hear that you attended. We always like to see people in the food business taking an interest in our efforts," Dr. Pohl responded.

Sage gestured to the empty chair at the table. "May I?"

"Of course! But, I warn you, we'll need an additional chair if Dr. Lane shows up as promised. One never knows with him." The smile on Pohl's face was indulgent. Sage wasn't Lane's only admirer.

Homer came to take the ladies' orders. Once he was gone, Sage told them about Mozart's bout of food poisoning. "We intended to request your assistance in identifying the problem, Dr. Hampton. But then Mrs. Clemens switched our dairy orders back to our original supplier. That seemed to do the trick. We've received no further word of a customer becoming ill."

"I'm not surprised it was the dairy," Dr. Hampton said. "We so desperately need an inspector for the city's creameries. The State's started inspecting the nearby farms but, once the dairy product is out of the farmer's hands, what happens to it? We don't know."

"Mrs. Clemens was with me at your lecture, Dr. Hampton. After hearing about the coal tar preservatives and how embalming fluid thickens milk and stops it from souring, we concluded she made the right decision. Those characteristics exactly described the dairy products we had been receiving from our new supplier."

"Who, may I ask, was that new supplier?" Hampton questioned.

"The Quality Emporium. Its owner was furious when we withdrew our business."

The look shared between the two doctors seemed knowing rather than surprised.

Observing it, Sage asked, "You've found problems at that business?"

Pohl said, "Far be it from us to cast aspersions, at this point. However, I believe Mrs. Clemens made an excellent decision to switch back to your former supplier."

Hampton leaned forward to say quietly, "I'd never drink or eat any dairy from the Emporium. There's a pound of Emporium butter in my ice box. It's been there for over a year. It has yet to spoil." Her small nose wrinkled in disgust.

"You talked about coal tar preservatives. I don't understand what they are or how they relate to food," Sage commented.

Hampton nodded. "It does seem a stretch, doesn't it? They are used to dye food, make it more attractive and to preserve it. I am sure you are familiar with creosote?"

"You mean what's used to preserve wood—like railroad ties? That's in our food? I thought creosote was an insecticide." When Hampton raised an eyebrow, he continued, "And, the embalming fluid. How does it work?"

"Formaldehyde is used for embalming because it hardens all biological matter and so prevents its decay. It can't be good for living matter. God knows what either one of those additives does to a human body's internal workings."

"Would those preservatives explain our customers' vomiting and diarrhea?" he asked in a low voice after glancing at those sitting nearby. This wasn't a good supper-time topic.

Pohl jumped in, also keeping her voice low. "The human body is quite miraculous. Most times it knows when it is being poisoned and does its best to eliminate the poison. So, yes, your customers' illness makes perfect sense.

"But, science doesn't know what impact small, repetitious doses of those preservatives have on the body. We suspect they undermine the body's ability to fight disease and, over time, it's anybody's guess what harm their buildup causes."

"Well, well," sounded a hearty voice from over Sage's shoulder. "It seems my favorite doctors are discussing my favorite topic!"

Sage looked up at Dr. Harry Lane. Jumping to his feet, Sage shook the doctor's hand. "Dr. Lane, it is good to see you again." His enthusiasm was unfeigned. Previously, Lane helped Sage and his friends rescue a young boy and his family from death and disease.

When Sage gestured Lane toward the chair he'd vacated, Lane raised a staying hand. "Please, Mr. Adair, don't leave on my account. I am gratified to see someone who wants to learn about our poisoned and diseased food supply. Fetch yourself a chair and join us."

"Harry, keep your voice down. We are sitting in a full restaurant after all. Once again, you've shown your lack of commonsense when it comes to polite table conversation," Pohl admonished as she dipped her head toward those sitting at the neighboring tables. Sure enough, Lane's words had effectively got their attention. They were staring at him with a mix of curiosity and alarm.

Lane looked momentarily contrite and lowered his voice. "Oops, sorry."

Once Sage was seated, Lane continued, "I refuse to believe that God Almighty intended grown humans to drink milk. No other animal drinks it after being weaned. Milk's a bad habit. Statistics show that half of the infants fed on impure milk die. Dr. Hutchinson has established that a teaspoon of impure milk contains millions of bacteria."

Lane was on a roll because he raised a finger to stop Pohl's attempted interruption and continued. "Even in a teaspoonful of good milk, there are still thousands of the little beasts. If we take the child and put him to drinking this so-called "good" milk he dies also at a higher rate than breastfed children. If we sterilize the so-called good milk he still dies at a higher rate. So, it's the milk and not just the microbes."

Sage's glance at the two women caught them rolling their eyes. Pohl noticed he'd seen and explained, "Harry has climbed atop his current soap box now that the problem of the night soil jars in the vegetable garden has been mysteriously resolved. Right, Harry?"

Her reference to the shotgun-blasted jars elicited silence and a sly smile from the People's Doctor.

Hampton leaned forward and said, "Harry, you've never given an adequate answer to the problem of the poor woman unable to nurse her child."

"She does what women have done for centuries—finds a wet nurse."

Hampton shook her head. "You must think wet nurses grow on trees. There aren't nearly enough of them available. It was a plentitude of serfs, slaves, and dire poverty that made wet nurses possible. It's no longer a solution in these modern times. Women are working outside the home and are unavailable to wet nurse. Even unemployed women aren't willing to take on that role."

Lane shrugged and took a sip of his coffee before changing the subject. "You know, Adair, I see your help as crucial to passing the pure food legislation."

"Me?"

"Oh, don't be coy, now. This restaurant is patronized by the richest folks in the city, many of them being our city fathers. And, you serve food. All of which means your words carry a lot of weight with those powers that be."

The two women nodded and in the ensuing silence, three pairs of eyes drilled into him.

He felt cornered. "Well, I guess that's so. I'd need to know a lot more to speak with any authority on the subject. I mean, I guess I know enough to talk about dairy thanks to our conversation tonight. But the pure food legislation is about more than dairy isn't it?"

Sage ended up being sorry he asked that particular question because it released a flood of facts. Way more than he wanted to know. They spouted examples until he wondered whether any food existed that wasn't adulterated, dirty, or diseased. When he asked that question, they agreed pure food was difficult to find. They filled his ears with so much disgusting information, that it sent him "a bit off his feed" as his mother noted in the days that followed.

Release came when he noticed his mother waving a flimsy slip of yellow paper at him from between the kitchen doors. He made his excuses, promising he'd consider becoming involved. Unsaid was his belief that involvement in such a progressive cause would damage his cover. Still, he intended to find out where Mozart's got all its foodstuffs. He also planned to use only those local suppliers who allowed him to inspect their facilities.

Mae waited just inside the kitchen. She handed him the paper. It was a telegram from Fong.

"I can't figure out your and Fong's code. Does it say what I hope it says?"

"Yup. If Hanke turns up, tell him Fong has Noah. If he doesn't turn up, send him a message. I might not be back until late."

He exited the kitchen and soon returned, wearing his rain slicker, boots, and a wide-brimmed hat.

"Where are you going?" she called after him as he headed out the back door.

"To find a horse," he threw over his shoulder as the door slammed shut behind him.

THIRTEEN

The situation in Victoria turned complicated. It was dusk and raining hard when Fong and Noah stepped through the back door into the noodle house kitchen. The owner took one look at Noah, his eyes grew big, and he rushed forward, his hands outstretched, trying to push them back out the door. "No, no white boy. Big trouble."

Fong replied in rapid Chinese, his words calming the man. Fong looked at Noah. "Show Mr. Tang paper from father."

Dutifully, Noah pulled it from his pocket and handed it to the man who glanced at it before going to the swinging door into the restaurant's dining room and hollering something in Chinese. A boy about Noah's age popped into the kitchen. He was handed the paper, the noodle house owner saying with pride, "Grandson read English good."

Upon hearing the boy's translation, his grandfather's attitude changed. "Okay. You stay in storeroom this night only. Tomorrow you go."

Fong nodded but returned to the alley doorway. From there he and Noah watched the storm roll in, its rainclouds black and heavy, pushed eastward by a vicious wind. Such weather never cleared in a single day. Until it did, they were stuck in Victoria. So was *The Freeman*, unless the captain was an idiot. That was one more reason to stay hidden until the gale departed. They dare not encounter any of that ship's crew.

He'd arranged for the fishing boat to anchor offshore every night. That couldn't happen this night. It was too dangerous to venture onto the sea in such a violent storm. Tomorrow night was the soonest they could rendezvous with the boat, but only if the storm abated.

The owner returned to shoo them into the storeroom. He came back a few minutes later carrying a second straw-stuffed pallet for Noah. Next, he brought some well-worn towels. That was followed by two bowls of noodle soup, cups, and a pot of tea. "You stay here. No go into restaurant."

His face was grim as he accepted Fong's coins. "You go tomorrow," he insisted.

Once they'd dried their hair, shed their soaked coats, and filled their stomachs, Noah asked, "How do you know my pa?"

"He is friend of Sergeant Hanke who is my friend too." Fong decided he might as well tackle the most important question.

"Tell me, Noah. How you end on whaling ship?"

"I was checking something out. Next thing I know, someone grabs me and slaps something cold and wet on my face. After that, I don't remember much until I woke up crammed into a wooden crate. They took me somewhere in a wagon. It took a long time. I was hungry, I needed to pee, and the cramps from being all squeezed up like that, made me want to bawl like a scared calf. Once the wagon stopped, they loaded the crate onto a boat. It was a small boat because the engine sounded right next to the crate. Anyway, the boat rode on the water because I felt it bobbing and heard water slapping its sides.

Once we docked, two people lifted the crate out. I knew it was two because I heard them cursing. The crate lid came off and they pushed that wet stuff onto my face again. When I came to, I was in the ship's hold. A few minutes later, they dropped Mr. MacBride down next to me."

"What happen after that?"

Noah's face stiffened with recollection. "Me and Mr. MacBride agreed we wouldn't cooperate. So, every time they made us climb on the deck, we crossed our arms and refused to work. They smacked us a few times. Nothing serious. We figured they didn't want to damage their future crew members."

He took a deep breath. "We agreed that once the ship sailed from Port Victoria, we'd start working because, otherwise, they said no work, no food, except for feeding us to the fish. That sailor, Jack, told us the ship's sailing straight to the Bering Sea. It won't touch land again until whale bits fill the hold."

Fong imagined the fear this young boy had endured. For certain, MacBride deserved rescuing. Without him, Noah Yoder might not have survived.

Noah's face scrunched and his words were earnest when he asked, "Mr. Fong. Why are some men so cruel? Are they born that way?"

Fong shook his head and after a moment said, "I tell you story about that. It comes from ancient wise man, name of Meng Tzu."

> Once big trees shade the hill outside city. They cool water that ran down the hill. Then people graze animals on hill. Animals eat all young shoots. No more trees grow. Next people want firewood. They lop off branches, cut down trees. Soon hill is bald. Later people think hill always bald. But that not true nature of hill.

Seeing Noah's confusion, Fong explained the message. "To have no morals not true nature. If person has no morals it because in life, morals lopped off just like trees on hill."

Fong watched Noah think and saw realization widen the boy's eyes "You're saying those sailors' lives were so hard that they became hard."

"Pretty much." Fong picked up the teapot. "More tea?" he asked.

Later that evening, after all the noodle house customers departed, Fong filled out a telegram blank that Noah had retrieved from the telegraph office on their way to the noodle house. Message written, Fong was handing the coded telegram and money to Mr. Tang's grandson when fists pounded on the restaurant's front door.

Taking the grandson's arm, Fong guided him to the alley door and pushed him out. "Run. Send telegram," he ordered. The boy hesitated then took to his heels, evading the grabbing hand of a policeman who'd just entered the alleyway.

Fong locked the back door and returned to the storeroom where he found Noah fast asleep on his mat. Fong touched his shoulder, shaking him awake. "Noah. Police here. You tell them I am family servant. Show them father letter. Say you run away. Do not tell them about the *Freeman* whaler. Captain maybe show false papers saying you agree to be on ship."

Noah was still rubbing the sleep from his eyes when the storeroom doorway was blocked by three policemen, their clubs at the ready.

The one in front looked at Noah and exploded with rage, his mouth big, and his face red. "You goddamn bastard!" he yelled. "Did you hook the kid on opium so you can sell him without a fuss?"

Noah snapped wide awake. "No, no!" he shouted too late.

The policeman rushed forward, followed by the other two. They quickly flanked Fong and grabbed his arms.

Fong stood unresisting, his face impassive, even as his internal focus sharpened. The shouting officer hauled back a fist and punched low and fast toward Fong's stomach. Drawing a deep breath, Fong relaxed in the split-second of the fist's first touch, only to instantly expel the air along with his Chi force as the fist followed through. He doubled over, acting as if painfully winded, but sent a wink at the horrified Noah from beneath the arm holding him.

The policeman grimaced and shook his hand as if it hurt, but still drew back his fist again.

Noah wasn't having it. He leapt forward clutching the arm, shouting, "No, no! Stop! Mr. Fong's my family's servant!"

The policeman hesitated, realizing the kid he thought drugged insensible was, instead, fully alert and furious. He dropped his arm. "You two handcuff and hang on to the Chink," he ordered his companions.

To Noah he said, "We'll sort this out at the station."

It was still raining outside. Unlike Fong, Noah was allowed to don a coat. Noah snagged a blanket and draped it around Fong's shoulders. The five of them exited the restaurant. An anxious Mr. Tang followed, repeating, "No opium. No bad man. Most honest business." Once they stepped outside, Tang locked the door behind them, his fearful face peering through the door glass as they headed down the sidewalk.

Fong felt sorry for Tang. The first chance he got, he intended to sort the situation out and prevent any harm to the noodle man. As the five of them headed toward the police station, Noah continued to insist Fong was his servant, pouring out a tale of running away and being rescued from his bad decision by the faithful Fong.

They were separated when they reached the station. Noah was ordered to take a seat inside a small room. Fong was escorted deeper into the building until they reached a long corridor lined with barred cells. They removed his handcuffs, unlocked a door, and shoved him into a cell that held Asians. In parting, the officer said, "You'll spend the night here with your own kind. Come morning, Captain Martin will sort things out."

It was cold in the cell and, despite the blanket, Fong was soaked from the walk between the noodle house and the station. After glancing around, he sat on a bench bolted to the concrete floor and studied his fellow prisoners. All looked Chinese except for one man. He had the smaller eyes, long nose, and lighter skin of a Korean.

Soon he learned that, with one exception, his cellmates were awaiting deportation. His skin crawled at the thought. He hoped the police captain wasn't stupid or too prejudiced to listen. The one exception to the deportees was a big Chinese man bragging about having killed another man.

Fong eyed the murderer and concluded there'd be a confrontation. If so, it needed to happen sooner rather than later. He wanted to sleep. He sighed, stood and grounded his feet the instant the man clenched his fists and stepped forward to growl in Cantonese, "You give me that blanket."

Fong looked at him and replied in the same dialect. "No. I will keep this blanket."

The big man reached for it and found his wrist captured. A painful twist drove him onto his knees with a thud. An elbow to his temple knocked him out. Fong stared at the others, ready should one of them jump to aid the downed man. Every face was grinning.

He realized that the fellow had been bullying his cellmates. Fong fished through the man's pockets. Whatever he found, he tossed it into the middle of the cell. There was a scramble as his cellmates rushed forward to recover their extorted possessions.

The man groaned. Reaching down, Fong grabbed an arm, giving it another sharp twist and getting a yowl in return. Fong flashed a toothy smile. "You sit in the corner and be good," Fong instructed. The man obeyed, crawling on all fours into the corner.

The night passed peacefully. The others made room on the bench, telling Fong to stretch out with his head pillowed on a jacket one of them insisted he use. Doubtless, they'd wake him should the bully stir from his corner.

Before closing his eyes, Fong fingered Laidlaw's paper inside a leather pouch still hidden in the waistband of his trousers. He hadn't shown it to the arresting officers once he realized they lacked the authority to hear and accept his explanation.

He closed his eyes against the glare of the single bulb in the corridor outside the cell. From behind his eyelids, he replayed his "capture" and plotted how he might have escaped from the three officers had that been his intention. Briefly, he imagined the pleasure of incapacitating the big coward who'd punched him. He released both thoughts, ruefully acknowledging that the last one was unworthy of a warrior. Next, his mind became serene as he envisioned, one by one, the faces of everyone he cared about—so many now. Finally, in his last moments of consciousness, he fixated on the one person most precious to him, his beloved Kum Ho.

FOURTEEN

Sage reached the stables on Second Avenue just as a cabby was harnessing his horse for the late evening trade. After the flash of a Double Eagle, the cabby agreed to drive Sage to Cedar Mill with the promise of another if he got there as fast as possible. The horse was soon trotting down the dark streets. The cab jounced over bricks and cobbles until reaching the steep cut leading up into the Tualatin Valley. Though Sage was grateful he wasn't riding a horse, he fidgeted at the cab's slow pace up the canyon's plank road. For a reason he couldn't name, his anxiety was increasing with every minute.

All that day, he'd worried about Eli Yoder. Losing his wife, baby, and son was damaging enough. To also be under the boot of the law might make Yoder snap. The fight with Block meant Yoder was nearing the end of his rope. Disheartened people often did stupid things.

Yoder's demeanor after Hanke bailed him out and brought him to Mozart's was worrying. Neither Sage's nor Hanke's reassurances about Fong's likely success seemed to ease the man's despair.

The horse picked up speed once the cab reached the top of the pass and began descending into the valley. Minutes later, they wheeled off the valley road and onto the planks heading toward Cedar Mill. Though the cab's pace was much faster than that of the huffing Clementine, Sage's anxiety stretched out the minutes, so it seemed to take forever to reach Cornell Road.

A sharp pain in his hand made Sage realize he was fearfully gripping the side rail. With relief, he spotted Yoder's narrow driveway. At his shout and sharp rap on the roof, the cabbie reined the horse onto the muddy lane where the going slowed. Sage wanted to jump out and run ahead but forced himself to stay seated. With his luck, his boots would get stuck in the muck.

At last, the cab pulled into the yard. Although a faint light shone from the house's window, it was the moving light inside the barn that made him jump down to run in that direction. Charging across the barn's threshold Sage's first sight was of Eli standing beside a cow, his arm across the animal's neck, his face against its muzzle. The cow was leaning into him as if trying to comfort.

Hearing Sage's entrance, Eli raised a bleak and tear-streaked face to look at him. "They've found Noah's body? The boy in Victoria isn't him?" He spoke in a voice bereft of hope.

Sage spoke quickly. "No! Noah's alive! Mr. Fong has him. Noah's okay. Mr. Fong's bringing him home."

As Eli's knees gave way, Sage leapt forward to help him down onto a nearby hay bale. Once both were seated, Sage kept his arm around Eli's shoulders, as sobs released all the despair and fear of the preceding days.

After a bit, Eli rose, patted the cow and whispered something into its twitching ear before leading Sage from the barn. Soon they were sitting at Yoder's kitchen table, mugs of hot coffee in their hands. Sage eyed the revolver lying on the table.

Eli looked at it as well before saying, "Thank god you came when you did."

"Yes. But, you know, that's never a solution.

After a beat of silence, Eli asked. "Are they still in Canada?"

"Yes, the telegram came from Victoria."

Sage saw fear again flash across the other man's face. "Don't worry. I have absolute faith in Mr. Fong's abilities. Besides, the worst is over. He's rescued the boy from the whaler. All that remains is crossing into the US and catching a train. Noah will be home in a day or two. The British consul here in Portland is prepared to intercede should they encounter any snags," he said, doing his best to make the return trip sound easier than was true.

Sage glanced around the kitchen, noticing it looked a bit neglected. "Look Eli, I think when you come to town tomorrow morning, you should plan on staying with us at Mozart's. That will be Fong's first stop with the boy. Fong has a third floor bedroom there that I know he'd want you to use."

Eli readily agreed with the plan. "My neighbors already offered to take care of our cows, milk them, and such. They'll be glad of the free milk. I'll go see them first thing in the morning, make my delivery to Purity Creamery, and then meet you at Mozart's."

Eli and Sage were sitting in Mozart's kitchen eating breakfast the next morning when the alley door opened. Looking up, Sage saw Hanke. Unexpectedly, there was no relieved smile on his face. That was puzzling because, the night before, Mae sent the message to Hanke that Noah was found. Instead of showing delight at that news, the big policeman looked grim. He even waved away Ida's offer of coffee as he advanced toward their table.

Sage stood. Something was wrong. He tried to ease the sudden tension. "Sergeant, why on earth are you upset? I thought you'd be overjoyed that Noah's safe."

Hanke ignored him and instead addressed his friend with formality, "Eli Yoder, I am arresting you for the murder of Aldus Block. You need to come with me." He took hold of Yoder's arm and pulled him up from the chair.

Sage intervened, his hand halting Hanke. "Wait a minute. Block is dead?"

"Yes, his body was found last night by the creamery manager."

"But I was with Eli last night, out at his farm. He couldn't have killed Block. He was with me!'

Hope flared in Hanke's eyes. "What time did you reach the farm?" he asked.

"About nine. I headed out there straight after receiving the telegram from Fong."

Hanke's face fell. "Block's body was discovered just before 7:00 p.m. So, Eli's not in the clear. There was plenty of time for him to reach home before you showed up."

"But I didn't kill Block. I didn't go anywhere near him once they let me out of jail!" Yoder protested.

Hanke sighed heavily, his face a miserable mix of sadness and regret. "I want to believe you, Eli. Unfortunately, the Chief is convinced you killed Block. He thinks you returned to finish what you started the day before. Nobody else has fought with Block lately."

Yoder yanked his arm out of Hanke's grasp. He rose to his feet, dignity in his raised chin and his words. "I'll go with you, Norm. But I swear, on my dear wife's name, that I know nothing of Block's death."

Sage was remembering the revolver sitting in the middle of Yoder's table. Thinking back, he was certain there'd been no fired weapon smell coming from its muzzle. "How was Block killed?" he asked.

Hanke hesitated before making a decision. "The coroner thinks Block was chloroformed while sitting in his office chair. While unconscious, someone tied his hands and feet. When he came to, he was forced to drink poison. He died in agony."

"Holy mother of god," Yoder breathed. "I could never do something like that."

Hanke stared at his friend. "Frankly, I can't believe that of you, Eli. I've been telling the Chief that. He insists your motive was that you believe Block was involved with Noah's disappearance. That's what you told me when I bailed you out yesterday. I couldn't keep that from the Chief after we found Block dead."

"I understand. And, yes, I believe Block was responsible. When I was sitting in that cell, thinking things over, I realized that his overreaction to my simple question of whether he'd seen or knew anything about Noah didn't make sense. It wasn't the response of an innocent man. He was way too defensive. I told you my suspicion hoping you'd find proof. That maybe you'd question him, dig a little deeper."

"Well, plan to explain all that to the Chief once we're at the station," Hanke said, his wooden delivery devoid of reassurance.

Yoder looked at Sage. "Mr. Adair, I beg you to please see to Noah's safe return. That's all that matters right now."

Hanke again gripped his arm. Yoder resisted moving long enough to say, "Mr. Adair, I never murdered Aldus Block. Please believe me. Please make Noah believe that."

That said, the two men disappeared out the back door.

"Well damn," Sage muttered as Hanke and his prisoner disappeared.

He was sitting in stunned silence when Mae entered the kitchen. "Fong's sheets are changed and the room is ready for Mr. Yoder if he'd like to take a nap. I'm sure he hasn't slept much these past few days." She looked around the kitchen. "Where is he? In the toilet?"

When Sage explained Eli's absence she dropped onto the empty chair and exclaimed, "Some days it doesn't just rain. Sometimes it floods, Sage." She patted his hand. "We'll sort it, Son. We always do."

She rose and spurred Sage into action, saying, "Best we get a move on. Time's a'wasting."

Sage was soon being escorted into Hanke's office. The Sergeant held up a hand to stave off Sage's inquiries. "I can't tell you anything about the case. My chief has warned me. If I want to stay involved in the investigation I can't share any information outside the department. And, I've got to stay involved to protect Eli. To make sure everything is done proper."

Sage put a hand to his chest, in a show of dismay. "Now Sergeant, it hurts to know that you think I come here just for information."

"Ha! I think that because you always come here to wheedle information from me. Take a seat," he instructed, pointing to the vacant chair before his desk.

Sage shook his head. "Nope, I'm not here for conversation. I was hoping you'd accompany me to the Quality Emporium. When I passed by just now it was closed. Through the window, though, I saw a fellow moving around inside. I figure he will say more if you're standing beside me."

Hanke's brow wrinkled. After cogitating a bit he stood and picked up his beehive. "I guess if all I do is accompany you, that can't be considered sharing information. Let's go before I change my mind." He stepped around Sage and exited the office.

They found the Quality Emporium still closed so they headed around to the loading dock's side door into the store. Hanke knocked and soon a man appeared to let them in. He had a sharp-nosed, weak-chinned, and bug-eyed face. Nerves seemed to be vibrating his rail-thin body.

"Ah, why are you here, Sergeant? I told you everything the last time. You okayed me to start making the store orderly." His attitude was a mix of mixed querulous and panic.

"No problem Mr. Deason. There might be a few more questions once I look around a bit more—if you don't mind."

Relief lowered the man's shoulders and he smiled, showing teeth overlarge for his small mouth. He reminded Sage of a frightened rabbit. "Oh sure, okay, go right ahead. I'm just trying to get some order in my cousin's paperwork. That girl didn't finish the job. There's still a lot to do."

"What girl?" Sage asked.

Deason started at Sage's sharp tone. He looked toward Hanke for an explanation.

Hanke sent a warning look at Sage. "Ah, I'm sorry, I forgot to introduce the two of you. This is Edgar Deason, he's now in charge of the Emporium. And, Mr. Deason, my companion is Mr. Blake. He is helping us with our inquiries."

"Oh, okay." Both looked at him. "Oh right," he said. "Umm, she always came in after I was gone for the day. According to Aldus, she was helping with the paperwork. I only saw her once because I come in at five in the morning and I'm gone by five at night. I'm in charge of taking deliveries, stocking the products, and working the register when he's gone. Anyway, Aldus usually closed the store a bit after six."

He paused for a minute. "I guess when I open the store tomorrow, I'll be running the whole shebang. Hard telling. Aldus had no relatives other than me that I know of. He's my cousin. His mother was my mother's sister. She's dead now—his mother I mean. The attorney for the store is checking for more relatives."

Sage pressed. "The woman helping Mr. Block didn't come in when the store was open?"

"Umm, Aldus kept the store open until sixish like I said. He wanted to catch those laundry ladies down the street when they got off work. So, I'm thinking she maybe worked between five and six, when things are slow. I'm thinking she used the counter for sorting, like I'm doing now because Aldus's desk is small and covered with stuff. There's a ton of paperwork that has to be sorted."

Hanke butted in, "Do you know if she came last night?"

"No, I surely don't. I skedaddled early because of a bad tooth." He rubbed the side of his jaw. "The dentist pulled it. Still hurts like the devil."

Hanke continued, "Can you tell us anything about her? What'd she look like? Do you think he hired her from an agency? Paid her with a check?

Deason looked taken aback by Hanke's peppering questions. He cleared his throat before speaking. "Well, she looked like a respectable lady. Not like some he brought in here after hours. She dressed plainly in decent clothes. I noticed she wore newish boots. And, ah, her hair was darkish with a little bit of red, if you know what I mean. She looked somewhere in her late twenties or early thirties. I don't know where she came from."

Sage returned to the hunt. "Did you hear her name?"

"Nah, Aldus called her a bookkeeper when I asked who she was." He pondered a bit before saying, "Usually, I never asked about the women he brought in here. But, unlike the others, she looked respectable like I said. To be honest, I first feared he planned to replace me with her."

"Do you think that was the case?"

"Nah, when I asked, he said she was just here temporary to sort out the papers for an hour a day," he glanced at the cash register counter along the side wall, near the front door. Paperwork covered every inch of it. "I know I shouldn't say it but, too bad the killer didn't wait until she finished the job. This is a real mess and the lawyer says it has to be sorted. I'm not good at doing this type of work."

"Is her name anywhere on those papers?" Hanke asked.

"Nah. First thing after the lawyer gave me the job, I tried to find her name and address. I figured he'd okay having her keep doing it. But, I couldn't find anything about her. Maybe he was paying her cash from out of the till."

"You didn't keep track of the till?"

"Nah. When he was gone, Aldus let me work the register. Otherwise, I mostly stocked shelves and kept the store tidy. All the ordering, accounting, and paying out was done by him."

Sage and Hanke looked at each other, neither thinking of any more questions. Following a quick tour of the store, creamery, and basement, they bid Deason goodbye. Just as they headed toward the side door, Hanke paused. "I say, Mr. Deason. My cousin's new to town. She's looking for employment. I bet she'd be interested in helping with that paperwork." He gestured at the laden counter. "I know she book worked at her father's general store, so she's more than capable."

"Why that's a wonderful idea. I'll ask the lawyer for his okay right away. Tell her to stop by tomorrow morning when the store's open. Tell her to just come on in. What's her name?"

A flustered expression passed over Hanke's face before it cleared, "Lucy, Lucy Cooper."

"Okay, then. You tell Miss Cooper I'd be beholden for her help. I'll pay her decent." The man's relief was palpable. He didn't want to do that paperwork.

Once outside on the sidewalk, Sage asked, "Lucy Cooper?"

"Well, she surely knows accounting. She runs a mighty successful business, after all." Hanke grinned. "'Course, it's up to you to talk her into doing it."

FIFTEEN

Loud voices and a nightstick rattling across the bars jerked him awake. Fong sat up to see the guards push tins of gruel through the feed slot. A cellmate brought him one, bestowing it on him with a respectful bow. Gratitude for the return of their extorted possessions continued. Fong smiled his thanks, flipped a roach out of the dish with a fingernail, and tried a spoonful. It was a tasteless paste. He offered the plate to the skinny man who'd delivered it. He accepted it with a surprised xie xie thank you.

The bully stayed on the floor in his corner, throwing sullen looks at Fong while shoveling in his gruel. The furtive glances others sent in the bully's direction indicated that, in the past, they'd been forced to surrender their portions to him.

He asked the man next to him when the detainees expected to be shipped out. The answer was a shrug and the comment that the 'round eyes' never told them anything.

Settling himself on the bench, Fong closed his eyes and focused on the in and out of his breathing until the sounds and his thoughts became mere wisps drifting into and out of his awareness. Soon he reached that quiet place of peace. It seemed like seconds later that the clatter of tin bowls drove him from the serenity of his meditation. He was surprised to realize he'd been so deep that the sound of the dirty dishes being pushed underneath the bars into the walkway never penetrated. It took the trustee tossing the empty tin plates into a metal pot to accomplish that.

Fong began conversing with the men around him and soon learned that he was in the company of an herbalist, carpenter, cobbler, bricklayer, teacher, and a multitude of other professions, all having traveled to the Americas to seek fortune and freedom not available under the Chinese Imperial dynasty with its petty functionaries and regional despots.

One man was of particular interest to Fong. He spoke a formal Mandarin dialect, telling Fong that he'd fled China because he'd been a minor government official supporting the 1900 Yi Ho Tuan peasant movement. Fong knew of that Northern China uprising. Led by the "Righteous and Harmonious Fists" the revolt failed. Westerners called their failed effort the "Boxer Rebellion" because so many of its participants practiced martial arts.

He'd followed the movement's progress closely. Initially, he'd admired their desire to rid China of foreign imperialists and the Christian missionaries' extraordinary privileges. Most objectionable was the privilege that enabled preying bandits to escape accountability, simply by feigning conversion to Christianity. Once protected by the missionaries, they couldn't be brought to justice.

In the end, though, he'd been dismayed by the movement's increasing reliance on mystical beliefs. Their failure became inevitable when the Fists laid siege to Peking, promising their followers that fighters would descend from the heavens to fight the armies of eight Western nations that had invaded China to protect foreign economic interests. As he foresaw, the foreign armies decimated the Fist fighters and installed their puppet ruler. Within a few months, the Fists vanished and the executions began.

"Are you not afraid of returning?" he asked.

The man shrugged. "The Canadians will ship us to British Hong Kong. From there, I plan to travel south to relatives in Shanghai rather than returning north to where I lived in the Yangtze River Valley. The South was never part of the uprising. I am willing to take the chance. I have been saving for passage home. Now, the Canadians will be paying for it. Unlike the rest of these men," he waved a hand at the others in the cell, "I don't like it here. I miss my beautiful China and its people."

Fong understood. Still, the man would face danger and despair over the changes in his beloved country. The Westerners' rabid looting, even of the Empress's Pekingese dogs, their stranglehold on the economy, and the increased Japanese influence were transforming China. Still, Fong wished the man luck. He understood. He too missed his home. Fortunately, his home was just a few hundred miles south.

Late in the morning, the guard came for him. He was led into a small room containing a table and a few chairs. Wind-driven rain splattered against the sole window. It was his first time seeing the weather since the night before. He was glad not to be out in it.

Minutes later a man wearing the same uniform as the arresting officers entered. The hat he removed and placed on the table, however, was flat rather than a beehive. Fong decided this man was the Captain Martin the officers mentioned.

"I am Captain Gabriel Martin. Do you understand English, Mr. Fong?" the man asked politely.

"Yes, Sir, I do." Fong responded.

"Tell me why you and Noah Yoder hid out in the back of a noodle restaurant."

Fong allowed himself a smile. "Boy run away. Father ask me to bring him home. Noodle house best place to stay with boy. Hotels will not rent room to China man with white boy. I need to make sure he not run away again."

"Okay, that makes sense. Did you give him drugs to keep him under control? The officers thought he looked drugged."

Fong didn't have to pretend shock. "Never drugs," he insisted. "When police come, boy asleep. Took time to wake up. That is all."

"That's what the boy says too. He is alert and eager to return home."

"In pocket there is paper." Fong started to raise his tunic to reach inside his waistband. Seeing the officer guarding the door stiffen, Fong froze and explained, "Paper hidden in trouser."

Martin nodded at the officer who stepped forward to reach into Fong's waistband pocket. He handed the leather pouch to the captain who opened it, withdrew Laidlaw's letter, and read it.

The captain fingered the wax seal and studied Fong. "Well, this does look genuine. I need to confirm its authenticity by telegram to Consul Laidlaw in Portland. It'll go through the British consul office here in Victoria. I expect verification to take at least today. In the meantime, both you and Noah must remain in custody."

"That fine. Weather bad anyway," Fong nodded at the rain hitting the window.

"I am sorry for the delay. But, Noah is just fourteen and there is a slight chance that you're working for a white slaver and the letter from his father and this letter here are both forged. We need to make sure."

Fong nodded. "Not a problem. Good you careful," he said and meant it. They both stood. Fong made a deep and sincere bow to the captain. He'd appreciated the captain's civility.

The captain returned the bow and saw Fong's surprise. He smiled. "I worked a stint in Hong Kong. I came to know many Chinese, some good, some bad. I try not to make assumptions."

Fong decided to risk the man's displeasure on two points. After all, some white men didn't take well to anything that smacked of criticism from a yellow man.

"Mr. Tang, he not involved. I just rent storeroom. He angry about boy. Told us to leave in morning."

"Yes, that is what Tang told my officers. More than once. If your story checks out, I promise that Mr. Tang will face no difficulties. "

Fong took a hesitating breath. "Sir, the big Chinese man, accused of murder. He in cell with others you send back to China."

The captain acknowledged that declaration with a frown, likely expecting a plea for mercy.

Fong looked the captain in the eye. "That man is a bully. He hurts other people. Takes their things and food."

The captain's lips tightened though he made no response before gesturing for the officer to return Fong to the cell.

Sage trotted up the long stairs and entered the police station. The rain pelted down so hard the drops bounced. He hoped that Fong and Noah weren't on a boat in it. Once inside, he furled his umbrella. Advancing to the desk, he told the officer, "I am here for Sergeant Hanke, he'll be expecting me."

Sage had visited the undertaker who doubled as the city's coroner. That man, named, Christopher Hadley, was welcoming having helped Sage the year before on a case involving children.

He was a kind fellow who'd agreed to serve as coroner after all the city's other undertakers refused the job. It was taking a toll on Hadley because, with every encounter, the man seemed more dispirited. It also explained that faint whiff of liquor coming off him.

Unfortunately, Mr. Hadley added little to Hanke's information, other than to say the friction burns on his wrists meant Block was tied to his chair and awake enough to fight dying. Also, he'd discovered a slight circular bruise on Block's temple and cotton fiber smelling of chloroform in his nose and between his teeth. "Though I can't say for certain, I believe someone slapped a chloroformed rag over his face from behind. He fought until he passed out. After that, he was tied up. When he came to, they forced him to drink embalming fluid."

"What was the circular bruise from?" Sage wondered aloud.

"A gun muzzle, I'm thinking. Looked like there's even bruising from the sight above the muzzle. Somebody pushed it hard against his head."

"It'd take some force to leave a bruise like that. You say formaldehyde's the poison someone used to kill him?" If so, it was yet another strange coincidence. They'd suspected that Block added formaldehyde to dairy products. Now it seemed that was the murder weapon.

He pondered awhile before saying, "I wonder if the murderer brought both the chloroform and embalming fluid to the Quality Emporium. Are they hard to transport?"

The coroner raised a finger. "Ah, but that's where you are wrong. According to Sergeant Hanke, the premise search found chloroform in his office and barrels of the embalming fluid in the store's cellar." A puzzled look crossed the man's face. "Can't say I understand the presence of either one."

The chloroform's presence was puzzling though not a total surprise. Unsavory people like Block sometimes found it useful. As for the formaldehyde. . . . "Well, I believe Block added the formaldehyde to the dairy products he sold."

Shock sent the undertaker's eyebrows up and made an "O" of his mouth. "But that's crazy. Formaldehyde is used to embalm dead bodies. Drinking it is insanity. I've exhumed bodies after fourteen years in the ground. The embalming fluid kept them stiff as statutes with no decomposition at all." The man's face fell into sad lines and he asked, "What is wrong with people? Why do they do these awful things?"

Sage touched the man's shoulder. "I've asked that question many times and never found a satisfactory answer. I just have to keep reminding myself that there are more people in the world like you, than not, Mr. Hadley."

In the ensuing pause they both mulled over that conundrum. Sage decided it best to enlighten the undertaker. "As for the formaldehyde, I'm learning that most of the city's creameries add it to food so it won't spoil as fast."

Sage also thought it a good idea to drum up business for the honest purveyor, and so added, "I buy from Purity Creamery because I've been told they never use additives and are squeaky clean in their handling of dairy products.

Now he and Hanke were waiting for Yoder to be brought up from the cells, Sage shared what he'd learned from the undertaker-coroner. When the door opened, Yoder stepped into the office and asked, "Has Noah come home? Is he here?" The farmer's eagerness was painful to hear.

Sage gently reminded him that Fong and the boy needed at least a day, maybe two, to make the trip. "Because of this storm that's moved in, it may take longer. You know how big these North Pacific storms get. We don't want them on the sea in this weather. Fong won't take the chance. He's a careful man."

"Yes, you're right. It's just I feel all jangled not knowing he's home safe."

Hanke jumped in. "Noah is safe with Mr. Fong. I'd trust that man with my life. And, I've done just that in the past, more than once."

Yoder's forehead crinkled at that declaration causing Sage to speak before the man could ask an awkward question. The fewer people who knew about Sage's crew of social justice warriors, the better. Hanke was so upset about his friend's predicament that he just might blurt something out that Yoder didn't need to know. "We better talk about Aldus Block's murder," Sage said.

Yoder nodded. "When I wasn't worrying about Noah, I was worrying about being accused of murdering him."

Hanke scooted his chair further back from his desk and his eyes narrowed as he studied his friend. He remained the silent observer, leaving Sage to ask the questions.

"Did any suspects come to mind with all that worrying?" Sage asked with little hope and so was surprised when the man nodded.

His hopes fell at Yoder's response.

"Bunches."

"Who, for example?"

"His workers. His competitors. Maybe he was pressuring other dairy-men to sell their milk to him. He was an unpleasant, dishonest man. Surely he made many enemies."

Hanke spoke up. "But you also think he was involved in Noah's disappearance."

"Yeah, I know. I know it looks bad for me, especially since I stupidly slugged him that morning."

Silence ensued until Sage got an idea. "Whoa up a minute. Is yesterday afternoon's newspaper handy, Sergeant?"

Hanke leaned over and fished *The Evening Telegram* from his wastebasket. He tossed the folded paper across the desk to Sage. Flipping through the sheets, Sage found the Police Beat column. It contained a small paragraph that Sage read aloud:

> Mr. E. Yoder, a Cedar Mill dairyman, has been arrested for assaulting the well-known owner of the Quality Emporium, Mr. A. Block. The men argued over business, according to Block. Bail will be set by the judge in the morning.

"Well, that is a damn lie," spluttered Yoder. "We never talked about anything to do with business. Block turned insulting the instant I asked about Noah."

"Yes, I believe you." Sage tossed the paper onto the desk. "Sergeant, you best keep hold of that paper."

Both men stared at him as if trying to fathom his reasoning.

Sage pointed at the newspaper. "That article is evidence that the murderer counted on having the blame land on Eli. This report of the assault gave the killer cover. It might be what caused him to act last night."

He looked at Yoder. "And you made things worse by telling your policeman friend here that you believed Block was responsible for Noah's disappearance, since, just hours later, Block was dead. Sergeant Hanke was required to tell his boss what you believed."

Yoder's lips twisted ruefully, "I know. Norm didn't have a choice."

SIXTEEN

Lunch was dry bread, hard cheese, and weak tea. Once again, the bully received no extra. His glittering eyes shot darts at Fong who rejected more than one offering of food. Noon meal over, the other inmates talked among themselves.

Fong waited on the bench, his thoughts reaching out to Noah with the hope that the boy was faring better than he was. At least Fong knew the boy wasn't in jail because every other barred cell was empty.

The corridor door opened and the jail guard entered, accompanied by two policemen. All conversation ceased as the guard unlocked their cell door and the two officers entered. The name they called made the bully clamber to his feet. Two seconds later, he was being frog-marched down the corridor and shoved to an empty cell. They slammed the door and departed. Fong smiled to himself. As he'd thought, Captain Martin was a decent man.

Once the jailer and officers left, the bully hollered threats at Fong, blaming him for the loss of his prey and their belongings. Fong bowed in the man's direction before returning to his meditation practice. It was a long day of enjoyable China reminisces and stories among his cellmates.

The first thing the next morning, they came for Fong. They returned his belongings before taking him to the captain's office where Noah waited. Captain Martin waved him into the vacant seat next to Noah. The boy looked alert and happy.

"How you been, Noah?" Fong asked, though the ease in the boy's face told him the answer.

"I've been great. Mrs. Martin, the Captain's wife, has fed me wonderfully and I even slept in a real bed."

The captain smiled at the boy. "Noah's been an excellent guest. My wife has enjoyed his company and his help around the house."

There followed handshakes, thank-yous, and heartfelt good wishes. Minutes later, Fong and Noah stood outside the police station, breathing air laced with a fragrant mix of salty seaweed and horse manure gently steaming in the weak sunshine.

"You okay?" Fong asked.

"Yes, the captain and his wife treated me kindly. But, I couldn't find out whether *The Freeman* sailed, so we better be careful."

Fong squinted at the sky now a clearing, pale, wintery blue. "I think whale ship gone. Tonight, we leave island."

"How are we going to do that? You don't have the papers to get back into the United States on the ferry."

Fong gave him a toothy grin. "You see. That small problem. Meantime, we find noodle house with no cockroach meat in bowl."

"Fong's been in Victoria's jail for the last two days," Laidlaw announced as he entered Mozart's just before noon. He grinned at Sage's stunned expression, adding, "Don't worry. He's out now and reunited with the boy. I expect they'll be home sometime in the next few days. They just have to get out of Canada and into the U.S. As you know, that's the last tricky part."

Laidlaw explained that he'd been away and hadn't received, until just that morning, the prior day's telegram asking him to confirm Fong's legitimacy. He'd been in Salem with his fellow foreign consuls, once again lobbying legislators for anti-shanghaiing laws. "It's damn discouraging, Portland's business lobby has so much more "pull" with your lawmakers than we do," he groused.

Glancing around the restaurant he gave Sage a sly smile. "Well, since I'm here, I might as well celebrate Fong's success at finding the boy. What does our admirable Ida have on offer today? I have a mind to enjoy her daily special, whatever it is, and maybe a slice of pie."

Sage grinned. "I expect you'll want me to keep mum about your little celebration if I happen to encounter your lady wife any time soon?"

Laidlaw chuckled. "I will expect nothing less from you, John."

Sage gave Ida Laidlaw's order, told his mother he was going, and headed out the door. It was time to take the next step in their mission to exonerate Eli Yoder.

Elvira opened the door to greet him warmly. "So nice to see you, Mr. Adair. What beautiful flowers you've brought. Let me take them. I'll put them upstairs in her bedroom as a surprise. She's in the back parlor doing bookwork." The corners of her mouth twitched in a wry smile. "I expect she'll welcome the break. You know how much she hates shuffling papers and calculating sums."

Well, that is damn inconvenient, considering what I plan to ask of her, Sage thought. He chuckled, handed Elvira the flowers, and headed down the hall toward his second favorite room in the house. The best thing about Lucinda's back parlor was that, unlike the front parlor, it displayed little bric-a-brac. Even better, a plentitude of pictures and mirrors hid most of its busy wallpaper. The fussy excess of Victorian décor was claustrophobic. That's why just a few good copies of old masters hung on Mozart's pea green plaster walls above plain walnut wainscoting.

He opened the door and stepped into the warmth radiating from the room's tall coal-burning stove. Lucinda looked the picture of elegance, with her erect posture and upswept chignon of honey-colored hair. Her face, however, was scowling as one hand pawed through the papers covering a table that usually held only liquor and glasses. In her other hand, a pencil eraser was tapping an irritated beat on the table's edge. She was muttering, "Where the tarnation is that pesky invoice? I just saw it!"

She looked up, her scowl transforming into a smile at seeing him. "Well, if it isn't my favorite visitor come to call. If I didn't need to finish this damnable accounting, I'd jump up to give you a proper welcome." Her eyebrow lifted coquettishly, making him laugh. She was good at making him laugh.

He glanced around the room. Evenings, the rugs were rolled up so her patrons could dance, with boozy shrieks and laughter, to music blaring from the gramophone's big horn. Those nighttime frolics took place in the light cast by Lucinda's newly installed electric table lamps—their glow softened by red gauze. According to Lucinda, everyone looked better through a haze of rosy light and alcohol.

Today, the room looked staid and middle-class. Every electric sconce and table lamp glowed brightly, every rosy drape was gone. Admittedly, Lucinda's electric illumination seemed useful. His own bookwork had to take place during the day, on the dining room table next to the front windows. Otherwise, Mozart's gas sconces were too dim and gave him a headache.

Slowly, he was beginning to accept the idea that they'd need to electrify Mozart's dining room. Maybe they could extend the electric wire, currently feeding the kitchen's sole electric globe. That'd make his mother happy. He just wished the innovation wasn't so damn dangerous. According to his firemen friends, electrified wires caused the most fires.

Lucinda tossed her pencil onto the table. "Given the time of day, I bet you've come with a request." The warmth in her look flushed the sting from her words.

He pulled up a chair. "Well, since the sight of you lifts my heart, why can't I be here for that pleasure alone?"

She shook her head. "Cut the blarney. You weren't raised Irish." She sighed again. "I hope whatever you want relieves me of this job for a minute or two."

"Well…," he hesitated.

"Oh, Lord, I'm not going to like this at all."

"Given your frustration today, I suspicion you're right," he admitted and began relating the most recent events involving both Yoders. He concluded his request with, "So, Hanke and I were hoping you'd be willing to play Lucy Cooper, Hanke's bookkeeper relative extraordinaire. There might be something in those papers that will lead us to his killer. We're positive it wasn't Eli Yoder." He quickly added, "It was Hanke's idea that you help sort out Aldus Block's paperwork"

A tiny smile quirked her lips. "Hanke's idea huh?" Though sounding skeptical, she continued, "I am glad Mr. Fong found the boy. You do realize that every time I become involved in one of your escapades things turn complicated? Millie Trumbull already has me doing more about that new pedophile house."

"She does? What are you doing? I thought your job ended when you discovered its location."

"You'd think that. And, that is exactly what I mean. But, no, the end is not in sight. She's not content with just shutting the place down. Now she wants to know the name of the man financing the operation. For sure it's not the cretin managing the house—that much I've discovered.

"As expected, she learned that, according to city property records, a shadow company owns it. She says its attorney won't name the company's owner. So now she wants me to ask the other madams if they know the owner's name. That means many visits and conversations. Still, I will do it."

Sage understood Trumbull's urgency. The last two houses closed when Trumbull's army of middle-class women paraded before them with picket signs. One house was subsequently leveled by fire. Just before the flames shot skyward, a Chinese man was seen scampering across the back porch roof, leaping to the ground, and slipping away through backyards. That man was never found nor arrested.

Trumbull was right, though. As long as backers want to finance such operations, those despicable houses would exist. Lucinda's willingness to help was understandable. She'd been raised in one of those god-awful establishments.

Still, Eli Yoder remained his priority

She studied his face and perceived his thoughts. "So, the plan is I become plain Lucy Cooper, offer my services, and plow through a mound of paperwork. I'm to see if there's anything in the Emporium's operation that might have triggered Block's murder?"

"'Yup, in a nutshell, that's exactly what we need. It's just a couple hours a day and only for a few days. Just long enough to for you to find anything that will help us identify Block's murderer." He wrapped an arm around her shoulders and wheedled in her ear, "Are you willing, Sweet Lucy? I don't think any danger is involved," he added reassuringly.

"Hah! You say that every time. And, we both know how that's gone in the past."

Sage departed Lucinda's to once again visit the Hadley mortuary. He stood in deep stillness until the bell above the door did its job. The undertaker popped out of an adjoining office.

"Why Mr. Adair, did you forget something?" Hadley asked.

Sage held out a bottle, "No. I wanted to bring you this raspberry brandy distilled near Oregon City. I thought that you might enjoy it."

The man flushed with pleasure as he took the gift. "I've heard tell of it. I will look forward to tasting it."

"I am also here to ask a question and make a simple request if you don't mind."

Hadley gestured Sage to a nearby chair and took one facing him. "I'll try my best to answer it."

"What I want to know is where might one buy barrels of embalming fluid? Do the city's undertakers sell it?"

"Oh, no. We use it. We would never sell it unless to each other. I can see an undertaker's eyebrows rising at such a request. There'd be talk. Anyway, most of us buy from a chemical manufacturing company in St. Louis, Missouri. That's the closest source and therefore has the cheapest freight charges."

"It's shipped on trains?"

"Well, yes. Those barrels are heavy. There's no other way to obtain large quantities of it. After what happened in the '03 Heppner flood, most of us try to keep more on hand than we need."

Sage was puzzled. He knew about the flood. Still, how was formaldehyde involved?

Hadley read his mind. "That flash flood killed over 246 people. There wasn't enough formaldehyde in our two states to embalm them. It was beyond terrible. We had to bury them immediately, with no ceremony. Families were distraught. Afterward, we undertakers decided to stockpile the product, in case of another disaster. Nowadays, most of us buy it by the barrel."

"Can a storekeeper obtain barrels of the stuff? Someone who's not an undertaker?"

"Well, since I am certain sure no undertaker sells it to them; I hazard a guess that, if a storekeeper has barrels of it, he ordered it direct from the supplier in St. Louis and shipped via the railroad. That's what we do."

"Suppliers will sell to someone who isn't an undertaker?"

The man's tone turned bitterly sardonic. "And, why wouldn't they? No regulation says they can't. It's just another case of the god almighty dollar making decisions."

Before Sage departed, Hadley let him sniff embalming fluid.

SEVENTEEN

A CRISP AUTUMN BREEZE TWISTED leaves from branches, sending them scuttling along the sidewalk. Lucinda Collins was relishing how anonymous she felt ambling along beneath the afternoon sun as the colorful leaves swirled against her ankles. Her face was scrubbed free of makeup and she was plainly dressed in a narrow-brimmed black hat, somber gray dress, black wool mackintosh, and neat black boots.

While passersby might sense they'd seen her somewhere before, they'd never recognize her as the city's most notorious parlor madam. Deliberately notorious because, sometimes, she and her ladies rode around town in a fancy open carriage, all decked out in finery and tittering whenever they snagged either men's admiring eyes or their women's disapproval.

A block from the Quality Emporium, she paused to eye someone upended into a garbage bin, his boots barely touching the ground. A tattered coat covered the man's rear end while one of his hands, encased in a fingerless glove, clutched at the bin's edge to prevent him from toppling all the way in. A ragpicker's cart, its cargo covered by a canvas tarpaulin, stood nearby with its long handle shafts resting on the street.

She stepped to his side and waited for the ragpicker to raise his head. When he did, he started, surprised to discover someone standing so close. The next instant, a grin split his neatly trimmed beard, flashing his sturdy white teeth.

"Why, Miss Collins. Fancy meeting you here! What a surprise. 'Beauteous thou art! Thou art no illusion—for I can touch thee with my mortal hand.'"

"Herman Eich, shame on you! Your flowery speech might distract Mae Clemens but not me. Sage sent you, didn't he?"

The ragpicker poet touched his heart in mock pain before shrugging and saying, "He asked me to remain nearby."

"You realize don't you, that Sergeant Hanke has already put the fear of god into the Emporium's new owner? He also told him that I'll only work between the hours of one and three."

"Ah, the Sergeant managed to impart that info to you? Sage wasn't sure he'd be able to."

"Hanke scared my cook witless when he showed up at the kitchen door last night. She thought it was a raid. At least he possessed the sense not to knock on our front door. Imagine my patrons' reaction." They both chuckled at the thought.

"So what are your instructions?" she asked.

"I'm to park the cart and rest myself outside the Emporium's side door. If you call for help, I'm to gallop in and save you."

"That's all? What if the person attacking me has a weapon? A gun for instance?"

"Well, then, I guess I shall throw canned peas at him."

Lucinda laughed. "That's not reassuring, dear Mr. Eich!" She glanced at the pale blue sky. "Well, at least it's clear today. You'll stay dry while you wait. I'm not worried about this assignment but, I will feel a measure of comfort having you nearby, canned peas, or no. You should know that I'll also be keeping my hat pin near to hand. In the past, I've used it to good effect." Again they both chuckled, this time at the memory.

She was still smiling when she entered the Emporium. After a momentary glance around, she strode to the counter where an exasperated man was pounding the cash register keys and cursing under his breath. From the sour expression on his matronly customer's face, his mild curses were offending.

He raised his thin face and, catching Lucinda's eye, said, "I'll be with you in a minute, Ma'am. This doodle-darn register drawer don't want to open."

"I'm Lucy Cooper, come to help. Let me work on it. I am familiar with that type of register." She moved behind the long counter and he stepped aside for her. A few pushed buttons later and the drawer shot open with the familiar ting. The clerk stepped over, made change, and bid his customer good afternoon. She compressed her lips, cast him a distaining look, and hustled out the door.

After glancing to confirm no other customers waited, he huffed with relief. "Boy! I'm sure glad you came along in the nick of time. That harridan was fixing to clobber me with her handbag. My name is Edgar Deason." He stuck out a hand that she shook.

She smiled, finding herself quite liking the fellow. "I hope that I'll be able to help you with your paperwork problem. I've quite a bit of experience in that area. Perhaps you'd like to show me where I'll be working?"

"Yes, yes. Let me show you. Since your cousin, the Sergeant, came by to say you could work only during the afternoon, I moved the paperwork into my cousin's office. I managed to wedge a table in once I pushed his desk against the wall. I hope there's enough room for you."

He led her from behind the counter to the rear of the store and up two steps into a small office space. It was in a shambles. Shelving overflowed with paperwork, tools, and a jumble of who knows what else. A folding table held stacks of paperwork. A desk was indeed, shoved to one side. Its top was hidden beneath even more paperwork. Lucky those drawers faced the room and not the wall, she thought. Still, searching the cluttered room was going to be challenging. She stepped forward, eager to start.

"I'm sorry about the mess. Aldus wasn't much into paperwork either. I just haven't been able to clean this up, what with the deliveries and waiting on the customers and all. I laid the current invoices and delivery receipts right there on the table, along with the payment ledgers. The lawyer needs everything entered in the ledgers according to date. I started but, I don't read real good. I'm okay checking deliveries in, but…," He shrugged his shoulders before pulling the room's only chair over to the table for her.

She removed her hat, coat, and gloves, took a seat, and flashed him a reassuring smile. "Don't worry, Mr. Deason. I've tackled far worse. I intend to make a good start today. It looks like you've already pulled everything needing entry. The first step will be to sort."

That morning Sage took one look at Mae and decided to stay through Mozart's noontime dinner hour. She was exhausted. No wonder. Fong usually cleared tables and performed a myriad of other tasks. His absence and Sage's sporadic attendance left just Homer to help in the dining room. Matthew, Ida's nephew, couldn't help right now because he was preparing for exams. Everyone agreed that took precedence. So, Sage worked through the noon dinner hour, helping to set up and acting as Mozart's maitre d' and busboy until the last customer departed.

At that point, two hours of relative peace lay ahead. Mae waved him toward the door, "Get going. Try to get back for tea time at four. Homer can't come that early today. It'll be a bit hard if I've got to do everything alone."

With a "Yes, ma'am," and doff of his hat, he headed out the door, to the sound of her chuckling. She was an amazing woman, steadily resolute, strong, and loving, despite all the lurches he'd left her in.

The Portland Hotel's dining room was also empty of customers. This time the new waiter, Angus Solomon's nephew, greeted and seated Sage and poured him coffee before fetching his uncle. As always, Angus was pleased to see him.

"Well, well Mr. Adair. I am delighted to see you here. Any news about the boy?"

Guilt pricked Sage and he mentally kicked himself. He'd forgotten to let Angus know about Noah being found. "Yes, thank god. After a bit of a kerfuffle, involving a couple of days in jail for Mr. Fong, he and the boy are headed back. We're unsure when they'll arrive."

Sage next told his friend the latest developments in Eli Yoder's life. Angus reacted how Sage expected.

"That is most distressing news. How might I assist?"

"Well, those barrels of formaldehyde in the Emporium's basement keep nagging at me."

The maitre d' didn't look surprised. "You know what that's used for, right?"

"We suspect Block added it to his dairy products."

"I am not surprised. I suspect he added it to more than the dairy. Purveyors of foodstuffs are adding formaldehyde and other poisons to other things as well. We just received a barrel of oysters. Our cook thought it strange they looked so fresh. Sure enough, the first order of raw oysters from that barrel laid one of the hotel guests out flat. He was so sick, we thought he might die. The hotel summoned Victoria Hampton; she's a chemist and a doctor. She took samples and, sure enough, those oysters weren't fresh. They were embalmed! It is becoming quite difficult to find pure food to serve."

The two men exchanged a look of consternation. "The situation tends to taint one's enjoyment in eating, does it not?" commented Angus.

A few minutes later, Sage was heading back to Mozart's the long way. Solomon planned to ask the train station porters to keep an eye out for barrels carrying the St. Louis Chemical Industry label and to write down the names of every recipient that wasn't a funeral parlor.

At this point, they had no evidence that the barrels of formaldehyde were related to Block's murder except for being used to kill him. Still, damned if any Portland baby was going to die because it drank embalmed milk. He wanted to know which creameries used it and stop them, even if it meant going all Carrie Nation and attacking the barrels with axes.

The Quality Emporium was quiet when he entered. A few customers browsed while Deason stacked shelves. The storekeeper was sharing a laugh with a customer. Sage strode the aisles as if hunting for something and finally settled on a pair of work gloves. Buying an eatable from the store was out of the question.

When he reached the counter Deason recognized him. "Well, hello there Mr. Blake." Sage was momentarily bumfuzzled. Blake? Then he remembered. Blake was the alias Hanke gave him when they'd met. "Hello, Mr. Deason. Are things going easier for you now?"

"Oh my yes! Sergeant Hanke's cousin is here plowing through that awful paperwork. She's in Aldus's office." He pointed at a door in the store's back wall. "She's real good-natured and seems to know what she's doing. She says she needs just today and tomorrow to get it done."

Deason leaned forward, genuine delight on his narrow face. "And the attorney came by to say that Aldus doesn't have any living relatives besides me. His pa died years ago and there is nobody alive on that side of the family. And on his ma's side, I'm his only relative. I know that for a fact." Deason waved his arm to take in the whole store. "So, it looks like I'll inherit everything."

Well, there's a motive, Sage mused. Inheritance was behind the case where Dr. Hampton was the prosecution's witness. The man had killed his wife to inherit her property and her sister who witnessed the murder. Still, Deason's enthusiasm could be considered exonerating. If he'd killed his cousin, would he be so open about relishing his good fortune?

He congratulated Deason, took his change, glanced around, and, not seeing Lucinda, left.

Once outside again, he spotted Eich sitting in the alley atop the store's loading dock, a book in hand. Doubtless a poetry book. The ragpicker was, himself, an accomplished poet. Upon spotting Sage, Eich ambled down the alley to meet him on the sidewalk.

"Herman, thank you for being here. Everything looks calm inside, I'm not sure that you need to stay."

"Ah Sage, I mind it not at all. I'd be worried if I didn't stay. She's a mighty fine woman, our Lucinda," he added.

Sage patted Eich's shoulder, feeling a surge of affection for the man and thinking Lucinda Collins wasn't the only fine person around. "That she is Herman, that she is."

EIGHTEEN

"Drat! That was close!" Lucinda mumbled, frustrated that Deason repeatedly checked on her progress. This last time, his shoe scuff on the office steps alerted her. She'd quickly slid a desk drawer shut. When his head poked around the half-open door she was standing, rubbing her back.

"Sitting too long?" he asked sympathetically before saying, "Miss Cooper, I was thinking to fetch you a coffee. How's it going by the way?"

She hoped her phony smile hid her annoyance. She'd refused the same offer just fifteen minutes ago. "Yup, my back's a tad sore. Anyway, I'm close to having the pile sorted. Once that's done, I'll start with the ledger entries. As for the coffee, that sounds wonderful. Black, please." She normally took cream in her coffee. Not here, though—knowing what she did about the embalming fluid.

Deason toddled off and soon returned with the coffee. After thanking him, she asked, "Do you also handle day-to-day operations in the creamery?" She made vague gesture in the direction of the double doors that led to the Emporium's creamery operation.

"Nah, my cousin never wanted me involved with the dairy processing side of the business. The creamery's going to be tough for me to oversee since I know nothing about it."

"Oh, my. So, your cousin handled the creamery all by himself?"

"Nah, there's a manager. His name's Allen Gribble. Surly sort of guy. I got to keep him on, leastways until I learn that side of the business. The creamery's the Emporium's real money maker.

I'll just bet it is, Lucinda mused. She gestured at the papers. "By day's end, everything will be sorted. That means I'll be ready to tackle the ledger entries tomorrow." She flashed him a transfixing smile. "Mr. Deason, thank you so much for the coffee. I best get busy now."

After a brief hesitation, he took the hint. "You . . . you are most welcome. I guess I better return to shelf straightening—no rest for the wicked as they say," he mumbled and made a clumsy retreat.

She shook her head. *Doltish, though kinda sweet,* she concluded. She eyed the invoices and receipts. They were sorted and most were already entered into the ledger. In truth, she could easily finish today but she needed more time to search.

She pulled out her gold pocket watch. Her thumb caressed the embossed dove on the lid before flipping it open to read the inscription inside, "Always, S." He'd given it to her the night he'd finally accepted that she would not marry him in the near future.

After noting there was still an hour before she could leave, she shut the lid and slipped the watch back into her pocket. Turning back to the paperwork, she shuffled the invoices she'd already entered in case Deason came to check on her progress. She gulped down half of the bitter coffee before turning back to the desk and easing out another drawer.

Short minutes later, when a stairway scuff again sounded, Deason found her sitting at the table, an ink pen in hand. This time he asked whether she wanted a coffee refill.

Shyly averting her eyes she asked, "Actually, Mr. Deason, I was wondering, where might the necessary be? All that coffee, you know."

His face blanked until he understood. "Umm. . . yes . . . the necessary! Umm, that'd be just inside the door of the creamery. Aldus installed a water closet and septic tank just last year. No more alley outhouse for us."

"Perhaps you might direct me?" she prompted since he remained in the doorway, staring at her as if her ears had sprouted flowers.

After she cocked her head in inquiry, he stirred and mumbled. "Why, umm . . . sure. Follow me."

This guy really needs to find himself a wife, she thought as she trailed him down the steps and through the double doors.

She gasped when they stepped into the creamery. She'd expected to smell sour milk but, an eye-watering stench like cat pee sent her hand flying up to cover her nose and mouth.

Deason noticed her reaction. "The smell's pretty bad, isn't it? My cousin said he got used to it after a while. I never have. I come in here to use . . ." He pointed at a nearby door.

She nodded and entered. She tried to hold her breath as she used the toilet. Pulling the long chain dangling from the elevated water tank, she glanced up and saw that the toilet cubicle was open to the rafters—no wonder it smelled so bad. Grabbing a handful of tissues, she eased the door open, hoping Deason had fled the stink. Sure enough, he was gone.

She paused before re-entering the store, breathed through the tissue, and surveyed the creamery. Somehow she'd pictured creameries as quiet, sanitary places full of shining vats. This place was anything but that. Rattling noise came from a spider web of belts stretching up to the rafters and down again. The belts were attached to various vats, pots, and barrels. A gas engine fumed away, making both noise and smelly exhaust, as it powered the small electric motors moving the overhead belts.

The barrel nearest her ceased rotating and a man appeared. Using a wooden paddle, he scooped out congealed fat that looked like butter and slapped it onto a big, flat disk that had grooves radiating out from its center. Once he finished spreading the fat over the disk, he lowered and clamped down a heavy-looking lid. Evidently that machine shaped the fat into butter cubes.

Another man wheeled up a dolly holding canisters. He dumped their contents into the churn. She recognized milk and lard, but not the other ingredients he added, like the bright yellow liquid and a second jar of something that intensified the cat pee smell. Her stomach roiled. It would be a while before she ate butter again.

She glanced around, noticing splashed milk and filth on the cement floor. Black crud crawled up the equipment legs.

A heavy-set man strode up to her, a scowl on his face. He didn't bother with niceties. "The public ain't allowed in here, lady. You best go back into the store," he rasped.

"You must be Mr. Gribble," she responded pleasantly, her tissue mask now down at her side.

"Don't matter who I am. You ain't supposed to be in here."

"I'm here assisting Mr. Deason with bookwork and ...."

"Well, there ain't no bookwork in here. You done your business," he gestured at the water closet, "so git yourself outta here."

She turned on her heel and pushed through the doors into the store.

"Now him, I don't like," she muttered. Still, she was smiling when she entered the cramped office. The Emporium creamery's filth and canisters of additives were curious. As were the two mysterious ledger entries she'd spotted. All and all, it was a successful day.

Sage stretched and turned to her. It was late at night. While business was still underway in the rest of the house, this room was a quiet oasis.

She rose onto one elbow. "Now, to tell you what I learned."

He chuckled. "Yup. I guess I'm ready to hear it. Now."

She laughed. "First, I don't believe Deason has it in him to hurt or kill someone, let alone torture them." Her lips twisted, "I can't say the same for the manager of the creamery, Allen Gribble."

"Why? What's he like?"

"He's a big bully. He almost shoved me out of the creamery. And I don't think the workers there like him either because one of them winked at me over Gribble's shoulder. It seems a terrible place to work." She described the filth and stink. "And, Lord knows what they added to that butter. I saw what looked like lard, bright yellow stuff, and something that smelled like cat pee."

"From what I understand, the yellow stuff is coal-tar dye. And, when I was at the funeral home, Hadley let me smell formaldehyde. It stung my eyes and stunk like cat urine. I only saw the creamery briefly and it wasn't in operation."

"I hope all creameries aren't like the Emporium's."

"We can hope they're not but, I'm beginning to wonder. The good news is that, when Mom went to reinstate our order, the Purity Creamery's manager gave her a tour. She said the production room smelled like fresh milk and the equipment was gleaming. She even said she wouldn't hesitate to eat off its tile floor—it looked that clean.

"So, how did Block get away with it?" she wondered aloud.

He turned on his side to face her. His finger traced her jaw before playfully tapping her nose. "You just asked an excellent question, my lady."

Her smile held the warmth of suns before fading. "One more thing you mind find interesting. Recently, two people made ledger entries. One seemed a female hand.

"That makes sense. Deason told us a woman was working on Block's account books."

"Well, in the last month, there are small cash outlays for something called "bookkeeping"—so that confirms that someone was doing his books.

She next imparted what she considered her most interesting find. "Also, every month, there's a cash payment for something labeled 'security.' Unfortunately, no name is attached to either the bookkeeping or the security entry."

"Water very cold," Fong warned. He and Noah were hiding beneath the stubby fir trees along the shoreline. The darker it turned, the colder it got. He hoped the boat arrived soon. A stiff wind was rising. Despite their new heavy coats and wool pants, they'd get too cold if they had to wait past midnight.

"What are you saying?" Noah asked, his teeth clicking together. "Colder than right now?"

"Afraid so." The time had come for instruction so Fong said, "You see lantern flash, you take off shoes, pants, and stockings. Put in bag. Tie around neck. Then we wade to boat."

The boy was quiet before he asked, "How deep is it? I don't swim too good."

Fong patted Noah's shoulder. "Water just hit top of legs. They say this best place for us to reach boat. Too shallow for boat any closer."

He felt the boy's shiver and reassured, "Boat cabin has stove, hot tea. We warm up. Think on that."

The minutes crawled by as the black vault arcing overhead sucked up all of the day's lingering warmth. The strengthening breeze began driving wavelets across the bay. A crescent moon behind racing clouds offered a chill, fitful light. Fong focused on his memories of being warm.

He pulled the shivering boy to his side. There was no resistance. Rather, Noah moved even closer. Voice muffled by Fong's coat, he asked. "How long must we wait?"

Noah's question triggered a decision. The captain of the boat was a member of a Chinese tong friendly to Fong's own. Honor required the captain to keep returning every night unless stopped by the weather or a message. Given the boy's shivers and the mounting cold, Fong made a decision. "Tonight we stay here until moon straight above. Then we go find warm place to sleep. Come back again tomorrow night."

"But, who'd take us in? That noodle shop man is mad at us. He won't let us stay there again."

In a tone carrying more confidence than he felt, Fong assured, "We think of something." In truth, he knew it would be difficult to find a place to stay. Especially at night. At the very least, it meant a long trudge across the city to the poorer district, a place of plentiful boardinghouses and few questions asked. Even so, they were an unusual pair and might encounter hostility.

He pulled the boy closer. "Maybe now you tell story how you end up on ship."

"Yeah, I guess I told you the last part first." Noah fell silent, gathering his thoughts. Finally, he cleared his throat and began. "You said you met my pa?"

"Father good man," Fong responded. Beneath his arm, the boy gave a small sob.

Gaining control, the boy agreed, "He is the best father ever!" before continuing, "Anyway, Pa took me with him to hear ladies' club speakers. He's the master of the Cedar Mill Grange," he added with pride.

"So, anyway, Pa and the Grangers are real mad about embalming fluid being added to milk so it won't sour. A while back, he and the Quality Emporium owner argued. I heard 'cause I was with Pa. He made me wait on the wagon so I couldn't hear their words but I thought maybe it was about the man poisoning the milk. Afterward, all Pa would say was that the man was ornery.

"The day they kidnapped me, I was heading to the kinetoscope parlor when I stopped to let this fellow pass in front of me. He was wheeling a barrel from a wagon down an alley and around to the back of the Emporium. I thought it was strange that he didn't wheel it through the side door 'cause that way was a lot closer.

"While he was gone moving a barrel, I stepped closer to the wagon so I could read the label on one of the barrels. It said "formaldehyde." That chemical was what they talked about at one of those ladies' club meetings. That's what they put in dead people.

"I didn't know what to do, so I waited. I pretended to look in a shop window until the fellow finished unloading the second barrel and drove off in his wagon. I snuck down the alley to the back of the store. There was another entrance there with steps down into the cellar beneath the building."

Noah gulped air. This next part was harder for him because his words came slower. "I figured I could help Pa and the Grangers if I found where the barrels went. At the lecture, those lady doctors asked folks to tell them if they saw someone adding bad stuff to food. So, I figured to look in the cellar window and make sure that's where those barrels went. I mean, how come a provision store and creamery needs formaldehyde? That's what I wondered.

"So, I was kneeling, looking through the cellar window, when a big arm wrapped around my chest and a hand shoved something cold and wet onto my face. I fought until I blacked out."

Fong felt the boy shudder and tightened his hold on him. When Noah spoke again, his words were subdued. "I came to later. Real dim light came through a small window meaning it was nighttime. Still, a bit of light seeped in, you know? Enough so I saw those barrels. I figured I was in the Emporium's cellar. I heard two men shouting upstairs. I couldn't tell what they were saying. Their yelling is what woke me up.

"I wanted to escape in the worst way. I tried but I couldn't because my hands and feet were tied and a gag was in my mouth. So, I lay there, worrying about what they planned to do with me. I must have dozed off because the next thing I knew, the window was bright and someone was dropping me into a wooden crate. The rest you know."

"You see man who attack you and shove you in crate the next morning?"

"I didn't see who caught me when I was peeking in the window. But, I saw the man who put me in the crate. He was big and his face was mean. I'll never forget him."

NINETEEN

Lucinda strode into the Emporium confident of finishing the job in less than an hour, which left her time to question Deason and snoop further. As usual, the storekeeper hovered around.

She didn't mind because she planned to quiz him about the two vague entries. Depending on how that went, she was also going to ask him what was being added to the dairy products in the creamery.

"Mr. Deason," she began when he popped into the office yet again, "There are two puzzling cash paid entries in the ledger. I think your attorney is going to want to know more about them."

Perplexed, his forehead wrinkled, and he stuttered, "What, what . . . I don't . . . what entries are you talking about? Don't we have invoices for everything?"

"I'm afraid not. One entry is called "bookkeeping," But there's no name attached. That's entered for the first time in last month's accounts."

"Did it come to much?"

"No, it was $8 a week for the three weeks. Nothing for last week."

"That's got to be for the gal helping Aldus with the books, I'm pretty sure of that."

"You don't know her name?"

"Nah, she always came in after I was gone."

"You never saw her? You never heard her name?"

"I just saw her once from a distance. She looked respectable. But I never heard her name."

"Okay, then. The other cash-paid entry with no invoice was for "security". It also doesn't show a person or a company's name."

That information triggered another perplexed frown. "Well, that's darn peculiar. Maybe my cousin bought some locks or something."

Lucinda shook her head. "Nope. Not unless he was buying locks every third week of every month for the last year. Also, it's a goodly sum, fifty dollars every month."

"Whoa, that's a lot!" Deason's surprised reaction was convincing. "That don't figure at all. Aldus was mighty tight with a dollar. I used to kid him about it. He didn't like me saying that."

"So you have no idea what the security expense was for?"

"I don't have a single, solitary clue. It makes no sense. There's no security here in the store or the creamery. Plus, no one's ever broke in or nothing."

The store bell tinkled, pulling Deason away.

Lucinda was frustrated. So far, the day yielded no new information. As she entered figures off the few remaining invoices, two male voices drifted in from the shop floor. The high pitch and rapid fire of Deason's words meant he was nervous. She rose and peeked out the door. Her heart stuttered. She'd seen the other man somewhere before. If she recognized him, maybe he'd recognize her. He'd know she was no country miss named Lucy Cooper.

She tried to think what to do. Her alarm shot up a notch when she heard Deason talking about the books and offering to show them to the man. There'd be no hiding her face if the three of them crowded together in this small space.

Gathering up her skirts she charged down the steps into the store, as if propelled by an urgent need. Face averted, she swished past the approaching men and passed through the swinging doors into the creamery. Once out of sight, she diverted into the toilet, slammed the door shut behind her, and took a seat. She needed to wait Deason's visitor out, stay out of sight until he took himself off. She wished she'd brought something to read. Lifting the edge of her long skirt, she masked her nose and mouth to lessen the creamery stink.

Some minutes later, the creamery doors swished open and the voices murmured right outside the cubicle. She froze, praying no one needed to use the necessary. Relief came when the voices moved deeper into the creamery.

She eased the door open. Seeing no one, she quickly slipped through the double doors. Rather than risking an encounter with the stranger, she fetched her purse from the office and scooted out the shop's side door and down the alley. Reaching the street, she crossed to the café half a block away. She'd watch from there. Once the stranger exited, she'd return to the store. Though, she'd need an excuse for having skipped out.

After fifteen minutes of her sipping weak coffee, the Emporium door opened and a man stepped out. He slapped a hat on his head and strode off at a fast clip, his back to Lucinda. That brief glimpse, as he exited, confirmed that she'd seen him before. She just couldn't remember his name or where she'd seen him. He wasn't a parlor house regular. Still, not everyone visiting the house bought time with her ladies. Sometimes, her customers wanted an evening of card games and brought friends. If that's when she'd seen him, it made sense his identity was elusive.

Whoever he was, his expensive coat, hat, and boots, as well as the glint of gold across his chest and on his fingers as he buttoned his coat, all proclaimed the man was wealthy. She sighed and stopped trying to force the memory. The name would come. It always did.

Minutes later, Deason delightedly accepted the cookie she brought him from the café. He didn't question her excuse of sudden hunger. Following her into the small office, he stepped close to observe Lucinda complete the final ledger entry.

"Who was that man, you toured around the shop and creamery?" she asked. "He looked somewhat familiar like I've seen him somewhere before."

"Oh, boy. That was the food inspector. Today was the first time I ever spoke to him. I was so nervous that I already forgot his name. He's been coming in every month but Aldus always dealt with him."

"He causes problems?"

Deason shrugged. "I don't think so. Maybe. My cousin always seemed upset every time he showed up. I thought Aldus was worried about passing the inspection."

"What does the food inspector inspect?"

"The creamery and, it seems the books. Leastways, he and Aldus always came in here and closed the door."

"Oh. Did he examine the bookwork today?"

"Yup, he flipped through the whole ledger. He told me it was all in order." Deason smiled shyly and added, "Thanks to you."

She pondered that information for a bit, thinking of the filthy creamery and its overpowering stink. "Did the inspector say anything today about the creamery's condition?"

Deason's lips twisted. "Well, he told Gribble to scrub the floors down. So, I guess that was a problem. He told me he's coming back next week to talk about making an 'arrangement'. I can't think what he means."

Talk about the creamery gave her the opening to ask her final question. "Mr. Deason, yesterday in the creamery, I saw them adding something to the butter vat . . . might you know what that was?"

He waved a dismissive hand. "Oh, that stuff's because we aim to sell the best dairy products. Aldus told me he'd discovered a secret ingredient. He refused to tell me what it was because I didn't work in the creamery. Told me that all I needed to know was that the stuff helped preserve the dairy. He said it keeps the milk, cream, and butter fresh longer. And, customers have told me the same thing—that our dairy products last longer than other folks' dairy products."

"Poor Edgar offered me a part-time job doing the books. I told him 'no.' I thought he was going to cry until I told him I might know someone who'd like a part-time bookkeeping job."

"What? You declined an opportunity to add more work to your day?" Sage teased.

"I'm overwhelmed as it is. I'm still rising earlier to meet with the other madams. You may recall I've been tasked with finding out who owns that new house." Her face saddened and she added, "I'm not complaining. I'm glad to help.

"Anyways, my stint at the Emporium is over. Edgar paid me and even added a bonus. I don't believe there is any more to learn there what with Deason popping in and out every five minutes. I peeked at prior years' ledgers and the monthly entry labeled "security" first appeared about two-and-a-half years ago. Also, while I was there, the food inspector paid a visit. He looked familiar. Edgar said he came every month to inspect. Today, all he did was tell the creamery manager to wash down the floors."

"It sounds like you like Edgar Deason."

She shrugged. "He's harmless—eager to please and scared of his own shadow. I doubt his cousin involved him in anything nefarious. Look at him cross-eyed and he'd spill the beans in a second."

"How are you going to find 'poor Edgar' a part-time bookkeeper?"

She smiled. "I already know just the person. One of my gals. She's eager to escape the business and she's smart. She'll learn simple bookkeeping in a few days. And, since it's part-time to start, she'll still be living here in the house so I can help her if she runs into a problem. Once she has that experience under her belt, she'll be qualified to look for something full-time. I told Edgar that I'd be sending my bookkeeping niece to him first thing next week."

"You look pleased with yourself."

"I am! I've been worrying about Christina because she has no skills other than the obvious. Fortunately, she's been learning to read, write, and calculate and doing quick work of it. I think she'll jump at the chance to change careers."

They continued sitting on the front parlor divan as day faded into dusk. He'd been watching from the front window when she returned from the Emporium, trailed by the faithful Herman Eich and his cart. Remembering that amusing sight engendered a powerful rush of affection for both his friends. Impulsively, he threw an arm around her and hugged her hard.

She startled, then laughed. "What just got into you?" she wondered aloud before asking, "Any ideas about what is going on?"

"Hopefully, when Noah returns, we'll learn whether the Emporium was involved in his disappearance. If so, that connection would be a double-edged sword. On one hand, it would make Block's murder somewhat justifiable. But, conversely, it reinforces the idea that Yoder did the deed.

"The bottom line, to use an accounting term, is that it's better if Yoder never steps foot in a courtroom. I believe him when he says he didn't kill Block. That means there's a murderer on the loose. We better find him or her."

"Any hope in that direction?"

"There are faint trails but nothing looks promising down any one of them."

"What trails?"

"Well, we can try to find someone who saw Yoder return home shortly before Block was murdered—say around six or seven. That won't reveal the murderer but a witness could get Yoder off the hook. It would take some of the pressure off us and force the police to keep looking."

Sage lifted a hand to show two fingers. "After that, I see two ways to go. First, we know Block was disliked. One reason being his bullying the area's dairymen into selling exclusively to him, thereby putting his competitors out of business. So, a dairy farmer or a creamery owner might have killed him. Another reason for his murder could be tied to the poison additives he was using—though that's a real long shot."

Sage dropped his hand. "All that means talking to a lot of people. If Yoder's out of jail, he can help by talking to the other dairymen. He's in the best position to discover who else Block pressured. Also, I'm going to talk to the Purity Creamery owner. I think he'll help. Ma told him that we're now urging people to buy from his creamery. He might know which creameries lost customers due to Block's tactics.

"And," he gave her shoulders another squeeze, "Thanks to you, we now know that Block was poisoning his dairy. Maybe someone died and revenge is the motive, pure and simple. The gruesome manner of his dying smacks of revenge. Though, I don't know how one could discover someone died because of Block's additives."

"Yeah, it's not like he advertised that his milk came with a dollop of embalming fluid."

Sage huffed. "More than a dollop, I'm afraid. Once Fong returns home, we all need to sit down and talk about how to proceed. Maybe he's thought of another angle to pursue.

"In the meantime, I best head back to the jail once Mozart's supper service winds down. It's a pretty far trek from Portland to Cedar Mill. I can't believe that no one saw Yoder heading home that day. I asked him to try recalling whether he saw anyone. If he did, I'll track them down. We need only prove he was on that road just before the Emporium closed at six o'clock. If we prove that, he's in the clear."

She patted his knee and stood. "I best go make sure all is ready for this evening's entertainment. Also, I want to talk to Christina and see if she'd be interested in learning how to keep books."

She kissed his forehead and moved toward door. When she reached the threshold she asked, "You said Fong's going to be back soon? I hope so. It seems like he's been gone a long time."

Noah's teeth were chattering like Mexican castanets by the time a bobbing light appeared offshore. It was near eleven, given the moon's location. To signal their presence, Fong lit the dry tender he carried.

They shucked shoes, socks, and pants, stowing all in burlap sacks tied around their necks. The instant they stepped into the icy water, every degree of heat whooshed away. Despite Fong's grasp on Noah's upper arm, the boy stumbled and got wet up to his waist.

Upon reaching the boat, the boy's numb hands fumbled as he tried to climb the rope ladder, his flailing feet fighting to find its rungs. Still, with Fong pushing and the crew above pulling, the boy reached the deck and was rushed into the cabin. Soon blankets covered their laps, hot tea was burning their tongues, and their numb feet were being toasted by a little pot-bellied coal burner.

When Noah's teeth stopped chattering, he asked, "How long until we are in the United States?"

"That depend."

"It depends on what?"

"Ocean, captain, if custom guard waiting when we dock."

"Are we going to wade in the water again?"

Fong grinned. "Best hope not. Your teeth not strong enough."

TWENTY

It was after nine before Sage covered the distance between Mozart's and the police station. He feared he'd miss Hanke. Sure enough, just as he reached the station the Sergeant was rushing down its steep outside stairs.

"Sergeant!" Sage called. "Might we speak a moment?"

Hanke stopped to say something to the police officer accompanying him. That fellow sped north, leaving the sergeant on the step. Something was up.

"Trouble?" Sage asked.

"Another ruckus at Erickson's."

Sage knew that saloon. It was the city's largest watering hole, block-sized and offering a stage where scantily-dressed dancers kicked up their heels. Itinerant workers, elite slummers, and working women crowded it seven nights a week. Most nights, problems were prevented by the hefty bouncers manning all four of the saloon entrances. A call for police assistance meant the ruckus was a big one.

"I was hoping to talk to Eli. It's important."

Hanke made an exasperated face before reversing course and mounting the stairs, saying over his shoulder, "There aren't enough men on duty to bring him upstairs. You'll have to talk between the bars."

Hanke ushered Sage into the station, introduced him to the desk officer, gave the officer instructions, and departed. Coming out from behind the desk, the officer opened the door. "You're lucky. It's still a bit before I've got to open up our jail hotel."

Sage knew what he meant. During the fall and winter months, the city allowed the homeless to sleep on the jail's corridor floors and in its empty cells. It was an uneasy berth because water seeped through the walls, sending icy rivulets across the cement floors. Still, if they avoided the damp, it was warmer and dryer than sleeping outside. In the morning, the jailers even served a meager mush breakfast that was better than an empty stomach.

The officer showed Sage Eli's cell and pulled a chair up to the bars before returning upstairs. Sage glanced around, gratified to note the adjoining cells were empty. At the corridor's far end, a large holding cell contained men snoring atop the bare slats of iron bunk beds. A whiff of soured alcohol drifted from that direction. Those were the city's drunks, which explained the lack of mattresses.

Eli Yoder was alone, a book in his hand. Seeing Sage, he placed the book face down on his bunk and hurried to the bars. Sage was glad to see that, unlike the fellows in the drunk tank, Yoder had a thin mattress and blanket—not to mention the book.

"Noah!" Eli exclaimed. "He's made it back?"

Sage shook his head, "Sorry Eli, they're still in route."

Yoder's face fell. He took a deep breath. "Is there any news of them?"

"No, not yet. I'm not worried. Fong is resourceful. I'm sure Noah is safe."

Yoder looked doubtful. He took a steadying breath and changed the subject, "I expect you wonder if I remembered seeing anyone when I drove home that night."

"Exactly. My dearest wish is for you to be out of here before your son returns. I figure that, given the recent weather," he gestured toward the little streams darkening the corridor floor, "the soonest possible time for that to happen is tomorrow or the day after. Fong won't chance an ocean crossing in bad weather. Remember, they'll be traveling from Victoria to the San Juan Islands and, from there, to the mainland. A journey like that can take a couple of days—provided there's good weather."

Eli sighed and changed the subject, "Well, the fact is, I remember seeing a wagon coming down the canyon on its way into town. I didn't know the driver but we tipped our hats to each other. He was a typical farmer hauling a load of crated vegetables. He must come from somewhere around Beaverton. If he was coming from further out, he'd ride the train."

"Had you ever seen him before?"

"A few times. Always between five and six in the afternoon. He might remember seeing me."

"Did you see anyone else? Maybe someone on the plank road to Cedar Mill or on Cornell Road near your farm?"

Yoder rubbed his bewhiskered chin thoughtfully. "You know, right after we mounted the planks, I remember hearing the lumber mill's steam engine coming behind me. It rolls along mighty slow. We all hate getting caught behind it" His face fell. "Ah, heck. I was probably too far ahead for the engineer to notice me."

"Do you know the time?"

"Oh, jeez. It was turning dark so I think it was near to six. Once I was bailed from jail, I looked for Noah, and I walked to the Annex to confirm the convention preparations. After that, I ate a quick dinner before heading home sometime after five . . . it was fairly dark."

Sage sighed. "Well, I plan to retrace your journey around the same time. Maybe we'll be lucky and I'll find the man hauling vegetables. And, I've met the driver of the lumber mill engine. It couldn't hurt to ask him if he remembers seeing you or your wagon."

A few hours before sunset the next day, Sage rented the stable's most docile horse. At least that's what the hostler promised. Since Sage didn't know the man's other horses the animal was being compared to, he remained skeptical. But, still, the horse didn't act skittish on their sedate amble through town or during the steep climb up Canyon Road. A hundred yards before the hill's crest, Sage spotted a large fir tree with overhanging boughs. Dismounting carefully, he led the horse under the tree to where dry needles covered the ground—adequate shelter if it rained.

He ducked under its boughs and faced the road. Behind him, Tanner Creek roared at full spate, carving the canyon deeper. It was close to five. If he was lucky, the vegetable farmer would appear within the next hour. If unlucky, he and the horse might have a dank, fruitless, wait beneath the tree. He pulled a carrot from his pocket and offered it to the horse. With quivering lips it gently lifted the morsel from his palm. Nice horse, Sage thought and scratched between its ears.

As they waited beneath the tree, Sage replayed his afternoon visit to the Woman's Club. He found Victoria Hampton in a small office on the same floor as the woman's club lecture hall. She wasn't alone. Three other women bustled about, clacking on typewriters, and shuffling papers.

Dr. Hampton recognized him when he paused in the doorway. "Mr. Adair, how nice to see you! I hope you're here to lend a hand to our pure food efforts!"

Sage was embarrassed. After they spoke at Mozart's, she and the others left hoping he'd lend assistance. He'd forgotten. "Oh, I'm sorry. I can't right now. Unfortunately, today, I must talk to you about something else."

He glanced around the room and she caught his meaning. "Come, we don't want to disturb these ladies. They're busy readying for the Grange convention."

"Grange?" he repeated somewhat stupidly. Because of Eli, he knew about the convention. He wondered how these women were involved.

Hampton answered his unspoken question. "Oh my, yes. The Woman's Club is going to provide hospitality to the women arriving for the convention. We'll have an excursion train outing and a few other events. But, you're not here to learn about that. Let's find a quiet place to talk."

She rose from behind the small desk and he followed her into the corridor. Reaching the lecture hall, she headed for a table and chairs near the door. Once seated, a young woman appeared, carrying a tray holding a coffee pot and mugs. She set them on the table before leaving and returning with a plate of cookies.

Hampton's voice was kind. "Thank you so much, Ruby." The woman smiled, dipped her head, and departed.

"I'd just asked Ruby to rustle up coffee and cookies for everyone so your timing is perfect," She pushed the coffee pot toward him. "Help yourself!"

"She looks young. Are all your volunteers that young?"

"No, most are middle-aged matrons. Ruby just started with us a few months ago. Her husband is often gone working on the railroad. She says she has too much time on her hands." Sadness flicked across the doctor's face before she continued, "She's been a great help in compiling our information. We need many facts to buttress our pure food lobbying down in Salem and with the city council."

"In a way, that's why I am here. I suppose you heard that Aldus Block was murdered?"

Hampton's lips compressed briefly. "Yes, I also read that a dairy farmer was arrested."

"Well, that dairy farmer is a friend and I am certain he's innocent. I'm looking into the situation. Perhaps you didn't hear how Block died?"

Hampton shook her head. "No, I'm too busy to read the newspapers. I learn most things by word of mouth."

"That's understandable. So far, the police aren't saying how he was murdered. But, I know and that's why I tracked you down."

Her eyebrow arched but she said nothing, waiting for him to continue.

Sage explained how Block died. A crash in the hallway punctuated the end of his recital. Hampton jumped up and rushed away. He heard her speak to someone just outside the door.

Returning, she smiled wryly. "Poor Ruby. She tripped and dropped the cream and sugar she was bringing us. What a mess. I told her we'd do without." Hampton sipped coffee before setting down her mug. "What a gruesome death. How do you think I can help?"

He explained about there being barrels of formaldehyde in the cellar beneath the Emporium and his certainty that Block was, indeed, adding embalming fluid to the dairy products he sold. She nodded along as he spoke.

"I take it that is no surprise to you?"

"It's what we suspected. We just needed proof."

"Doesn't the food inspector take samples? I know he visits the Emporium. Besides, you're a chemist; can't you take and check food samples for poison?"

"If someone brings me a sample, through official channels, I always check. Only an official sample results in an official response. Still, for my own information, when I can, I collect samples. Those are what I talked about in my lecture the other day. But, I've never visited the Emporium."

She paused, turning the mug round in her hands. "And, yes, the State inspector is supposed to take and test samples. Of course, that requires him to inspect the facility. At present, the city has no food inspectors and there's just the one State inspector. So inspections are happening but they are few and far between and . . . ," her words trailed off, her lips clamping shut on what she'd been about to say.

"What are you saying? Are there no inspections going on?"

"I'm uncomfortable talking about this. Dr. Pohl and Dr. Lane are members of the city health board. Both of them are better qualified to discuss the inspections that are occurring presently."

She leaned forward, her face earnest. "Please remember the city is served by just a single State inspector who must visit the hundred or so farms that source the dairy products coming into the city. He also tries to inspect all of the city creameries that process and sell those dairy products—they number close to thirty. That doesn't include the countless dairymen selling milk, cream, and butter off the back of their wagons.

"Plus, there are non-dairy items in hundreds of food stores and meat markets to inspect. That workload is doubled because the State inspector has to go back to every site to confirm that they've complied with his orders. His workload is overwhelming and impossible to complete. That's why we're fighting for money to hire a city inspector and why we want to enact stricter laws with high fines for repeat violations."

She swallowed more coffee and continued. "I want to be more involved. My problem is my workload. In addition to my medical practice and volunteering at Valentine Pritchard's Free People's Dispensary Clinic, I also work as a chemist, performing lab tests on various hospital specimens. So, what little help I can give to the pure food fight generally happens in the evenings or when an hour opens in the afternoon, like today."

That ended his visit. And he left feeling he'd learned nothing new.

Now, waiting beneath the fir boughs, Sage felt like the dripping, gloomy canyon was mirroring his dismal mood. His only hope was that this wait would yield an alibi for Eli Yoder. Overhead, the drizzle became a downpour, penetrating the fir needles and driving him deeper under cover to plant his backside against the tree trunk.

"Least we not have to wade," Fong told him as they slogged along an inland path beneath a downpour. Upon reaching Orcas Island, the fishing boat had tied up to an abandoned dock. There they spent a dry, warm night huddled in the cabin together with the captain and his two crew members while rain pounded the roof overhead.

At daybreak, as the clouds overhead began turning a sullen gray, they'd stepped onto the rotting planks and cast off the boat. It was taking its catch around the point and up the slough to the cannery at Deer Harbor, leaving Fong and Noah to head overland to the village of Orcas Landing. It was a short distance and they hope to arrive before the ferry steamer's first sailing of the day.

"You're going on the steamer with me, right?" asked Noah. The dark circles beneath his eyes evidenced a restless night spent crammed into the boat's tiny cabin.

"I do my best." Fong patted the bag holding his well-to-do clothes. "We play by ear. If lucky, the crew man will remember me and not alert customs. Otherwise . . . ." He shrugged his shoulders and added, "We 'wing it' as my friends say."

He flashed a set of rather large teeth in a reassuring smile. "We reach Anacortes, hop on train, and you home lickety-split."

The boy grinned though his eyes stayed anxious.

TWENTY ONE

THE RAIN PAUSED JUST AS a wagon crested the long hill down into town, the setting sun riming a man's shape atop a wagon seat. Sage slipped Jack London's *Sea Wolf* into his inside coat pocket, glad to abandon the frenzied mutiny underway in London's latest adventure story. After ensuring the dozing horse was securely tied, he stepped onto the plank roadway—his empty hands out to his sides to appear unthreatening.

The man hauled his horses to a stop, set his wheel brake, and stared down from beneath a wide-brimmed hat. Behind him the wagon bed held crates piled high with kale, lettuce, chicory, chard, cabbage, cauliflower, broccoli, kohlrabi, leeks, and onions. This could be the man Eli saw.

Sage doffed his hat. "Excuse me, Sir," he called. "I am hoping you saw someone on this road four evenings ago, about this same time."

The farmer looked puzzled. "Why might you be asking me?"

Sage considered how much to say. He couldn't taint the man's answers. On the other hand, this man was understandably cautious. Too little information and he'd turn unhelpful. Sage chose disclosure. "My friend, Eli Yoder, says he saw someone hauling vegetables into town at that time. Assuming I find the person he saw, that'd be enough to get him released from jail. Right now, they think he killed that creamery owner, Aldus Block."

At the mention of Block's name, the farmer's nose wrinkled in distaste. He stared off into the middle distance, searching his memory. Switching his attention back to Sage, he said, "Block was not a decent man. I don't know your Mr. Yoder by name but, if his horse is a handsome bay Morgan with a black mane, and he was hauling empty milk cans in his wagon, why yes, I did see him. We nodded and touched hats at each other when he pulled off the road to let me pass. Didn't exchange any words. I was running pretty late, it was nearing six o'clock when I rolled into this here canyon."

Joy surged through Sage and he asked the next most important question, "Would you be willing to tell the police that?"

"I guess so. The problem is, I got to deliver these vegetables and I'm already late because I waited for the rain to ease. Our co-op members expect payment tonight. These are their vegetables as well as my own. They're waiting on my return."

"Could you deliver the produce and then stop by the police station?"

"You say this fellow Yoder has been accused of murder? I've not heard his name before. Just who is he?"

"He has a dairy farm out Cedar Mill way. He's also the master of the Grange in those parts."

That information seemed to firm up the farmer's resolve because he nodded decisively. "Well then, I guess it's my duty to tell what I saw. Is there someone I should ask for at the police station?"

"Sergeant Norm Hanke. Tell him John Adair sent you and tell him what you saw."

"You're Adair?" At Sage's nod, the man responded, "I'm Jebediah Shaw, a member of the Beaverton Farmer's Coop. My farm's near Sylvan. I'm the fellow who takes our co-op's products to market—maybe three times a week. Sometimes, if it gets too late or wet, I spend the night at my sister's and return home in the morning. That's what I was planning to do and why I was on the road a bit late when I saw your friend, Yoder."

"Eli will be grateful that you took the time to help. I need to track down a second person who may have also seen him that evening; otherwise, I'd go with you to the police station. You need to ask for Sergeant Hanke. If he's not at the station, tell the officer at the desk that you have important information regarding the Block murder but that it is for the Sergeant alone."

Seeing the man's puzzled look, Sage added, "Hanke's heading the investigation and will know what to do with your information. Otherwise, you might waste your time telling the wrong person."

That explanation seemed to satisfy Shaw. "Alrighty then, I better get to cracking," He released his wheel brake, shook the reins, and clucked his horse into a walk.

Sage watched the wagon rumble downhill for a moment then ran for his horse.

He was in luck. Upon reaching the plank road leading to the Cedar Mill lumber yard, he heard Clementine huffing just ahead of him. Peering through a sudden deluge, he saw the steam engine moving in a steady chug toward the foothills. His heels nudged the rented horse onto the plank road. They needed to catch Clementine and find out whether Smoke saw Yoder's wagon ahead of him on the evening in question.

The horse picked up his pace, moving into a steady, smooth canter. Gratified, Sage leaned forward to again scratch the animal between the ears. "That's another carrot for you, old girl."

Within a few short minutes, they came up behind Clementine, close enough that Sage's hail stopped the big wheels' turning.

"Why howdy, there!" Smoke called. "You riding that horse will break poor Clementine's heart. She's a jealous lady."

Sage laughed, glad that Smoke remembered him. "Miss Clementine, I do beg your pardon. You are a very congenial and much safer ride. Today, though, I needed speed, hence this pitiful horse."

Smoke chuckled. "You want to climb on up, outta the rain?" He gestured to the metal rungs leading up to the platform.

"Would that I could but I can't. I'm in a hurry. I wanted to ask you whether you saw anyone ahead of you on this road four evenings ago, somewhere around six o'clock.

Smoke thought a moment. "That'd been my last haul of the day. The boss don't like Clementine being out once it's dark. Truth be, I ain't too fond of driving her that late either."

He again lapsed into thought, only to grin when realization hit him. "Why, I did see a wagon when we first rolled onto the planks. He started right ahead of me before pulling too far ahead to talk. Clementine, she always takes it slow and easy."

"Can you describe the person driving that wagon?"

"Don't have to. It was that dairy farmer, Eli Yoder. Nice fellow. We chin wag now and again. I seen him and his wagon before. I'd know it anywhere. Miss Clementine's pace gives me lots of time to notice things.

"Didn't talk to him that day though. Like I said, he got too far ahead. But there was still a bit of light in the sky 'cepting I know it was a bit after six 'cause we was racing the dark."

Sage wanted to whoop with relief. Two witnesses. He'd found two witnesses! "Would you be willing to tell the police you saw Eli that evening?"

Realization brightened Smoke's somewhat sooty face. "My Lord, is that when that store owner died? The one they say Yoder murdered?"

At Sage's nod, Smoke straightened. "Well, then, let me deliver this load and I'll ride into town pronto quick."

"It'll be full dark," Sage cautioned.

"That's okay. My trusty horse, Timmy, finds his way into the city with no problem. But, Clementine here, she takes a while to make it to the lumber yard. Expect to see me at the police station in about an hour and a half. I'll try to make it in less time. Depends how muddy the roads are, what with today's rain and all."

With that, they parted, Clementine huffing away. Sage reined his horse homeward, his heart singing for the first time in days. If justice prevailed, they'd free Eli Yoder tonight.

Sage was climbing the steep steps into the police station just as Jebediah Shaw was descending them. Mid-stairway, the two men paused to exchange words.

"I just finished signing my affidavit, Mr. Adair. Sure seemed like your Sergeant was real happy to hear my information. A bit odd, that."

The farmer's face held a question that Sage answered. "He never believed Eli Yoder was guilty. The whole situation has been made worse by the fact that Yoder's fourteen-year-old boy was missing."

"Was missing?"

"Yup. Shanghaied onto a whaler. He's been found and rescued up in Canada."

"By all the saints. That's a lot for a body to bear. It makes me doubly glad that I knew something real helpful—at least that's what the Sergeant kept telling me."

After saying goodnight, Shaw raised his hat, descended to his empty wagon, and climbed aboard. Sage continued his climb and entered the station.

When Sage entered, Hanke was in the lobby. He greeted Sage with a big grin. "You did it, Adair. Given Mr. Shaw's information, the Chief should release Eli."

"We need to wait an hour or so because I discovered a second witness. It's Smoke, the engineer of that steam engine we rode into Cedar Mill. He's coming into town to talk to you."

"Two witnesses! Boy oh boy, that's just dandy. Wait here. I was on my way to fetch Eli from the cells. I can't wait to tell him the good news. It'll be a bit before we can release him. I'll need to hand carry both affidavits to the Chief's home since he's already gone for the day."

Hanke's tone held a touch of satisfied malice. Evidently, the police chief's pooh-pooing his defense of his friend had rankled. That made the two witness affidavits sweet vindication.

They waited until the steamer's crew moved to cast off before emerging from the surrounding woods and hurrying down the ramp to board. Fong was wearing his fine suit. Noah was as tidy as possible following his night aboard a fishing boat. Each clutched a ticket that Fong had purchased on his outbound trip. Noah was to act as if they were strangers.

Their luck held. The crewman took their tickets and gestured them onto the steamer. Once aboard, they made their way past barrels of lime and crates of canned fish to enter the passenger cabin.

Few seats remained inside. Having already explored the steamer on his outbound trip, Fong sat on a far bench and eyed each of the passengers from beneath the brim of a hat pulled low. Noah moved around, gazing out the port holes and wandering the deck while the steamer made its slow, circuitous route, stopping at Lopez and San Juan Islands, before turning toward the mainland.

As they steamed toward the Anacortes dock, Fong rose and sought out the one crew member he'd chatted with on his outbound trip to Orcas. Before leaving Portland, he'd visited the man supplying Chinese laborers to the Columbia River canneries. That fellow told him the name of his counterpart doing the same job in the San Juan Islands—a man named Chun Ching Hock.

When boarding the boat at Anacortes, Fong had introduced himself to the crewman overseeing the boarding, telling the man he was a new associate of Mr. Chun.

That fellow instantly straightened and became friendly. "We see Mr. Chun quite frequently on this boat. He has business dealings with all the canneries on the islands. Glad to see he has some help. He's a nice man. Generous, very generous."

Fong knew what that meant. As he was leaving the steamer at Orcas Island, he made sure that he was also, "Generous, very generous."

Fortunately, the same crewman recognized him as they docked at Anacortes and jumped to man the gangplank as Fong approached to disembark. "Good morning, Mr. Fong. I trust your business went well?"

At Fong's smiling nod, the man continued. "Mr. Chun will be happy. Please give him my best regards."

After being "generous" a second time, Fong stepped onto the dock.

Immediately, a man exited a small shack and strode up the dock toward the steamer. His shiny billed cap, wide gun belt, and knee-high leather boots meant he was an immigration inspector. He stopped ten feet from Fong. "Halt," he ordered, raising a hand.

Fong stopped and kept his face impassive. Despite the chill fall air, sweat trickled down his back, and every nerve in his body alerted. He was ready, if necessary, to knock the inspector onto the planks and run for dry land. He and Noah discussed that eventuality. If Fong needed to evade capture, they'd meet at the back of the train station. Once there, Fong would somehow sneak onto the train. If he didn't escape, Noah had enough money to board the train, ride into Portland, and make his way to Mozart's Table. That was their emergency plan.

He resisted showing relief when the crewman stepped behind him to lay a hand on Fong's shoulder. "This here is Mr. Fong. He works for that labor contractor, Chun Ching Hock. As you know, Mr. Chun is a big man around these parts with important friends. Mr. Fong's alright! He's no immigrant. I know him well. Let him pass." The crewman rubbed his index finger and thumb together in the universal sign for money.

For a moment, the inspector looked like he'd resist until a calculating look narrowed his eyes. He surveyed Fong from head to toe. After what felt like a long time, he dropped his hand and stepped aside, motioning for Fong to continue on his way.

Fong slipped a few more coins to the crewman, gave the inspector a brusque nod of thanks, and strode up the dock. Noah waited at the top, a big smile on his face. Fong grinned in return as he stepped onto land. Passing the boy, he warned, out of the side of his mouth, "Best hurry. Don't want to miss train."

TWENTY TWO

Yoder's release was delayed. The chief was visiting a relative in Vancouver when a vindicated Hanke tried to deliver the alibi affidavits. So, Eli Yoder spent one more night in jail. The next morning, Sage was in the police lobby when Hanke brought Eli up from the cells. His face shone brighter than the sky outside, though that wasn't saying much since the morning's sullen clouds lay thick and low.

That morning began with a coded telegram from Fong. Once outdoors, with Yoder at his side, Sage turned toward the train station. The other man staggered when he realized their destination. Sage took hold of his elbow to keep him upright, saying. "If the train is on time, we have about an hour's wait. I figured you'd want to be on the platform when it pulls in. In the meantime, I thought we'd eat breakfast in the station café."

It seemed an endless hour. A distracted Yoder ate sparingly while constantly glancing at the big wall clock. Ten minutes before the train's scheduled arrival they stood on the platform. As he stared up the tracks, Yoder's expression teetered between hope and fear.

At last, a whistle tooted, signaling that the train was crossing the river. A minute later a huffing rumble heralded its approach. Seconds later, the engine rounded the final bend and slid into the station.

Sage thought Yoder might levitate out of his boots in anticipation. His son must have been in a similar state because the second the train braked to a halt, a young boy jumped off the second-class car even before the porter lowered the stairs. With a whoop and a shouted "Noah", Yoder ran.

The boy, seeing his father, shouted "Pa", and also charged forward, arms outstretched. The two met in a hug that lifted Noah high into the air.

In the meantime, a well-dressed Chinese man quietly descended from the same car. When his eyes met Sage's they both grinned. Their greetings were more subdued—just a hearty handshake and squeeze of one another's shoulder.

Late that afternoon, Sage climbed the narrow stairway to the second floor offices of the Boards of Health. Midway, he had to step aside for a well-dressed stranger hurriedly descending. As he passed, the man politely tapped his hat brim.

It had been a wonderful morning with their arrival at Mozart's sparking a celebratory air among all. While wolfing down a meatloaf sandwich, Noah recounted some of his adventure. Soon thereafter the dairy farmer and his son departed to collect their wagon and horse from the livery stable and head home. Eli vowed he'd be keeping his son close by "for a good long while." They would stop at Noah's school only long enough to show his classmates and teacher that he'd returned safely.

While walking to the Board's office, Sage asked himself why he felt compelled to pursue the reason behind Block's murder as well as the problem of impure food. And, why his mind persisted in trying to link the two.

Before leaving Mozart's he'd discussed the situation with his mother and Fong. Hanke reported that, with Yoder now exonerated, the police intended to focus on finding Block's mysterious female bookkeeper. The three of them agreed that their job was done. Sage said they'd fulfilled their promise to Hanke and could return to their everyday life.

A heavy silence followed this declaration, during which Fong and Mae exchanged smirks. Mae finally said, "Hah. If you believe that's what we're going to do, you're fooling yourself. For you to stop nosing about would be as likely as snow in July." She smiled and patted his arm. "It's okay, Son. I understand because I'm also keen to know who killed that despicable man and why. We sure can't trust the police to find the answers."

Sage opened his mouth to argue but shut it when he saw Fong nodding his agreement. He grinned and conceded, "Okay, you two. You're right. We might as follow it through and figure out who murdered Block. So, what's our next step?"

"You say Dr. Hampton act like she know more than she say," Fong observed.

"Yeah, she was evasive when I asked her why Block's creamery wasn't being cited for being filthy and using embalming fluid. She gave me a long spiel about how one inspector is trying to handle the work of ten. When I pressed her further she told me to talk to Dr. Pohl. She said the doctor was the best person to answer my questions about Block."

"Well, then, maybe that's where you need to head next." Mae said, before giving him a stern look and adding, "You can visit the doctor once the noon dinner hour finishes. We'll still be short of help because Mr. Fong needs to go home to see his wife."

So here he was, temporarily freed from his Mozart's chores and hoping to find Esther Pohl in the nondescript, two-story brick building housing the Board's offices. The second-story hallway was dim, a single skylight providing the sole light. After squinting at every door plaque, he found the one announcing the shared office of both the City and State Boards of Health.

He found two women inside, one of them Dr. Pohl. The other was Mrs. Evans, the president of the woman's club. They were leaning forward across a desk and talking with quiet intensity. At his entry, they sprang apart as if he'd caught them wrong-footed.

Sage doffed his hat. "Ladies, I'm sorry to have startled you. Good afternoon Dr. Pohl and Mrs. Evans."

Recognition lit Dr. Pohl's face and she jumped up to round the desk, her hand out-stretched. "Oh, that's quite alright. We thought you were the Commissioner returning because he'd forgotten something. You probably passed him your way into the building," she added.

Her fluster under control, she continued, "But, forgive me, Mr. Adair. Please take a seat. How wonderful to see you, though this is a bit surprising. Are you here to file a food complaint? Do you need the services of our inspector?" she asked, while retaking her seat behind the desk.

Sage sat on a nearby chair and shook his head. "No, I've no complaints. Mozart's experienced a problem but we located its source and eliminated it. So, at present, all is well at the restaurant."

She raised her eyebrows. "So, why might you be honoring us with your presence this afternoon? I don't mean to be rude but Mrs. Evans and I are rather busy. We must prepare for a meeting that is quite important."

Sage raised a hand. "In that case, I'll make it quick. I'm here because the source of Mozart's difficulty was Aldus Block's dairy products." Evans gave a faint gasp and the two women exchanged worried looks.

"Is this about his murder? Because I assure you . . ." Pohl began quickly.

"No, no. It's not about that. At least not precisely, though it might be related." The puzzlement on their faces was understandable. He was sounding dithery. He cleared his throat and strove for clarity, "First you need to know that the cellar of Block's Quality Emporium contains barrels of embalming fluid. We've determined that Block was adding it to his dairy products. That's why my customers took sick. When we switched back to the Purity Creamery our problems stopped—no more sick customers."

He paused and realized there was a complaint, of sorts, to impart. "I think the current manager of the store knows nothing about it. I am positive, however, that the fellow managing the creamery knows and is still adding formaldehyde and other things to the dairy. My thought is that maybe you'll want to remove those barrels before someone else sickens."

Anger flashed across the doctor's face and her tone was resolute. "I will confer with the police immediately. Those barrels will be seized. Thank you for telling me." From the set of her rather square jaw, that particular conversation was going to occur sooner rather than later.

"Sergeant Hanke is familiar with the situation at the Emporium," he said. "That's the officer you'll want to talk to.

"But, there's something else you need to know. When I learned about Block's barrels I decided to discover where he bought them. I think a chemical manufacturing company in St. Louis is the supplier. To that end, I've arranged for the Union Station's porters to note when barrels from that company arrive and to note who's receiving them. Obviously, not all the formaldehyde being shipped in is for funeral homes. When I obtain a list of the non-mortuary recipients, I'll forward it to you."

"Why, that's wonderful!" exclaimed Mrs. Evans. "Esther, what a leg up that will give us! Why didn't we think of that?"

Pohl raised a cautionary hand. "Indeed, such a list will be quite helpful. Of course, it's possible that the barrels' contents are divvied up and sent to more than one place. Maybe Block was a distributor. Not every creamery can afford to buy or store barrels of embalming fluid like Aldus Block did."

Sage saw her point. Maybe their first task was to follow the barrels to the distributor and see where the chemical went from there—a perfect task for Fong or Eich. Dagnabbit, nothing's ever simple, he thought before moving on. "All of which brings me to the question I came to ask. How was Block able to get away with it? Block's creamery is a big operation. My source tells me that it's filthy and stinks. Yet, I am also told it's inspected every month."

This time the look exchanged by the two women was full of meaning though what that meaning was, Sage couldn't say. They didn't look surprised.

"When you say 'stink' I think what you mean is that it smells like cat urine and chemicals," Pohl said.

"Yes, that's it exactly. When I smelled embalming fluid at Hadley's mortuary it made me think of cat pee. My source was in the creamery and said that the odor was eye-stingingly strong. And, my source also saw them dumping something that looked bright yellow into the butter. How was Block able to do that without getting closed down by the inspector?"

Pohl stayed silent, apparently deep in thought. At the same time, Sarah Evans wordlessly studied her folded hands. These two knew something.

When Pohl looked at Sage, she met his eyes directly, "Mr. Adair, that question is what we've been asking ourselves. Block was murdered before we were able to answer it. Please, I entreat you to keep your Emporium-related questions to yourself for a bit longer."

"There's nothing more you can tell me? You obviously know more."

This time, he saw regret in her expression. "I'm sorry Mr. Adair. Presently, I am not at liberty to discuss this particular matter further." Determination compressed her lips, meaning it was pointless to press further.

Sage sighed. He'd encountered similar brick walls in the past. "All right then, ladies, I will take my leave. Thank you for your time." He set his hat on his head and headed for the door only to be halted by Pohl saying, "Portland's Board of Health is supervised by the State Board of Health. Maybe you best talk to someone at the State Board."

"Who at the State level is the most helpful? The Commissioner?"

Evans' cough failed to mask her derisive snort.

Pohl shot a quelling glance at the other woman and said, "I think the person you should talk to is Dr. Woods Hutchinson. He's Secretary to the State Board and is involved with its daily activities. Perhaps you remember him? He spoke at the lecture you attended. He's as concerned about food purity as we are."

Sage recalled the narrow-faced man. And yes, Hutchinson's speech was laden with passionate frustration. "Alright, I'll talk to him. How do I find him?"

"He'll be working here in the office the day after tomorrow. Right now, he's out in the field trying to buttress the efforts of our sole inspector. As I said, Dr. Hutchinson cares."

Sage exited, pondering what Pohl said and what she'd not said. Sarah Evans' involuntary, contemptuous snort was also noteworthy.

On his way down the narrow stairs, he stepped aside again. This time for a woman who was rapidly mounting them. Although her head was down, something about her seemed familiar. He immediately forgot the encounter because there were more pressing things to think about.

"Please partake of the tea and cookies, my dear. I made the cookies myself. We don't hire help. Mr. Trumbull and I like to keep our home private, without the folderol of strangers underfoot, listening to what we say and seeing all that we do." Millie Trumbull waved a hand around a parlor cluttered with stacks of papers and books.

"You are a busy woman," Lucinda acknowledged.

Millie's face sobered. "My dear Lucinda, I hope you don't take offense because I asked you to meet privately, here in my home. I just can't include the other ladies. I'm sure you know, better than I, just how hypocritical and judgmental others can be."

Lucinda's smile was genuine as she reached across the small table and squeezed the other woman's hand. "No, Millie. I am not offended. I am honored that you'd invite me into your home. And, I understand why we must keep our connection secret."

She spoke truthfully. This was her first invitation to a "proper" matron's home. So, being here was, indeed, an honor. Besides, Lucinda also wanted to keep their connection secret. Millie Trumbull was leading the progressive fight against child abuse as well as a host of other social ills. This made her the enemy of Lucinda's wealthy customers. She'd heard more than one shout derisively, while in his cups, "Hold on to your wallets gents, here comes Millie!" It would be disastrous if they discovered Lucinda Collins consorted with their enemy.

"Well, Lucinda, if I may correct you. . . I feel our "connection" has blossomed into a friendship. I hope you feel the same."

Tears smarted in Lucinda's eyes. She'd become very fond of this hard-charging, plain-speaking woman.

Millie, noting Lucinda's emotional reaction changed the subject. "So, my dear friend—did you find out who funds that damnable house?"

"I believe so. I am certain of the name. Unfortunately, it may create a real conundrum for you."

Millie's brow lowered, "For me? Why is that?"

"I believe the investor's a rather large donor to the Children's Aid Society. You're on the board of that organization, right?"

Millie collapsed against the back of her chair. "Oh my lord," she breathed.

"He's also a frequent visitor to my house. Though, once his involvement becomes public, I guarantee he won't be welcome in the future," she let that declaration trail off at seeing Millie's distress.

Millie's cup banged onto the table. "We must stop him. The house must be closed. I don't care who he is," she declared.

Lucinda realized that she'd been holding her breath hoping for that response while fearful that its failure to come would kill their budding friendship.

"Who is he? What's his name?" Millie demanded.

When Lucinda told her, the color drained from Millie's rosy face. "Oh, me," she muttered and flapped a hand as if cooling a flash of heat. Seconds later she turned still and silent. In that silence, the mantel clock's rich chimes marked the hour.

Millie cleared her throat and said, "I am shocked. His wife is a member of our woman's club. She's a volunteer at our children's home. And, you are right; he's a big donor to the Children's Aid Society. Now, I'm wondering why."

Lucinda had been wondering that herself and named the possibilities she'd considered. "Well, perhaps he feels guilty. Or, maybe he's shopping for potential victims. Or, maybe his wife makes him donate because she knows what he's doing or, just because she believes in the cause. We may never know."

Millie remained pale. "Do you think she knows?"

Lucinda shrugged her shoulders. "Even if she doesn't, I'd bet money that she suspects something's wrong with him."

Millie stood. "This discussion requires more tea," she said, snatching up the teapot and heading toward her kitchen. When she reached the threshold she stopped and Lucinda saw determination stiffen the woman's back. She turned and said with narrowed lips, "I promise you one thing, my girl. We will make it so uncomfortable for him that he'll skip town. And," here her finger jabbed the air like a vengeful god's, "I will make sure his name and description are known by every woman, in every woman's club, in the entire country. There are almost half a million of us, now." With that, Millie disappeared down the hallway.

TWENTY THREE

Female laughter echoing up the stairwell woke Sage the next morning and drew him down into Mozart's dining room three flights below. There he found his mother, Lucinda, and Millie Trumbull sitting at a large table, partaking of coffee and biscuits. Before he could ask what they found so funny, the kitchen doors swung open as Fong and Eich entered. The gang was all there except for Angus Solomon. Just as Sage mentally marked that absence, a knock sounded on the restaurant's locked front door and Solomon joined them.

It was obvious the women had summoned the men folk to this morning meeting. It was equally obvious that none of the four men knew its purpose. But, the women's laughter and smiles suggested it was a celebratory occasion.

When Millie Trumbull was introduced to Eich, Solomon, and Fong, she didn't bat an eye nor comment on the group's motley composition. She stared a little bit longer at Fong until her eyes sparked and a tiny smile tugged at her lips. She'd just realized who might be the "unidentified" Chinese man responsible for turning the fancy pedophile house into ashes.

"Okay, ladies. Might you explain why you summoned us here?" Sage asked.

Mae stood saying, "Before we share our good news, I'll fetch coffee and treats for you fellows being's how it's a mite early." She vanished into the kitchen and returned holding a loaded tray. Eich leapt up to take the tray and carry it to the table.

After distributing cups of poured coffee and passing around a plate of biscuits, Mae said, "How about you start, Lucinda dear and let Millie finish the story." For some reason, the three women laughed again as the men exchanged perplexed looks.

Lucinda nodded and laid out the steps she'd taken to discover the new pedophilia house's location. "It was right in the middle of the Negro district. I guess the idea was to plant it someplace where it'd go unnoticed by the town's so-called 'respectable people.'"

That comment elicited more chuckles from the women followed by Mille saying, "Boy, that sure backfired!" which brought forth another gale of feminine chortles.

The men just stared, spurring Millie into telling her part of the story. "Once we knew the location and the name of the money man behind the despicable operation, I held a meeting of the women I call the 'Old Guard'. Their picketing helped close down that last house. We determined that, this time, we needed to do more than just parade around with our picket signs. We decided to storm the battlements so to speak and rescue every single child being held there. That called for more, let us say, 'lively' participation." Her description triggered another round of chuckling among the three women.

Sage believed he spoke for the other males when he repeated, "'Lively'? You ladies carried guns or something?"

Millie gave a vigorous shake of her head. "No, not a single gun." She leaned forward as if about to share a secret, her eyes dancing. "You, see, some of my Old Guard also belong to the Ladies Temperance Union. One of them suggested that we mount a joint effort since those ladies are skilled at what do you suppose, gentlemen?"

Angus laughed and provided the answer, "Barging in with axes raised."

"Exactly. So that is what we did. We formed quite a little band of women marching down the sidewalk. It was noisy enough that neighboring women came out on their stoops to discover what was happening. They were already furious about the house and joined us! It was wonderful."

Lucinda interrupted to say, "I couldn't be part of the gang so I watched from a carriage, half a block away. I tell you, it was a sight to behold. At least twenty-five women stormed the house, some of them carrying axes and hatchets."

Sage shook his head as he asked his mother. "I suppose you took a front-row seat also, Mrs. Clemens? I wondered about your absence following yesterday's tea time."

She shook her head. "No seat for me! I was at the front. Millie let me knock on the door. When no one answered, I tried the handle. It was locked. So, I stepped aside and let the Temperance ladies go at it. A few swings of the ax and Bob's your uncle, we were inside."

Sage scowled. "You could have been hit with a shotgun blast for god's sake."

"And, that is why we didn't tell you what we planned to do," Mae told him.

"Why didn't you tell me that you'd done this last night?"

"Because our action had two parts. So, keep on a'listening," she instructed and nodded for Millie to continue the story.

"Once the door was breached, we stormed inside. The creature inside the house pointed a gun at us. He lowered it once he saw all those women and their axes." Millie gave a gleeful cackle.

"Once in, we executed our raid. Some of the women climbed up to the second floor, some scoured the ground floor rooms, and another group searched the cellar. All and all, we found seven children--three boys and four girls. Lickety-split a few women got them dressed, out of the house, and into Lucinda's carriage. They're all safe at the children's home."

It sounded like a chaotic, exciting scene. Sage noticed the other three men were also appreciating the tale. "What happened next?"

The three women exchanged grins. It seemed the best part of the story was yet to come. Lucinda took up the account. "First, some of the ladies rushed the children down the steps and into my carriage. After that, three men scooted out of the house," here she paused to suppress another chortle. Once she gained control, she finished quickly. "They were shoeless and stark naked except for flowered curtains wrapped around their waists. Best of all, Mae got that *Journal* reporter there with his Brownie camera.

Mae jumped in to declare, "That reporter's bulbs were a'flashing like lightning round a mountain top!" Guffaws filled the dining room.

Once calm descended, Sage asked. "However did you women make that happen? And, who were the three men?"

Satisfaction suffused Millie Trumbull's face. "One was the operator of the house. He's the one who dropped his gun on the floor pronto quick. Right away, a temperance lady, with a few feints of her sharp ax, scared him into dropping his britches and doffing the rest of his clothes. The other two men the same thing once we shooed them out of the closets where they were hiding.

"And, my goodness, how they whined and sniffled." It was evident from her expression that pity had not slowed the ladies' actions. Millie sobered and gave the reason for their hardheartedness by adding, "One of those little girls looked to be no more than six years old. And, one of the boys, no more than eight."

"What happened after that?"

Millie shrugged. "Let's just say that house is pretty uninhabitable—every window is broken and every room is bare. What wasn't removed was smashed to bits. The neighbor ladies never want to see such an operation in their neighborhood again. They'd already been trying to figure out how to get rid of it. That's why they jumped on our bandwagon so fast."

Millie's forehead wrinkled. "You know, given how churchgoing those folks tend to be. I am surprised at the stupidity of those scoundrels—situating a house like that in their midst."

Fong cleared his throat. "They learn lesson now." His comment triggered more laughter.

Sage stirred from his reverie and said, "Mae, what did you mean about it being a two-part action? What's the second part and when is it going to happen?"

She smirked and wagged a finger at him. "Well, while you snoozed this morning, we did what needed doing."

Millie cleared her throat to take over the telling. "We invaded the real estate office of the man responsible for funding the house. No axes this time. We were just fifteen upstanding, well-known, civic-minded, angry women, most of whom he knew."

She sighed. "I can't say I felt good about that experience."

Lucinda reached over to squeeze Millie's hand. "It needed doing," she told the woman. "Think of the alternative for the children."

"Yes, I know. I don't feel bad about him. But, his wife is a nice woman and I feel sorry about how our ultimatum will affect her life."

"What 'ultimatum'? Sage asked.

"We told him what we knew. We gave him two weeks to leave town and never come back. We also said we'd be notifying every single women's club in the country to be on the lookout for him. Of course, he'll likely change his name. So many of those scoundrels do."

"How did he react? What did he say?"

"He cried. Kept saying he couldn't help himself. He begged us not to tell his wife. That last is why I feel so bad. I hate to imagine what is going on in their home today. Whatever is he going to tell her?"

Lucinda broke the ensuing silence. "Maybe he will tell her the truth, give her the choice to stay or go. She has a right to know. What we need to remember is that seven children are no longer living in hell. We gave them a better chance at life. They are what matters—not the adult man exploiting them or his wife who's kept her eyes shut."

That afternoon there was a rain break. Weak sunlight glittered on the wet pavement as Lucinda and Christina headed toward the Quality Emporium. This was to be the young woman's first foray into the bookkeeping profession. She'd proven herself a motivated and adept pupil. After a few days, she'd grasped the fundamentals and was ready to tackle the Quality Emporium's books, with Lucinda providing backup.

Lucinda told Christina about the food adulteration because it didn't feel right to leave her in the dark about what they suspected was happening in the Emporium's creamery. Because she also didn't want the young woman to stumble into a bad situation with the man managing it, she warned Christina that Gribble had a threatening and nasty attitude.

She quickly assured Christina that was most unlikely that Deason, the new proprietor, knew anything about the creamery's dairy adulteration scheme. "First of all, he's not the sharpest needle in the pincushion. Second, Block kept most everything from him—just used him as a clerk, stocker, and errand boy. And finally, I just can't see him being a part of nefarious goings on. They'd never trust him not to blab. Aside from being not too bright, he's an inoffensive sort of fellow. My gut tells me he'll be horrified to learn what his cousin was doing."

She eyed Christina. "You can't call Deason handsome or good-looking. But, if a woman wants stability, kindness, and adoration in a marriage, Edgar Deason is a good choice. He'd be so gratified to find love, he'd keep his wife atop a pedestal for her entire life."

Christina made no response though, when Lucinda glanced at her, she noticed the girl looked thoughtful.

Rather than being repelled by the idea of working in a shady operation, Christina was intrigued. The girl was already excited about tackling her first accounting job. To think she might also help uncover evidence of poisoned food upped her enthusiasm.

With the Emporium in sight, Lucinda held the other woman's arm to make her stop and face her. "Christina, you listen to me carefully. You are heading into the lion's den. One man has been murdered there. A young boy was kidnapped from there. He ended up on a whaler bound for the Bering Sea. You must act like a demure, ignorant girl from the countryside. Under no circumstances are you to go into the creamery, unless it's to use the necessary. And if you do, step in and out as fast as you can. Do not look around. Do not act curious. Do not talk to that man Gribble. If he comes toward you, scoot. "

"But, what if I see something?"

"You keep your mouth shut. Ask no questions. Not a single one, you hear me? And, wait to tell me about it when you're back at the house."

Christina gazed into the distance.

"Promise me, Christina. Promise me or else this is all over. I will not introduce you to Mr. Deason. I will not let you work there. It's too dangerous if you don't do as I say."

The girl's solemn brown eyes focused on her mentor. "Okay, Miss Collins. I promise to keep my nose out of everything but the bookwork." An impish smile lit her delicate face, with its wispy frame of light brown hair, as she added, "While I consider whether Mr. Deason is husband material."

Lucinda smiled, let go of Christina's arm, and started walking. "Oh that poor, poor, man, he has no idea what he's in for," she said, making Christina laugh.

TWENTY FOUR

"Talk about killing two birds, with one stone," commented Sage to Mae and Fong when he joined them in the empty dining room. It was late, and everyone was tired. They hadn't the chance to talk following their morning meeting because the day rolled out like a runaway wagon down a steep canyon. "We returned Noah to his father and, we found and rid the city of a horrible place. We should take satisfaction in that."

"Hit two birds, one stone maybe. But most bad bird flap free."

"You are right Mr. Fong. A murderer is still running loose in the world," Sage agreed.

Mae slapped her palms on the table, stood, and declared, "Well, then, I guess we best get some rest so that, tomorrow, we can figure out how to trap that damn bird."

"That Mr. Deason sure is attentive," Christina commented early the next morning "He's at my elbow at least thrice an hour asking, 'Do I want coffee, do I want tea, do I have any questions' and so on." They sat at the kitchen table, peeling apples. That was the deal they made with Mrs. Miller; if they peeled the apples, she'd make the pies.

Lucinda recalled Deason's tendency to hover. "Yeah, I found it hard to shoo him away. And, since I wanted to search Block's office, there were a few close calls. I wasn't able to finish."

"Well, there's no problem now. He's asked me to go through and organize all the office paperwork. So, tell me what you'd like me to find and I'll keep my eyes open."

Christina reached for another apple and raised her chin, her eyes bright, as she said, "Mr. Deason asked me to work there for two hours every afternoon, five days a week."

It was obvious that Deason's request pleased her. "He says once I'm done with the book entries and straightening the office, I can teach him how to order supplies. He's only stocked shelves and inventoried. He doesn't know a thing about purchasing. Of course, neither do I but I figure you can teach me."

Lucinda smiled at Christina's newfound confidence. "Absolutely. I'll be happy to teach you. My friend, Mae, knows even more about ordering supplies. I'm sure she'd also be happy to help. Are you staying away from that Gribble fellow in the creamery?"

"Boy, I am sure glad you warned me about him. He's a nasty sort." Christina's face adopted a thoughtful look followed by a tiny smile.

"What's so funny?" Lucinda demanded.

"Well, I think that Edgar trails me whenever I go to the necessary. He stands right behind the swinging doors into the creamery. Whenever I go back into the store, he's always fussing around the shelf right inside the doors. And, twice now, he's burst into the creamery the minute Gribble has tried to chat me up.

This time, her smile was open as she told Lucinda, "It's kinda nice having a fellow wanting to protect me for a change."

Lucinda imagined how that felt for Christina. As a girl she'd seen her father beat her mother to death, after which he'd sold eleven-year-old Christina to a whore house and disappeared. That girl was now twenty, but a world-weary twenty. She is sweet, smart, and deserves better, Lucinda declared to herself.

"Good Lord, that must have been something to see," Lucinda mused. "Sort of a David and Goliath facing off."

Christina chuckled. "The first time Edgar charged through the swinging doors, I was shocked. He stood right up to Gribble. Told him to stay away from me and to never talk to me. That was something to behold. He's puny compared to Gribble. The second time Gribble stopped me, Edgar told him that he either leave me be or he'd be looking for a new job."

"Oh, my. I don't think Mr. Deason knows a thing about managing a creamery."

This time, Christina laughed. "That's what Edgar said." She went quiet and when she spoke again, her tone was somber, "You know, you were right. Edgar is a to-the-bone sweet man whose feelings are clear as a glass of spring water." Christina's head was down, her eyes on the apple she was peeling. Lucinda noted the smile tugging at the young woman's lips and how her tone softened when she'd called him "Edgar." Lucinda felt optimistic. Maybe Christine's new career was going to turn out even better than hoped.

Once again, Sage entered the Boards of Health office. This was the day the State Board's Secretary was supposed to be in. And so he was. After Sage identified himself, Dr. Hutchinson ushered him into the inner office. "Please, Mr. Adair, take a seat. Esther's shared what you are doing to help us out with the formaldehyde problem," he said, gesturing to the visitor's chair across the desk from him.

"I understand you've spent the last few days acting as a food inspector. Checking on dairy products once again?" Sage asked by way of introducing the topic.

"Hah. I wish. Our one local inspector has his hands full checking the farms, creameries, stores, and milk wagons. His workload is impossible. I try to tackle everything else—which is also an impossible task."

Hutchinson gazed at the grey sky beyond the nearby window before turning to face Sage. "Let me show you what I found during my last two days of inspecting the city's provision stores. Unfortunately, this morning, Dr. Hampton's chemistry magic confirmed my suspicions." He leaned down and hefted a small wooden crate onto his desk.

Sage suspected a lecture was in the offing.

Hutchinson lifted a tin can out of the crate and set it on the desk. The can was open and empty. "Read the label," he commanded.

"The label states the can contains chicken," Sage noted.

Hutchinson frowned and countered, saying, "Hampton's test found not a smidgen of chicken. It was all cheap, fatty pork and heaven knows what else."

Next, a sausage slapped onto the desk. "The report on this came an hour ago. It contains various kinds of meat scraps and sweepings off the packing house floor. Worst of all, it also contains rat feces and borax."

"Borax?" exclaimed Sage.

"It's added to keep it from rotting naturally. Given all the crap it contains, borax is a necessity."

Next, the crate yielded a jar labeled "Pure Honey". Hutchinson declared that all the jar contained was dyed glucose made from corn-starch. "Not a drop of honey in it!"

The so-called honey jar was followed by another labeled "Pure Strawberry Jam."

"What do you suppose is in this jam?" Hutchinson queried.

"Not strawberries," Sage guessed.

That earned him a nod. "You are correct. Not a single berry of any kind. It's a mix of glucose, apple peel scraps, plus two chemical additives that are dangerous to health: red dye and salicylic acid. The first additive is to fool the customer and the second is to keep it from ever spoiling."

A bag of hard candy next smacked the desktop particularly hard. "This candy, something people give their children, contains both lead and arsenic for the sole purpose of making it colorfully attractive to the little tykes."

Hutchinson tossed the candy back into the crate and opened a drawer. He drew out a piece of blank paper and laid it on the desk. After lifting a tin labeled "Loose Tea" from the crate he sprinkled some of its contents onto the paper. With a long, thin finger he separated the various bits. When he was done, he'd made two piles. One was some kind of leafy substance. By this point, Sage wondered whether it was actual tea. The second pile, however, was clearly not tea. No doubt about that. Sage leaned forward for a closer look, unsure of what he was seeing.

Hutchinson enlightened him. "To make the tea weigh more, so you pay more, they added brick and wood fragments. And, don't go thinking coffee is any better. Lots of times all the coffee tin holds is a combination of ground peas and acorns with charcoal added to make it look coffee-dark."

Charcoal? That bit triggered another question from Sage. "At the lecture the other day, Dr. Hampton mentioned coal-tar additives. What are they? How can something made of coal go in our food?"

"Glad you asked. Of course, Dr. Hampton, being a chemist, has a better handle on what they are. As I understand it, coal tar dyes, like that in the phony honey I showed you, are artificial coloring agents. They are made by combining the various aromatic hydrocarbons found in coal—like toluene, xylene, and benzene. They are obtained through distilling bituminous coal into coal tar—every one of them is a poison.

Because of coal-tar dyes, your pound of butter will appear an appetizing buttery yellow."

Sage remembered Lucinda saying she'd seen a yellow liquid being poured into the Emporium's butter churn.

Hutchinson's face twisted in disgust as he added, "I'm sure I need not tell you that animals, including humans, don't voluntarily or knowingly ingest coal or any of its byproducts."

"I must say, the situation is far worse than I could have imagined. What are you going to do about those products?" Sage asked, waving a hand at the crate.

"Everything in this crate came from a single store," Hutchinson said and waved at eight more small crates piled against the wall under the window. "Every one of those crates came from a separate store. Every one of them contains poisoned food."

Hutchinson put his elbows on the desk and used his palms to rub his temples. When he dropped his hands and raised his head, frustration marked every line of his narrow face. "We can't keep up with it," he said. "In my spare time, I will return to each store with a letter telling them to remove the mislabeled brands from their shelves or face a lawsuit for fraud. At least the district attorney's on board for that. He's also promised to channel every case to Judge Bergquist. In my opinion, he's the only honest judge in the city.

"Hopefully, those shopkeepers will be able to recoup their losses from the manufacturers. If not, then they'll be forced to absorb the loss. That'll tie the Commissioner's knickers in a knot."

"You mean he'll be upset that there's so much impure food on our store shelves?"

A disgusted gust of air escaped Hutchinson. "Good Lord, no. He's a political animal who was appointed to his position. I am not. I was hired by the men sitting on the State Board. Never the twain shall meet, so to speak. He hates it when I or Dr. Pohl 'rock the boat' and make it uncomfortable for business."

Hutchinson drew a deep breath preparatory to another informative spiel. Sage settled back in his chair.

Hutchinson leaned forward over his desk to say, "Food and Dairy Commissioner Hemsley recently held a press conference to tout the area's dairy and creamery industry. He noted that butter, cheese, and milk generated local wealth and lauded the fact that the county's purveyors were growing in number and size. He made a special point of declaring that every single new cow created additional tax revenue. Worst of all, he told the press that Portland's dairy products are of the 'first rank in milk and butter quality' despite every test showing the exact opposite." His fist hit the desk and Sage suspected the good doctor had an urge to plant that fist in Hemsley's face.

Hutchinson's outrage wasn't fully vented because he continued, "Whenever I turn up to lobby for increased State or City inspection, testing, and fines, Hemsley shows up to contradict me." Hutchinson's face split into an impish grin. "Of course, now I return the favor. Whenever he appears in public making his erroneous claims I dispute them. Though, there's no way to counter his lies when he bends people's ears in private. He belongs to clubs to which I'm never invited. And, he plays golf at that exclusive club south of the city. Needless to say, I'm not welcome there either."

Sage frowned and asked, "Why on earth is Hemsley taking that position? It seems the opposite of his professional duty."

Hutchinson's lips twisted in disgust before he said, "Last March, at a conference of national public health officials, I made the case, using verifiable test data, that little of Portland's dairy products are fit for consumption—given the high levels of microbes, preservatives, pus, and just plain dirt they contain. As soon as I sat down, Commissioner Hemsley jumped up to declare that Portland's dairy products are 'simply fine.' Next, he stated 'Besides, 'the public doesn't demand good milk.' Those of us in the know gasped at the audacity of his claim. Even so, he managed to confuse the heck out of the attendees."

"So, again, why is Hemsley defending impure food?"

"Because he views everything from the commercial standpoint of his wealthy business friends. The rest of us look at it from a sanitarian and health professional viewpoint. Hemsley judges milk as being good so long as it's rich in butterfat. What matters to us, on the other hand, is whether that same milk is full of poisonous additives, dirt, pus, or extreme levels of bacteria. Those measurements are what matter most!"

Sage started to rise then recalled the question he'd planned to ask before being sidetracked by the good doctor. "Dr. Hutchinson, the Quality Emporium operation has several problems. We suspect both embalming fluid and coal tar dye are being added to its dairy products. God knows what's in the store's jars and cans. I know some of that stuff is bought in bulk and put into Emporium-labeled jars. How in the world did Block's dairy products and the rest pass inspection?"

Hutchinson again switched his gaze to the window, his jaw twitching as if he were struggling to make a decision. Returning his attention to Sage he said, "Wait here." before going into the outer office. There came the sound of a drawer opening and paper riffling before he came back, paper in hand.

Once again behind his desk, he said, "Mr. Adair will you promise, on your oath, to keep what I am about to tell you a secret? If you don't, it could damage or destroy the case we are building. And that would be a very bad thing for this city and state."

"We?"

"Doctors Pohl, Hampton, and myself. I share this office with Commissioner Hemsley when he deigns to ignore his club and golf frivolities for a few brief minutes. So, we keep this hidden in the city's part of the office. It lists the businesses Hemsley insists on personally inspecting."

"Of course, I promise," Sage vowed, making the ancient sign of the cross over his heart even as his conscience twinged. His oath had to be a partial lie. If his team needed to know something, he'd tell them.

Hutchinson handed him the list. As Sage eyed the names he realized Hemsley was inspecting most of the city's largest creameries and dairy purveyors. One of the names on the list jumped out at Sage—Quality Emporium. He cast a questioning look at the good doctor. "So, he's the one who has been inspecting the Quality Emporium?"

"Yup. Once, I tried to inspect Block's operation. He threatened to throw me out on my ear. As it was, he gave me a not-too-gentle push out the door, shouting that he was already putting up with a monthly inspection and he'd be damned if he'd pay more."

Sage thought about that a bit before the last words hit him. He repeated, "Pay more? You charge for inspections?"

"That's what I picked up on too. And, hell no. The current regulations have no provision for inspection fees. The inspection costs come out of the State budget. Like I said, that list you're looking at is every business Hemsley insists on inspecting himself. He's forbidden any other inspection of them either by me or by the dairy inspector. Of course, he can't stop a customer, like Dr. Victoria Hampton, from purchasing and testing samples. We don't like what she's finding."

They stared at each other for a beat, no words necessary. Sage rose and handed back the list, feeling as grim as Hutchinson's face looked. "I best be going. There's work ahead for both of us. I expect that we'll be talking again soon. Thank you for the education. I won't forget this visit," he said while shaking Hutchinson's hand before departing.

TWENTY FIVE

While they were setting up for the noon service, a knock sounded at Mozart's front door. Sage was closest so he answered it and was surprised to see Dr. Hampton standing outside beneath a dripping umbrella.

He opened the door. "Come in, come in." Once she'd furled the umbrella and shed her overcoat, he guided her to a table where his mother was already setting down a coffee pot and four cups. A somber Hampton sat, accepted the coffee, sent a smile of thanks toward Mae, and turned to Sage. "I'm sorry to bother you this morning. A Sergeant Hanke at the police station told me to come see you. He didn't say why. The matter is urgent and he was insistent."

"I understand. The sergeant is a good man. I'm glad you came. What is the problem?" Sage said and beckoned Mae and Fong to join them at the table. If Hampton thought that strange, she didn't show it.

"The police arrested one of our volunteers. Her name is Ruby Fowler." She looked at Sage as she said, "You may remember her. The other day, when we met at the woman's club, she brought us coffee."

Sage thought back. He had a vague recollection of the woman. "Do you know why the police arrested her?" he asked.

Hampton breathed deeply before saying, "Well, it's a bit of a story. It's about Aldus Block's murder."

Sage exchanged looks with Mae and Fong. He suspected he knew where this was going. "Continue, please. Hanke sent you to us because he knows we're trying to find Block's killer."

"Okay, then. Now I understand his insistence. He kept saying his hands are tied and yours aren't.

"Initially, I met Ruby when she came to me because her baby son became ill. After he died, she volunteered at the woman's club because she wanted to help with our pure food efforts. But, her goal was quite specific. She was convinced that her son died because of Block's milk. She wanted to prove he was adulterating it."

Hampton glanced at the three of them as if weighing whether to make the next statement. When she did, her delivery was matter of fact. "Ruby is one of those women unable to nurse so she relied on cow's milk. The inability to nurse remains a great embarrassment to her, as it does to so many women incapable through no fault of their own."

Sage felt a mental jolt as he remembered Harry Lane's rant. He repeated it, "Dr. Lane claims that even a teaspoonful of good milk has lots of bacteria. I remember him saying that children drinking that good milk also die—despite the milk being sterilized."

Hampton nodded. "I've told him about the bacteria levels I've been seeing in the city's milk. Still, you need to realize that the bacteria in pure milk are harmless.

"Anyway, Ruby's baby failed quickly. He'd caught diphtheria, the city's most common deadly disease. Maybe he was infected by dirty milk. We'll never know. But, I became convinced that the milk Block sold to Ruby contained embalming fluid. It certainly displayed the key characteristics—it was thick and didn't sour. If so, that additive so weakened the poor child that his body couldn't overcome the disease. I was upset by the baby's death. I told Ruby my suspicions about the milk. I wanted to ease her guilt."

Hampton paused to blink away the tears in her eyes. After swallowing to control her emotions, she continued, "Sadly, the complications she experienced during the birth rendered her incapable of bearing another child. To add to her pain, Ruby's damn fool husband blames her for the baby's death because she couldn't nurse. Even worse, he's gone all the time, working on the railroad. So, she's left alone with her guilt and despair."

She exhaled heavily and added. "I feel responsible because I put her in the position to be arrested. I was so worried about her state of mind after her baby's death that I urged her to volunteer with us, to help us catch Block and whoever else was involved."

Mae spoke for the first time. "That was the exact right thing to do. I suspicion she's the young woman who was doing the Emporium's bookwork"

That earned her a glum nod as Hampton said, "You're right, Mrs. Clemens. We gave Ruby one of those new Kodak Brownie cameras and taught her how to use it. She took photos of the books and of the creamery."

A memory jolted Sage. That was why the woman he encountered on the stairs at the Boards of Health seemed familiar. He'd seen her at the woman's club serving coffee. "Mrs. Fowler is also working on the Hemsley project with you, Dr. Pohl, and Dr. Hutchinson, isn't she? Those photos are evidence against the Commissioner as well as Block."

Alarm stiffened Hampton's face. Sage rushed to reassure, "Please don't be concerned. Mrs. Clemens, Mr. Fong, and I are trying to find out what's been going on at the Emporium. We think it might be related to Block's murder. And, we know about the adulteration.

"When I told Dr. Hutchinson that, he told me about the three of you compiling evidence against Block and Hemsley. Although he swore me to secrecy, I shared that information with these two," here he gestured at Mae and Fong, "because they are integral to our efforts. Believe me, they are trustworthy. This isn't the first time we've worked to bring down a corrupt government official."

Hampton mulled his words over for a long moment before saying, "Alright, then. The answer is 'yes'. Ruby's photos prove that Hemsley is derelict in his duty when it comes to inspecting the creamery and store. The place is filthy."

"So, how did the police discover the mystery bookkeeper was Ruby Fowler?"

Hampton fished in a skirt pocket and pulled out a bit of newsprint. "Perhaps you didn't see this in last evening's *Telegram*. This notice was on the paper's front page."

> Anyone knowing the identity of the woman recently working at the Quality Emporium is asked to please immediately contact the police.

"One of Ruby's neighbors is married to a police officer. Ruby told the woman she was working part-time at the Emporium. Even worse, the woman knew that Ruby believed Block's tainted milk caused her baby's death. Though the neighbor didn't make the connection between the murder and the new job, your Sergeant Hanke sure did. To his credit, he seemed genuinely dismayed when he arrested Ruby. I think that's why he sent me to you."

Mae took charge, leaning across the table to ask, "Tell me, Dr. Hampton. Do you believe Ruby Fowler chloroformed Block, tied him up, held a gun to his forehead, and forced him to drink the formaldehyde?"

Dr. Hampton shuddered. "After Mr. Adair told me how Block was murdered, I pushed the thought of it out of my mind because it would have been a terrifying way to die." She went silent for a beat, before shaking her head, straightening, and declaring, "To answer your question, Mrs. Clemens, I am absolutely and positively sure Ruby had nothing to do with Aldus Block's death.

"And not just because Ruby is a good woman. When it happened, I asked her if she knew anything about it. She was adamant that he was alive when she headed home that day. She told me that he was acting 'twitchy' and made her leave early. Knowing how he was killed, I'm even more positive she was not involved. She doesn't have it in her to do something like that. She's a gentle gal."

Hampton looked at each of them in turn and said, "If anything, Ruby was dismayed by the murder. She knows we're close to proving Hemsley's crooked. Block's death means we lost a potential witness. Our goal is now at risk because we planned to get Block to turn on Hemsley. Without Block, it'll be harder to prove the case against him. Ruby came to believe that Hemsley's most responsible for the death of her son. She also told me she thought the creamery manager, Gribble, murdered Block. She's convinced that man is both cruel and corrupt."

After Mae, Fong, and Sage shared a look of agreement, Sage plunged ahead. "What you say makes sense. Don't be too sure that all is lost when it comes to catching Hemsley," Sage commented. "He's greedy. We know he recently visited the Emporium because we have someone on the inside. We suspect he will try to extort the new proprietor in the same way he extorted Block."

Sage glanced at his two comrades who were already giving small nods of assent. As his mother often said, "In for a penny, in for a pound", so he continued, "We will discover whether Hemsley demands bribes from the Emporium's new owner. Furthermore, we plan to take certain other actions, ones helpful to your case against the Commissioner."

Mae jumped in. "And while we're at it, we'll prove Ruby Fowler's innocence. We've done it before." She smiled, adding, "More than once."

Fong spoke for the first time, "Many times, we aim for sun and hit moon too."

❀　❀　❀

Hampton gone, the three agreed they better take the next step and, as Mae said, "Time to give that rotten scoundrel a good poke to see which way he jumps."

Sage agreed. "We best poke him sooner rather than later. That means a trip to Salem since Hemsley's main office is there and he isn't due back in Portland until next week, according to Hutchinson."

Sage was unfamiliar with the town fifty miles south, not having visited the state capitol in years past. Fong suggested Sage speak to James Laidlaw. The British consul frequently traveled to Salem in his heretofore fruitless effort to win anti-shanghaiing legislation.

The noon dinner service over, Sage headed to Laidlaw's tiny office. He, Mae, and Fong agreed that Laidlaw needed to know what their mission entailed. Sage knew the three doctors would object to him sharing that information with yet another person, but this was a "needs must" situation. They needed Laidlaw's help in confronting Hemsley.

Once Sage related the sordid story, Laidlaw was aghast. "So that's why my morning coffee tastes like it came from the bottom of a dirty bucket." His lips twisted. "I suppose you're not here just to turn me off my food. What do you need me to do?"

"Well, maybe nothing. Any chance you are going to lobby legislators in Salem tomorrow?"

"I am. Once again my fellow consuls and I intend to cajole and threaten. Not that we stand a chance against your commercial men. Still, we keep trying. We've managed to finagle a meeting with the governor. Mayhap he's starting to come round to our way of thinking. We want to push him a bit further in that direction. With your permission, I'd like to tell him of young Yoder's abduction, leaving out the connection to Block and the Emporium, of course."

"I'm sure Noah's father, Eli Yoder, would want the governor to know what happened to his son. You might tell the governor that he met him when Yoder lobbied him about proposed pure food legislation."

"So, what else do you want me to do while I'm down there?"

"If you don't mind, I'd like to go with you. And, once we're in Salem, I hope you can obtain the addresses of Hemsley's office and his home. I intend to confront him. We want to see how he reacts."

Laidlaw looked thoughtful. "Well, we have sincere sympathizers in Salem. They'll supply that information, I'm sure. But, I must caution that I'm not confident your plan is in your best interest. Our Commissioner of Health employs some pretty rough-looking characters."

Sage thought about that. "I'm glad you warned me. I will take precautions; maybe bring my own tough characters as backup."

Laidlaw laughed. "Let me guess—the formidable Mr. Fong and that enterprising ragpicker, Mr. Eich."

Sage grinned in return. "You'd be surprised what those two can do."

The next morning found Sage sitting in first class, on the first train south. He was in the good company of Laidlaw and three other foreign consuls. Fong and Eich rode the train as well, though in the less comfortable second-class car. The plan was simple: Get to Salem, get the addresses, and have Sage confront Hemsley while Fong and Eich lurked outside. Should a problem arise, they were to find a solution.

Mae remained behind to handle Mozart's noontime trade with Homer's help. Sage promised to return in time for the supper session. Skepticism raised her eyebrows as she said, "Goodness, me. I wonder where I've heard that before. I can't remember a single time when things spun out like you planned. Trouble sticks to you like a bug to flypaper."

TWENTY SIX

It was a pleasant journey in the company of the foreign consuls. Their witty observations of American ways mixed admiration with wonderment, except where shanghaiing was concerned. On that topic, they echoed Laidlaw's frustration.

"I haft to tell my captains to take great care if they sail into Oregon. Some captains refuse and go to Seattle instead," the Swedish consul declared in the singsong accent Sage often heard from Knute, the husband of Mozart's cook, Ida. The consul's jaw set as he determinedly declared, "That is exactly what I will tell the Governor."

The train steamed into Salem's wood-frame train station right on time. The building was charming rather than grand like Portland's huge station. Designed in the Queen Anne style, its turned pillars held up a porch roof fringed by tiny spindles while overhead, small-windowed gables jutted from its steeply pitched roof.

When they stepped onto the platform and rounded the station's end, Sage was gratified to see waiting, a rather decorative electric trolley.

Minutes later, Sage, Eich, and Fong dropped off the trolley in front of an ornate Victorian pile that was the county courthouse. The consuls continued on to the State Capitol building. Since they had a few hours before their meeting with the Governor, Laidlaw promised he'd use that time to learn Hemsley's office and home addresses. Meanwhile, his fellow consuls planned to twist the ears of Portland's uncooperative legislators. Interestingly, they said the rural representatives were the biggest supporters of the anti-shanghaiing legislation. The consuls explained that support was because their constituents' sons were sometimes shanghaied when visiting the big city.

Once on the sidewalk, Fong left them to seek out some "cousins" in Salem's nearby Chinatown. Sage took that to mean that some of Salem's Chinese belonged to Fong's tong, a brotherhood society that had members sprinkled up and down the West Coast. More than once, the tong cousins had proved helpful.

Eich and Sage entered a café across from the courthouse where they'd await Laidlaw's return. By the time Fong reappeared and sat at the table next to them, Sage felt like his "back teeth were a'floating,'—yet another of his mother's memorable sayings. In a low voice, Fong said, "Cousins on alert. Ready to help."

When he arrived, Laidlaw imparted discouraging news. First he laid a piece of paper on the table and said, "These are his addresses. His office is in the Catlin building on State Street. His home is out on Asylum Road. I'm told you can't miss it because it's big and white and has no close neighbors. I'm also told he lives alone with only a day cook and sometime cleaner."

"Asylum?" Sage echoed.

"The Oregon State Insane Asylum sits out there amid the same fields. You can't miss it. It's a red brick building sitting midst expansive grounds that are enclosed by a white fence. If you take the trolley as far as the asylum, you will have just passed Hemsley's house and need to backtrack."

"I'm guessing he'll be here in town, in his office," Sage suggested.

"Well, that is the bad news I carry. His secretary was alone in the office. She said she thought Hemsley might return there in the late afternoon. My sources at the capitol saw him heading out toward the golf course with some Chamber of Commerce fellows. So he's probably not at home. All of which means you three have to wait around in the hope he returns to the office after his golf game."

Laidlaw stood, clapped his bowler on his head, and wished them luck. He departed quickly saying he feared he'd be late for his meeting with the Governor. Glum silence followed his departure. Hemsley's golf game meant long hours of doing nothing and a late return to Mozart's which carried the very real risk of triggering Mae Clemens' ire.

"Well, the secretary being in his office makes it impossible to nose around there. So, what say we take a trolley ride out Asylum Road?"

Sage suggested as he pushed back his chair and rose to his feet. The other two smiled and rose also.

Once on the sidewalk, Fong asked, "You going to poke nose around inside house?"

"Yup, I'll sneak in while Eich distracts whatever servant might be around. This is a small town. I doubt he keeps his doors and windows locked. You can watch for Hemsley and his pals."

The house stood surrounded by fields as Laidlaw had described. In the near distance a three-story brick building sat in a park-like setting, fronted by a low, white fence. Sage momentarily paused to consider it, giving a mental shudder at what might be happening behind its institutional walls.

Sage and Eich next strolled past the house, while Fong melted into the dense shrubbery at the driveway's foot. From the road, an empty stable was visible, its doors open wide to show neither carriage nor horse. Sage trotted up the cobbled drive and along the side of the house. From there, he peered around the corner and watched as Eich strolled up to the front door, knocked, and waited.

A few more vigorous knocks summoned a woman. She stepped out onto the porch, an apron tied tightly around her rotund figure, a smudge of flour on her cheek. "What is it you're wanting?" she demanded, clearly irritated by his interruption.

"I'm sorry ma'am. I was told Mr. McCarthy lived here and it is he I am looking for," Eich answered upon doffing his hat.

"Well, he don't live here. Whoever told you that he did, didn't know what he was talking about. This is Mr. Hemsley's house. Be off with you now!"

Sage watched as Eich strolled back toward the street. Before disappearing into the shrubbery Eich glanced in Sage's direction and raised a single finger. Sage agreed. The fact that the cook answered the door meant she was probably alone in the house.

He found the side door to the stable yard unlocked. When Sage slipped inside, his nose was assailed by a mix of beeswax and fried bacon. A nearby archway opened into a parlor. Moving toward the back of the house, he tried the one closed door, hoping it wasn't locked. The knob turned easily. Stepping inside, he softly shut the door behind him, and glanced around. This was Hemsley's home office. It contained only an armchair beneath an electrified lamp and a desk with a swivel chair. The room's only window offered a view across an empty field.

Sage crossed to the desk and began opening drawers. From the bottommost, he retrieved two bank books. One was from a Salem bank. A glance told him that it tracked Hemsley's household expenses and salary deposits. The second bank book was more intriguing. It was from a Portland bank and showed random, significant deposits with no withdrawals. The account seemed highly suspicious. Sage was sliding the drawer closed when a throat cleared, snapping his eyes up.

A man stood there, dressed in pajamas and a robe. He looked easy to overpower except for the revolver aimed at Sage's chest.

"Who the hell are you?" he demanded.

"I thought you were golfing," Sage looked for an escape route as Fong's often repeated adage, "First run away, second fight," raced through his mind. But, neither running nor fighting was a viable option now. In such a small space, Hemsley couldn't miss.

Hemsley gestured toward the desk chair with his shiny gun. "Sit," he commanded before saying, "Golfing was my plan until I felt ill. My friends dropped me off. I was fixing to go to bed when I heard a knock on the front door. I came downstairs just in time to see you disappear into here."

Sage sat. Damn, best-laid plans and all that. In his mind, he heard the echo of Fong's oft-repeated admonition about using heightened awareness. Once again, in his eagerness, he'd failed to survey his surroundings.

"I asked you who you were! You better answer before I shoot you for the burglar you most definitely are."

"Name's John Miner," Sage answered.

"Well, John Miner, what the hell are you doing reading my bank books?"

Sage was dismayed that Hemsley had seen him paging through those records. Even if he miraculously talked his way out of this situation, the man would be on guard.

Hemsley waggled the gun. "I asked you what you're doing here."

Sage took a breath while flailing about for a lie that might work. For sure, he couldn't mention the three doctors. "Well, I heard that you're a rich man a tad on the shady side. So, I thought a little blackmail might be possible provided I could discover your secrets."

Hemsley lips tightened and he was about to respond when carriage wheels rattled across the courtyard cobbles. His lips tightened in a grim smile. "Well, I guarantee you're going to be damn sorry that idea ever entered your head."

There was a bang as the side door opened and closed. Hemsley backed to the door, and without taking his eyes or the gun off Sage, he opened it and called, "Stibert! Come in here!"

There was a scuff and thud of footsteps down the hall and Hemsley stepped forward, out of the way, as the door opened to admit a big man. Sage's heart sank. This wasn't looking good. Fong couldn't know they'd discovered him. He'd expect Sage to hide somewhere when he heard the carriage arrive. There'd be no quick rescue by the 'Chinese whirlwind' as Sage liked to call him.

Hemsley said. "Look who I just found trespassing, going through my desk."

"Whoa, boss, who the heck is he?"

"Just a petty crook needing to be taught a lesson." Hemsley fell silent, apparently contemplating just what that lesson might be then his face cracked into a wolfish grin.

More footsteps sounded in the hallway outside and another man stepped into the room. "The horse is in the stall, already chowing down on the hay," he said before falling silent upon seeing the frozen tableau before him.

Hemsley glanced at the new arrival and said, "Bardy, is your brother still working down the road?"

"Ah, yah, Clem still works there," the man answered, puzzlement slowing his words.

"Is he interested in making some extra money for that growing family of his?"

"Well, sure. Clem always needs more money. The forty bucks a month salary ain't enough. Especially since he likes to play them cards. His wife is always on him about that but it don't do much good. I've . . ."

"Good Lord man, I don't need to hear your brother's life story. Bardy, go hitch the horse up again. Stibert, go get some rope. We need to tie up this miscreant. I think he's quite insane."

Sage wondered at Hemsley's choice of words and at the grins on both men's faces.

Fong and Eich stood near the shrubbery but stepped out of sight at the sound of a carriage approaching. They glimpsed two men on the seat as the vehicle went up the driveway. Both looked rough. Fong and Eich shared a look and Eich voiced Fong's thoughts. "Neither one of them looks like a gentleman. So, neither one is Hemsley."

Fong agreed, saying, "Maybe they not go inside to office. Or, Mr. Sage will hear and hide. No problem yet." They watched as one man entered the house while the second one unharnessed the horse before also going inside. Soon, that last man rushed back out and hitched the horse up again. Fong smiled. "That is good. Men are leaving. Sage can sneak out once they are gone."

He was wrong. Five minutes later they saw Sage hustled from the house and wedged into the carriage between the two men. The horse was whipped into a fast trot down the driveway. Before either man in the shrubbery could move, the carriage entered the road and sped away. Eich and Fong sprang after it though there was no hope of catching it.

The carriage didn't travel far, turning as it did into the asylum's driveway. A guard sprang to swing the gate open, letting it zip through. Seconds later, the carriage wheeled around the south end of the building and disappeared.

Fong spun about, running away from the asylum toward a nearby copse of trees standing inside the asylum's boundary fence. He vaulted over the fence and disappeared among the trees.

Eich stood beside the dirt road, unsure of what to do. His eyes followed the Chinese man's small figure as it slipped from tree to tree, heading toward the place where the carriage had vanished.

TWENTY SEVEN

"I SAID, WALK DOWN THAT ramp." The gun barrel jabbing his spine hurt, so with hands bound and feet hobbled together, he shuffled down the steep ramp between the two narrow gauge steel tracks running beneath the basement door.

He and Stibert waited at the bottom until Bardy, who'd dropped off the carriage somewhere, swung the door open and Sage was shoved inside. Before them a tunnel stretched a long way into gloom, the two parallel rails glinting beneath widely spaced, low-hanging electric light globes. "Get your butt on the floor," Stibert ordered, shoving down on Sage's shoulder. The cement was cold and so was the whitewashed wall against his back. Sage drew his knees up to his chest for warmth.

Stibert lit a hand-rolled cigarette before commenting, "You moved fast, Bardy."

"Yeah, well, I worked here for a bit so I know how to get around the building."

"Steady job. Surprised you quit."

"Got fired when that Harry Lane was superintendent. He wanted to clean things up. He tried to stop the contract fiddling everyone knew was going on. Caught me selling meat out the back door." Bardy snickered. "They fired his butt not long after that. He learned you don't piss off the politicians, not when money's going into their pockets."

Sage felt a prideful stir at learning that the man he admired was as honest as he believed. But, what the heck were these two waiting for?

Did they plan on hanging about here? As if to answer him, clattering sounded at the tunnel's far end.

Bardy stared in that direction. "That'll be my brother, Clem," he said to Stibert.

The rattling sound increased as a man turned the distant corner. He was pushing a wheeled cart along the rails. As cart and man passed beneath a light globe, Sage saw that the cart was made of sturdy wood slats, its corners reinforced with metal braces. Reaching them, the man came to a halt, lifted the cart's wicker lid, reached inside, and pulled out a bed sheet and a wad of dingy canvas trailing a number of straps.

Oh crap, Sage thought and edged toward the outside door. He stopped when Stibert shoved the cold muzzle against his temple. "Look buddy, don't try any fancy moves. You go along with us and you won't die just yet. You cause problems and I'll pull this trigger. We're so far away and deep down that nobody's gonna hear the shot."

Sage froze, and the gun stayed against his head while Bardy and Clem loosed the ropes tying his wrists and shoved his arms into canvas sleeves. The men's experience showed. In a trice, he was buckled into the jacket, his arms crossed over his chest, and the sleeve ends buckled together behind his back. Sage was angry, frustrated, and embarrassed at his predicament. It soon turned worse.

"You remembered to bring the silent cloth, Clem?" Bardy asked.

The other man nodded, reached into the cart, and produced a layered gingham strip that he tossed to Bardy. Seconds later it covered Sage's mouth and was knotted behind his head. "Don't want you making a fuss," Bardy told Sage. Turning to Clem, he asked. "You ready a room for him?"

"Yup. Second floor, far end of the new wing. Ain't nobody staying down there. How long's he going to be here?"

"No more than a few days, like before. The Boss says first we prepare things so everything goes smooth."

Well, that sounds ominous Sage thought. He hoped Fong and Eich were planning to execute an extraction from this place right quick.

Clem reached into the cart one more time and handed Bardy a white jacket. "You best wear this. I'll need your help settling him into the room. If we move fast, we can get him locked away before anyone sees. Everyone's in the dining room eating their noon dinner. The other attendant is out sick today. No one else is up there today 'cept for the crazies and nobody listens to them."

The two men exchanged nods, and at the count of three, hefted Sage off the floor and dropped him into the cart, on his side, his legs bent up to his chest. The sheet was spread across him, and the wicker lid latched down. Clem's voice sounded overhead as he said, "Mister, you stay quiet on our little trip and I'll untie the jacket and take that gag out once we're in the room. You don't and I promise the days ahead will be mighty uncomfortable."

With that admonition, the cart started rolling. Sage's nose was pressed against a wood slat that stank of lye soap and dirty linen. Light from the overhead globes flashed through the tiny gaps in the wicker as the cart trundled along. Sage counted a single turn before it halted. A metal door clanged and there was the bump of a threshold. Clem said, "Bardy, you stay with him. Make sure there's no fuss. I'll meet you up top. Keep the door shut. I'll open it after I'm sure nobody's in the hallway.

The metal door clanged again, followed by a mechanical rumble and vibration. It was an elevator that shook and hummed until bumping to a stop. They waited. Then, as his legs began to signal severe cramping, the door clanged, the cart bumped, turned right, and began to roll on a smooth surface.

This was a peopled place, with muffled yelling and at one point, laughter and conversation. All the voices sounded male. A food smell wafted into the cart and Sage's stomach gurgled. Soon the chatter was gone, there was the rattle of keys, and the cart banged into a door frame while bumping over a threshold. He heard a door swing shut. The cart lid raised and the sheet covering him was yanked off.

"Okay, Mr. Miner, this can be done easy or hard. You help us stand you up or we'll just tip the cart over and dump you out. I promise that will hurt," Bardy said.

Sage braced his hobbled feet against the cart's side and pushed while the two men held the strait jacket at the shoulders and pulled. Soon Sage stood upright in the cart. They reached under his arms to lift him out to stand on the floor.

He winced as the feeling returned to his legs. He was in a narrow, clean room, furnished with a white-painted iron bedstead and night table. A print of Mount Hood decorated one pale green wall. The brown wool blanket on the bed looked rough but warm. A window at the bed's head provided the only light. Beyond its small panes, gray clouds roiled.

Bardy untied the gag and Sage spat it out. The two men stood looking at him. Bardy said, "I sure wish you hadn't been caught pawing through the Boss's papers. What a damn fool thing to do." Genuine regret colored the man's words.

He continued, "Your choice is to keep wearing the jacket and be tied to the bed or cooperate and find yourself free to move about the room. Either way, the door will be locked. And, even if you yell, folks will figure you're just another crazy. There are lots of yellers in here. My brother will say an out-of-town sheriff brought you in late last night. That happens all the time. Ain't that right, Clem?"

The other man nodded and echoed, "All the time."

Bardy looked Sage straight in the face and asked, "So, are you going to behave if we take you out of that contraption and don't strap you to the bedstead?"

Sage hated the idea but, at this point, the wisest move was to wait on Fong and Eich. He'd glimpsed them following the vehicle. They'd seen the carriage round the building's corner so they knew he'd been taken inside. If he wasn't liberated in the next 24 hours, he'd plot his escape.

"I'll do as you ask. No need to tie me down."

His captors exchanged looks. Bardy nodded and Clem bent to remove his hobbles. Next they released the buckle at his back. Once he'd uncrossed his arms, they opened the front buckles and removed the jacket. He rubbed his aching arms and shoulders.

Without another word, Bardy, his brother, and the cart vacated the room. The substantial door closed, keys rattled, and the lock snicked shut.

Eich was standing watch beside the asylum's fence when Fong reappeared at his side. "They took him inside building, down in basement," Fong reported. "We better rescue him. Need cousins, I think."

Eich agreed and soon they were aboard the trolley heading toward the town center. Reaching it, Fong led the way. Bilingual calligraphy on windows and signs hanging over the sidewalk announced their arrival at Chinatown's six blocks. They entered a laundry. The Chinese counterman and Fong rapidly exchanged words. The man came from behind the counter and gestured for them to head outside. Two storefronts later, he led them into a Chinese pharmacy. There the floor-to-ceiling glass-fronted shelves standing against the side walls displayed jars and boxes, some familiar, some not.

Again, Chinese words flew through the air before the white-coated man behind the counter opened an inner door and invited them inside. Once across the threshold, Eich saw they'd entered the man's living quarters. In perfect English, the man said, "Please, gentlemen, kindly take seats here at the table. I will ask my wife to bring us tea."

Fong replied, in his less perfect English, "I sorry, Dr. Wo. Matter most urgent. There is no time for tea." He turned to Eich. "I apologize, my friend. It go quicker, if I use Chinese to tell problem and find solution."

Eich nodded and said. "Of course."

There followed Fong speaking rapidly, his voice sharp with excitement, his gestures expansive. The other two men expressed shock and alarm. The three animatedly conferred until they reached an agreement. The man from the laundry exited, while Dr. Wo vanished through an inner door leaving Eich and Fong staring at each other.

Fong said, "We make plan. Dr. Wo and Mr. Sun come with me to asylum. They visit there many times. Two dozen Chinese patients live there. They ask patient pretend questions. I translate into real questions. Find out where in building is Mr. Sage."

Eich realized his presence was unnecessary to carry out the plan. "I think I better find James Laidlaw. I'll tell him what has occurred. Maybe he'll know if there is an easy way to free Sage. But, won't it be hard to find things out from the inmates? After all, they're there because their minds are troubled."

Fong smiled. "You part right. Some need much meditation to find reality. Others, problem is drugs or drink. They not crazy. Fingers crossed, one saw something."

The door opened and Dr. Wo stepped out, his white coat replaced by a somber business suit. Once outside beside the bustling street, they met a grim-faced Mr. Sun who'd also shed his work clothes for prosperous business attire.

Eich bid them goodbye and set off for the capitol, feeling optimistic about the three men's likelihood for success. Fortunately, he spotted Laidlaw and his fellow consuls descending the steps just as he approached the temple-like portico of the imposing three-story, iron-domed building.

Eich let his expression convey urgency, bringing Laidlaw immediately to his side. "Herman, what's wrong?"

Briefly, Eich explained. In response, Laidlaw pulled out his pocket watch and checked the time. Turning to the others, he said, "Go ahead and lunch without me. There's an emergency. I need to send a telegram." Without waiting for their reply he stepped to the curb and signaled a nearby cab. As the two of them clambered aboard, Laidlaw shouted to the cabby, "Get us to the telegraph office, fast as possible."

Once underway, with the horse moving at a fast trot, Laidlaw said, "Mr. Eich, it is my understanding that Mr. Adair and Dr. Lane are friendly acquaintances, is that correct?"

Eich agreed. "Yes, I believe they are. You think Harry Lane can help?"

"Well, he was superintendent of the asylum for four years. And, I believe he's friends with the current superintendent, John Calbreath. If he'll come here on tomorrow's morning train and Mr. Fong learns where in the hospital Adair is imprisoned, his rescue is guaranteed.

"I doubt that Dr. Calbreath knows his facility is being used as an impromptu prison. He'll believe Dr. Lane, at least enough to mount a thorough search, even if solely to disprove the accusation. Still, if Fong's friends pinpoint the exact location, even better.

Eich thought for a beat, before saying, "I think if we free Mr. Adair, we must keep secret, the fact of his abduction and rescue. There is quite a bit at stake."

TWENTY EIGHT

The asylum's guard greeted Fong's two companions with a respectful nod and opened the gate for them. Fong now wore the baggy trousers and tunic of a field laborer. When they entered the asylum's reception area, the man at the desk jumped up, knocked on an inner door, and within a minute, the superintendent arrived to greet Fong's companions with an outstretched hand, saying, "Dr. Wo and Mr. Sun, our Chinatown mayor, welcome. It has been some time. As always, we are honored to see you here." In the pause that followed the handshakes, he sent a questioning glance in Fong's direction.

Dr. Wo took charge. Pointing at Fong he said, "Dr. Calbreath, this is Mr. Ming Zhao. We are here hoping to see one of your patients, Mr. Lingyun Chen. Unfortunately, we bear sad news for Mr. Chen. A letter came to Mr. Sun from Mr. Chen's home village in China. The letter says that Chen's elder brother has died and that the family wants Mr. Chen to return. Unlike myself and Mr. Sun, Mr. Zhao speaks the man's dialect so we want him to translate. It is our hope that hearing his own dialect will ease the conversation given that the news we bring to Mr. Chen is both important and painful."

Calbreath seemed touched as he said, "Oh, I am most sad to hear that. If Mr. Chen chooses to return home, I will facilitate his travel as best I can. He is well enough to make the journey. As you know, his downfall is liquor, nothing more."

Calbreath addressed the man at the desk. "Evan, please escort these gentlemen to the second-floor dining room. After that, fetch Mr. Chen from wherever he is working today."

Another round of handshakes followed. Calbreath returned to his office after saying he remained available to provide further assistance. Evan rose to lead them into a back hallway. Soon the four of them stood crowded together in an elevator that juddered and rumbled up to the second floor.

When the doors opened, Evan stepped off and turned north along a corridor with many doorways opening off it. Rounding a corner, they saw yet another corridor, one lit by electric globes overhead and a window at its far end.

It looked unlike any hospital Fong had ever seen. Pictures decorated the hall walls above comfortable rattan chairs that stood on either side of a colorful rug running down the hallway's entire length. Fong eyed the numerous closed doors, wondering which one imprisoned Sage. The receptionist paused, noticed Fong's gaze, and said, "Most of the patients are working in the kitchen, garden, or the laundry. Those men that aren't well enough are locked inside their rooms. They'll be let out in a few hours for evening supper and socializing before the bedtime lockdown at 6 pm."

He gestured toward a room on their right. "You'll need to wait here in the dining room. I'll go fetch Chen. I believe he's helping in the kitchen today. He is a good man. I'm sorry to learn of his brother's passing."

The long room was mostly filled with two long rows of dining tables and chairs. A conversation area with armchairs and a small game table filled the near corner. The three men remained standing as they waited.

Chen arrived with the receptionist who said, "The rules require that I wait for Mr. Chen and escort him back to the kitchen. Patients are not allowed to wander freely. Recently, one of them took the elevator down into the tunnels and escaped that way. We're a bit short-staffed today. One floor attendant is ill and the other is outdoors, supervising the men doing yard work. So, please make this a quick visit because I must return to the front desk." He crossed to an armchair, obviously intending to remain during their conversation.

The four Chinese men exchanged bows before sitting at the nearest table. Chen took the empty seat next to Fong and across from Sun and Wo, the slight squint of his intelligent eyes the only sign of his anxiety.

Wo took charge, speaking in his perfect English, "This is Mr. Sun. I am sure you know him from his many visits here at the hospital. And this other gentleman is Mr. Zhao. He is here to translate because he comes from your part of Northern China." The last two sentences were lies for the benefit of the attentive Evan.

Wo nodded at Fong who made a show of translating what Wo said. He spoke Mandarin because Sun told him that Chen was a scholar trained in the classics. "Please do not be concerned. We have come to ask for your help. But, to see you, we must pretend we come bearing bad news about your family. Mr. Sun says that you were both a teacher and an actor in our home country and that your support of the failed popular rebellion forced you to flee. He also informed me that you understand and speak English quite well."

The man nodded and Fong continued, "For our ruse to work, we must act as if you cannot. Is that acceptable? Do you understand what it is we are asking of you?"

When Chen nodded cautiously, Fong continued. "I will ask you questions. You must act as though I am telling you the bad news that your elder brother has died. Will you do that?"

Again Chen responded with a nod, his face assuming an alarmed expression, even as his dark eyes twinkled. Relief swept through Fong. This was, indeed, a smart and talented man.

Fong spoke again, his tone somber, as if delivering bad news, "Now, I will ask the questions. Please convince our watcher that you are distressed by what you are hearing."

"Ah, so!" exclaimed Chen as his face transformed into one of misery and fear.

At this point Wo jumped in. "Please tell him that with his elder brother passing, the family is without its head. The family wants him to return to China to take on his duty," he instructed in English.

Fong nodded before making a show of translating Wo's words. What he said was, "Today, a man was secretly brought into the hospital. They brought him in through the tunnels. Was anything unusual noticed earlier today?"

Chen threw his hands in the air and shouted, "Ah, no!" Clapping those hands over his face, he rocked as if grief-stricken, while the words spoken from behind his fingers were, "I saw nothing because I work in the kitchen during dining hour. Later, others told me they saw something unusual. While they were eating, they saw the attendant and a strange man wheeling a laundry cart down this hallway toward its far end."

Fong edged closer to ask, "Did anyone see what was in that cart?"

Chen kept rocking and answered in a distress-filled voice, "No. The cart squeaked like it carried something heavy. When it returned right away, it rattled light, as if it was empty. They thought that curious. It was not the time for a laundry delivery and a full cart cannot be emptied that fast."

"Did they happen to notice whether the attendant wheeled the cart into a specific room? Or, which attendant pushed that cart?"

Chen dropped his hands, letting Fong see the tears wetting the man's face as he said, "They told me that one man was curious and peeked out the door. He watched them roll the cart into the end-most room, on the other side of this hall. They call the attendant 'Clem Bardon.'" Distaste briefly twisted the man's expression. He had a low opinion of Bardon.

Fong made a show of giving Chen's shoulder a consoling pat as he told Wo and Sun in Mandarin, "Mr. Chen has given us what we needed. We know where they have Adair imprisoned. With luck, he will still be there tomorrow morning. I will stand watch outside tonight in case they try to move him."

He turned to Chen and bowed deeply. "Thank you very much, Mr. Chen. Your information just saved a good man's life."

Chen nodded woefully, though he replied, "It was my great pleasure gentlemen. They assigned me to peel a mountain of potatoes so your visit has been a refreshing respite."

Fong added, "Mr. Chen, you are a most accomplished actor."

Chen's eyes twinkled in his sorrowful face as he replied, "That is a fine compliment since I do not enjoy the pleasure of having a family. I have been alone in the world for many years."

Fong replied in English for the benefit of the watcher. "Mr. Chen says that he cannot return to China at this time. He asks that we write his family and tell them so. He will also send them a letter in a few days if Dr. Calbreath allows."

With that, the four men at the table stood and exchanged subdued bows. The watching Evan also rose and shepherded Chen out. When he returned, the four of them descended to the main floor. The Chinese men exited the building and headed for the trolley stop at the asylum's gate.

Laidlaw, Eich, and Fong ate dinner in a Chinatown noodle house. After sharing news and plans, they separated. The next step depended on Dr. Lane and what he was willing and able to do. He'd telegraphed he'd arrive on the morning train from Portland. So, Eich, Laidlaw, and Fong would meet at the train station and await his arrival. They parted.

Eich and Laidlaw planned to spend a comfortable night in a modest hotel near the train station. Soon the two of them were sound asleep, worn out by the day's excitement.

Fong, on the other hand, had plans that didn't involve sleeping. Mr. Sun insisted on giving him a heavy quilted tunic and woolen blanket. With these, Fong returned to Asylum Road where he found a decent shelter—one that offered a certain ironic pleasure. A snug roadside hut with a fitted door stood at the foot of Hemsley's driveway. The Commissioner wanted to be comfortable while awaiting the trolley. Small windows in the end walls provided views looking both directions on Asylum Road.

Once Hemsley's house went dark, Fong exited the nearby shrubs and made himself a cozy nest inside the hut. Wrapped in the blanket, stretched out on the bench, he watched the asylum's gate throughout the long night. Come dawn, he was certain no one had whisked Sage away.

TWENTY NINE

Eich and Laidlaw intercepted Harry Lane when he stepped off the train. He looked tired and rumpled, his thick dark hair sporting its customary disarray above his long, narrow face.

"Thank you for coming," Laidlaw said as they shook hands.

"The telegram gave me no choice. You said the situation was urgent and Adair needed help. He's a good man, Adair."

"Once we're in the carriage, Mr. Eich here will explain." Laidlaw guided Lane around the station's end to a waiting carriage. Lane climbed in first, pausing at seeing Mozart's kitchen help swaddled in a blanket, asleep in a corner. Fong's eyes opened and he straightened, a toothy grin brightening his face. "How good to see you, Doctor!" he exclaimed.

Lane recovered from his surprise. "Good morning, Mr. Fong! Fancy seeing you here! I must say, Mr. Adair has a most interesting coterie of friends."

Laidlaw climbed in last after instructing the driver to "Head to the insane asylum."

Eich didn't waste time. "Dr. Lane, the situation we confront involves corruption, adulterated food, and the murder of Aldus Block. John Adair and others are investigating all three issues. Yesterday, Mr. Fong and I witnessed Mr. Adair being abducted and forced into the insane asylum. We've learned that the State Dairy Commissioner, Abner Hemsley, is deeply involved in the nefarious scheme.

Lane huffed in disgust and shook his head. "Well, that doesn't surprise me. I despise the man. He's more a hindrance than a help when it comes to keeping our food healthy."

Eich gestured at his companions and explained, "We requested your help because of your relationship with the superintendent, Dr. Calbreath. Adair needs rescuing. And the rescue needs to occur in such a way that it doesn't alert the malefactors."

Eich described the two men who taken Adair into the asylum basement, adding, "We also know the name of the asylum employee involved in the abduction—Clem Bardon." Eich noted Lane's eyes narrow in recognition but went on, "Somehow, you have to convince Calbreath to get Bardon out of the way without arousing Bardon's suspicions. We must find Adair and sneak him out of the building without anyone seeing. Fortunately, Mr. Fong discovered the room where Adair's imprisoned."

"Whoa, that's a tall order you just issued. Let me think about how to achieve all that." The creak and rattle of the carriage and the thud of the horses' hooves filled the next few minutes.

At last, Lane straightened and said, "It is fortunate you summoned me. I think I know how to go about it. Calbreath is a good man. But, I'll need to tell him the truth, explain what is at stake. Once I do, I know he'll help us and keep his mouth shut."

Upon reaching the asylum gates, Lane slid the window open as the guard stepped forward. "Hello there, Mr. Casey! Glad to see you are still on the job. Hope you and the family are keeping well!"

The guard grinned and unlatched the gate, pulling it open as he said. "We are all well, fat, and sassy Dr. Lane. It is mighty good to see you! We all miss you!"

Their carriage rolled up to the front portico to drop Lane off. He instructed the driver to take the carriage the length of the south wing, turn left, and, upon reaching the east end of the north wing, halt the carriage and wait.

The receptionist jumped to his feet when he recognized the former superintendent entering through the front door. "Dr. Lane, what a surprise. Are you here to visit Dr. Calbreath?"

"That I am, Evan. Is he here in the office or should I look for him at home?"

"He's in the office, Sir. He's just returned from seeing his daughter off to school. I'll tell him you're here."

The man disappeared into the superintendent's office. He soon reappeared, a smiling Calbreath on his heels. "Harry, how wonderful to see you. What brings you to our fair city and the hospital?"

Calbreath caught the telling glance Lane directed at the receptionist. "Come through, we'll have ourselves a good visit—it's been a while. And, you're in luck. Evan just delivered a fresh pot of coffee from the kitchen."

Once the two men entered the office, Dr. Lane shut the door and got down to business, "John, I have it on excellent authority a kidnapped man is hidden away in the hospital. He's a friend of mine. I want to rescue him."

Calbreath flushed scarlet, protesting, "My goodness! I find that hard to believe, Harry. If it were anyone else saying that, I'd say he needed treatment."

"Yeah, I had a hard time believing it myself. There's a lot involved. It's complicated," Lane said, "We better sit down while I explain." He told Calbreath of the Hemsley investigation, Adair's abduction, and how the Chinese men used yesterday's visit to pinpoint Adair's location within the asylum."

"You say Clem Bardon's involved?"

"Yes. I can't say I'm surprised. I believe I fired his older brother years ago. Caught him selling asylum food instead of feeding it to the patients. They call him, 'Bardy Bardon'. Given a witness's description, I suspicion Bardy helped to carry out the abduction and he's involved his brother Clem."

"We've had doubts about Clem," Calbreath confessed. "Patients complain that he's unkind and Evan, out there, doesn't seem to like him either. You say Adair's rescue has to happen without Bardon knowing about it. I'm not sure how to do that."

Lane smiled. "Well, I've pondered that little problem longer than you. Tell me, have you received any telegram regarding an impending judicial commitment? Say one from rather far away? Those were weekly occurrences in my day."

"Why, yes, there's a transport waiting in Klamath Falls," Calbreath answered, looking puzzled until realization hit. "We'll send Bardon to help with that transport instead of the fellow I intended to send. Everybody already knows that sheriff needs additional help from an asylum attendant with this particular patient. Bardon will be gone at least four days, possibly longer depending on the weather."

Calbreath jumped up to open his office door. "Evan, please call a cab and then go wake up Devon Hunter. Tell him he'll be attending on the North wing, second floor in half an hour. Once you've done that, find Clem Bardon and bring him to my office. While I'm talking to him, collect the train ticket and travel money from Render Davis. Tell him someone else will be going in his stead and that I'll talk to him later."

Lane and Calbreath chatted about the changes made in the institution since Lane's tenure ended over ten years prior in 1891. Calbreath complimented Lane, saying, "Your idea for creating Cottage Farm has proved a stupendous success. Quite a few patients live there now. It gives them a leg up when they transition back into their home communities—many fewer are returning here."

The door opened and a large man, wearing a white attendant's coat, entered. Lane thought about how much he resembled his brother, Bardy. The man's gaze twitched between them as he wiped his hands on his trousers and said, "Superintendent, you wanted to speak to me?"

Calbreath smiled and said, "Don't be alarmed, Mr. Bardon. I am afraid, though, that you will need to go upstairs to your quarters and grab some traveling duds. We've received a telegram from the Klamath Falls sheriff. He's holding a forensic patient the judge has ordered be transported to the hospital. He's being committed until he's well enough to stand trial. The sheriff has requested an attendant from the asylum. He doesn't think it's a good idea to transport the man alone. You'll need to take a straitjacket."

Panic jumped in the man's eyes, "But, but, I can't...I thought you wanted to send Render Davis," he protested.

Calbreath cut him off. "Davis can't go. He's taken ill. You can and you will. Evan has called a cab. I expect you to be waiting on the front porch in five minutes."

Bardon's face flushed. Lips compressed, he turned on his heel and headed out the door, slamming it behind him. The two doctors traded satisfied grins.

Ten minutes later, they listened as the cab rolled away down the drive. Once those sounds faded, Calbreath stood. "Shall we?" He opened his desk drawer and took out a big key ring.

As they left the office, Calbreath told Evan, "I'm going to give Dr. Lane a bit of a tour. He hasn't seen our new paint job or the new extension on the men's wing."

They set off down the ground floor hallway, first passing the dayroom. Lane paused in its doorway, admiring the sunlight pouring in through the bay windows and noting the embroidered pillows, rocking chairs, lacy curtains, watercolor pictures, colorful hooked rugs, and an upright piano in one corner, all of it making the place look homey. "My goodness, you've made this room so comfortable and pleasant. I see you've kept the lady patients busy with needlework. Is this room much used?"

"Yes, for the most part, the men on this floor are civil commitments, some are even here willingly. The room's well-used during their free time." As they continued down the hall Calbreath took obvious pride in the facility's improvements. Still, he graciously added, "I'll never achieve what you managed to accomplish in just four short years. Every time I flip a switch, I'm grateful for the electricity you installed, not to mention the Cottage Farm, and the two additional wings built on your watch. Why, for the first time since it opened, this hospital has a surplus of rooms!"

That last comment reminded Lane of their mission. He quietly mentioned that one of those "surplus" rooms likely held Adair. That observation spurred their steps to a faster pace and soon they were turning the corner into the new wing.

Again, Lane paused to admire. "The white paint, furniture, and decorations make it much nicer here. These hallways always depressed me. They were so institutional and dreary looking. I always wanted to paint and improve them. Time just slipped away from me." He gave a lopsided smile as he added, "As did my employment."

Calbreath, basking in Lane's praise, said, "Next year, when the weather improves, I plan to set the men to painting the outside of the building white as well. I find the red brick too institutionally forbidding."

Though Lane wasn't sure he liked that idea, he murmured his approval. They reached a stairway at the corridor's end and climbed to the second floor. Calbreath unlocked the nearest door and slowly pushed it open. He gestured for Lane to follow him as he stepped inside.

Minutes before, the door had opened and a hand swiftly reached in to deposit a pitcher on the floor so carelessly that water slopped over its sides. Sage was lying on the bed and before his feet touched the floor, the door was slammed to and the lock clicked shut. He spent a few minutes puzzling over what that meant. Since then, he'd drank the water only to wish he had something to read that would take his mind off his empty stomach.

He'd spent a restless night. Because the window lacked curtains, the cloud-teased moonlight kept flitting inside the room like a live thing, making sleep even more elusive. Sleepless and bored, he mulled over Noah's and his kidnappings, impure food, and Block's murder.

Once the sky began to lighten, he fell asleep. In the first seconds of waking, certainty took hold. Hemsley masterminded a corrupt bribery scheme involving impure food. He was up and pacing the room as he put all the puzzle pieces together.

Hemsley had either ordered or committed Block's murder. Noah and Sage had threatened Hemsley's scheme so he tried to get rid of them. It was indisputable exactly what Hemsley was doing to fatten his wallet.

And there was evidence to prove it. A simple comparison of his bank deposits to the financial records of the businesses he personally inspected would make Hemsley's corruption provable. Portland's extorted businessmen would be willing witnesses against him. They'd say Hemsley forced them to pay, despite there being no proof of wrongdoing. They could claim Hemsley extorted money from them by threatening to issue false violations that he'd then use to shut them down.

The tricky part lay in finding evidence to prove Hemsley responsible for Block's murder. Of his thugs, Stibert was certainly capable of murder. Bardy, not so much. Still, it was doubtful that Block would turn his back on those two or give them the chance to slap a chloroformed rag on his face. And, was it in their nature to think of forcing him to drink the formaldehyde? Did Hemsley come up with that idea? And, if so, how could they prove it?

After taking at least twenty turns around the narrow room, he again heard a jingle of keys and the metallic click of the door lock. In a second, he stood pressed against the wall beside the door. The time had come to take out the one man, Clem. Once he escaped the room leaving Clem locked inside, he'd find a way out of the hospital.

The door swung open. The arm of the person pushing it open was clad in a suit, not the white of an attendant's uniform. Whoever it was, the man was in for a big surprise. Sage grabbed the arm and yanked, flinging the man forward into the room. A stranger's startled face zoomed past while Sage reached to grab a second man, still in the hallway, but froze when he heard a familiar guffaw. Sure enough, there stood Harry Lane, in the doorway, laughing so hard his hand clutched the frame to stay upright.

"Harry!" Sage exclaimed. "You're a sight for sore eyes!"

Lane managed to gasp out, "Adair, you certainly have a knack for ending up in strange predicaments. You just threw the asylum's superintendent on the floor. Dr. Calbreath, meet John Adair, adventurer extraordinaire."

Calbreath regained his footing and his dignity. "Save your witticisms for later, Harry. We best be on our way before the replacement attendant turns up."

Soon the three of them were back in the stairwell. Reaching the ground floor, Calbreath pulled a large key ring from his trouser pocket and opened the outside door. A carriage, its horses shifting in the cold, waited nearby. The pacing driver saw them approach and clambered onto his seat.

Calbreath clapped Lane on the shoulder saying, "Harry, you better tell me how this all works out. If Bardon comes back, I'll feign total ignorance of Mr. Adair or where he might have gone, though it's unlikely Clem will ask me. As for you, Mr. Adair, I wish you all the success. I thank you and your people for your efforts."

Wide grins greeted Sage when he climbed into the carriage. Laidlaw, Eich, and Fong waited inside.

" It took you long enough," he teased, adding, "Mr. Fong, you look like hell."

Fong replied, "You not caught in first place, maybe I get sleep."

THIRTY

"WHAT THE HELL!"

Both men retreated a few paces before the anger, even though a big desk stood between themselves and Abner Hemsley.

"Where is he? Doesn't your brother know what happened to him?"

Bardy held up a calming hand. "Boss, that's the problem. Clem's out of town. I went to a nearby saloon and bought a feller a beer. He works at the hospital. He told me the superintendent had Clem out of the building and into a hansom in less than ten minutes. There was just enough time for him to fetch a change of underwear before he was gone. All his wife knows is that Clem was sent to Klamath Falls. He ran in and out of their rooms above the administration offices too fast to say anything more.

"Klamath Falls! Why send him there?"

"It's a forensic transport. Some judge down there says the person is too crazy to go through a trial so they're sending him up here to the hospital. When a local sheriff asks for help because the person's unruly, Calbreath sends someone with a strait jacket to assist with the transport. Another fella was picked to go but he took sick."

That was a long speech for Bardy. When he paused to breathe, Stibert stepped in. "We got the hole dug out there in the old Mission's woods. Close by the other one."

"Stibert, you idiot! What good is a hole in the ground when we don't have a damn body?" Hemsley shouted, his fists pounding the desk again, his face livid.

Bardy cleared his throat. "Umm, I snuck into the hospital late last night once I couldn't find Clem. I went to the room where we stashed that Miner fella. The door was locked. I knocked, real soft-like. Nobody answered or knocked back. I heard nothing moving around inside. Clem probably moved Miner someplace safer before leaving—someplace even more secret. I can't search that big hospital without someone noticing me. When Clem comes back, he'll show us where Miner is. We can still get rid of him like we planned."

"And just when is your brother supposed to return?"

"Well, if there ain't no hitches, it'll be a few days at least. He'll be taking the train down to Ashland and a stagecoach ride over to Klamath Falls. It's gonna be the same trip back. How long it takes depends on whether they catch the northbound train right quick or if they have to wait."

Hemsley's lips were a narrow slash in his face as he issued orders. "Bardy, you stay here in case Clem makes it back sooner. If he does, you take care of Miner on your own. Tell Clem to help you." He jabbed a finger at his other henchman, "And you, Stibert, plan on coming to Portland with me tomorrow."

He ignored their murmurs of assent as he dropped his head into his hands. muttering, "Hells Bells. This is bad. I don't like this at all!"

His two minions seized that opportunity to slip from the room.

"Are you positive Hemsley will arrive here tomorrow?" Sage asked the assembled doctors at their impromptu meeting. They stood leaning against the counters of Victoria Hampton's chemistry lab—there being a marked shortage of chairs in the room.

Sage, Lane, Laidlaw, Fong, and Eich all agreed, during the train ride up from Salem, that they had just a few days to obtain the proof against Hemsley because they didn't know how Hemsley might react upon learning his captive escaped. If smart overruled greed, the man would flee. Even if he struck around, he'd be on his guard.

Sage surveyed the assembled doctors, Pohl, Hampton, and Hutchinson. They were there in response to Sage's urgent summons. Once he'd told them about his abduction in Salem, they expressed astonishment at the lengths Hemsley went to, just to rid himself of a petty criminal who searched his desk. They agreed his behavior and his bank book, coupled with his insistence on personally conducting certain inspections, was proof enough of his extortions. All that remained was the unanswered question of whether he also murdered Aldus Block.

It was Dr. Esther Pohl who answered his question about Hemsley's schedule with contempt adding bite to her words. "Oh, he'll be here, no worry there. In the late morning, our dear Commissioner will be speechifying to the Chamber of Commerce. No way he'll forego the chance to assure the businessmen that our fair city's food is safe. The men of the Chamber, with their money and political clout, offer the perfect opportunity for him to further his political ambitions."

"That must be frustrating," Sage commented dryly.

Hutchinson jumped in. "Well, it is also an opportunity for us. One of the Chamber's members is taking me to the meeting as his guest. I plan to stand up and dispute what Hemsley says."

"Will he inspect the Emporium this trip?" Their answer was critical to their complex plan because it required Hemsley to try and collect a bribe from Deason.

"Oh, I know he intends to go there following a lunch meeting he's scheduled with a few of the Chamber's bigwigs. I took a look at his calendar before we came here. He entered 'Emporium' for the afternoon," Pohl said.

"I don't suppose he wrote down a time?"

"No. Though, I think we can manipulate the time. We'll tell him Dr. Lane has called a meeting and wants Hemsley to be at the office around 2 p.m. Since Lane is a member of the State Board of Health, Hemsley daren't refuse to attend even though he hates Lane."

"Did Lane actually call a meeting?"

"No, Harry's too busy. He's got double duty today treating the patients he rescheduled so he could rescue you. For sure, Hemsley will wait around for at least an hour because Harry often arrives late for meetings. So, Hemsley likely won't get to the Emporium until around 3 p.m. Will that give you enough time?"

"Yup. That'll work. Thank you very much! With luck, Hemsley will be in handcuffs by tomorrow night." An optimistic Sage picked up his hat and headed for the door. Still, he paused, halted by a niggling thought he fought to grasp.

Only after he shrugged it off and reached for the doorknob, did the recollected words surface. It had been when Clem asked his brother how long he'd be hiding Sage in the hospital and Bardy responded, "No more than a few days. Like before. The Boss wants us to make the same arrangements."

Sage turned back toward the doctors to ask, "Did anyone around Hemsley disappear unexpectedly?"

The three looked puzzled before Hutchinson said, "Why, yes. Hemsley's assistant, Samuel. Smart chap. Very eager and hard-working. Last time I visited Hemsley's Salem office Samuel was gone. He's been replaced by a rather dimwitted woman. I asked Hemsley where his assistant was and he hemmed and hawed before telling me that there'd been a sudden illness in Samuel's family. He told me that Samuel departed for California on short notice with no plan to return."

It was a brief walk across the park from Hampton's apartment to Lucinda's door. When he laid out the plan, Lucinda didn't hesitate. "I'm positive Christina will help, especially if I tell her what's at stake, It's pretty clear that she's developed a genuine fondness for Edgar Deason."

"I thought Christina is bright. Wouldn't him and her be a mismatch? From my experience with him, Deason might 'have a tough time teaching a hen to cluck,' as Ma likes to say."

"I know. He doesn't seem the brightest. I think what is important to Christina is his innocence and that he is a genuine person with a good heart. She says he's started to extend credit to widows, something Block never did. Christina grew up surrounded by evil, conniving people. Edgar may not be bright, but he is to-the-bone decent in his way, and transparent as a glass of mountain water. She's learned in the hardest way possible that someone like Edgar Deason is a rare treasure."

"Alright, let's ask her to help. If she's willing, that's a better way to go than having you turn up at the Emporium to substitute for her. If the two of them are forming an attachment, he might be agreeable to doing whatever she asks. Besides, if he's as decent as you think, he'll want to help." That task handled, he departed. There was much to accomplish before day's end.

Sage soon reached his next stop, the police station. Sergeant Hanke jumped up from his desk to shake hands. "Boy, are you a sight for sore eyes! I stopped by the restaurant yesterday and found Mrs. Clemens in a bit of a tizzy since you and Fong had been gone for two days. I even offered to help out." He chuckled. "Smart woman. She rejected my offer. Bet she figured I'd break stuff. My ma always said I've got as much grace as a drunk in a china shop."

He stood contemplating a memory before saying, "Anyway, Mae maybe didn't need my help. I saw that young kid, Matthew clearing tables. Still, I wager she was relieved when you walked in the door. Is Fong back too? And what happened to you? Was it related to Block's death? I surely hope so because I'm at a dead end where his murder is concerned. The Chief's keen on charging that young gal, Ruby. Me, I can't believe she's the killer. Even the DA has trouble buying the idea that someone so small overpowered a big, ornery, galoot like Block."

When Hanke paused for breath, Sage said. "Whew, you asked a lot of questions. I'll answer the most important one. Before I do, may sit down? I've been walking all over town."

"Sure, sure. Sit," Hanke said as hope widened his eyes. "You really can answer the most important question?"

"Yup. I'm near certain we've discovered Block's murderer and the reason why he was killed."

Hanke, who'd also sat, half rose again, demanding, "Are you serious? How sure are you? Tell me you're not joshing."

"No joshing involved. We're near certain we've found the man responsible for Block's death. He might even be the actual killer. But, the problem is, at this point, we lack proof. We've come up with a plan for getting that proof but we need your help."

"Who's the killer? Why?"

Sage related all that happened in Salem. He followed up by stating their theory as to the who and why of Block's murder. After a beat, Hanke jumped up, exclaiming, "Dadgum, what you say makes perfect sense. You just wait here, Adair! I'll be right back! The Chief needs to hear this!"

An hour later, Sage considered things well underway as far as the police component of their plan went. Reaching the street, a sudden downpour soaked him while he searched for a cabbie willing to undertake the long drive to the Yoder farm and to wait in the cab until Sage wanted to head back into town.

They reached the farm after a few alarming slews of the cab atop muddied surfaces. Before listening to Sage's proposal, Yoder insisted on the cabbie taking a seat in the kitchen, and on feeding him hot coffee and a sandwich.

Once that kindness was accomplished, Eli, Noah, and Sage gathered around the stove in the parlor. The school day was long over and Sage was gratified to see Noah's rosy face showed no trace of his ordeal. The boy professed to be "beyond happy" he was home and back in school.

Sage told the father and son about the recent events. Yoder shook his head in disgust. "Well, I am not surprised that greed is at the bottom of the whole mess. To think those rascals almost killed my Noah makes me mad enough to spit nails. But, Mr. Adair, you didn't ride out here in this rain and muck just to tell us that story. Is there a way we can help you bring this Hemsley fellow to justice?"

Not for the first time, Sage felt an intense liking for the farmer, saying, "There sure is, Eli. We need Noah's help. There won't be any danger. And, you'll be right beside him."

By the time Sage returned to town, the Emporium was closed. They'd have to wait until morning to put the last piece of their plan in place. Mozart's supper hour was already underway. His mother's face showed weary relief at the sight of him when they met in the entryway to exchange words in near whispers. He felt guilty. She was the toughest woman he'd ever known. Still, the last few days of worry and work showed in her thinner, paler face. Still the smile she gave him was so brimming with love that tears sprang to his eyes.

"Hey there, Ma. I'm so sorry to be late," he said.

"Pshaw, it hasn't been bad. Fong's here again so that's been a great help. You best go change into your meet-and-greet duds because the rush is just starting."

As he headed for the stairs, she asked, "Is everything set?"

He nodded. "Yup, almost. We just need to get Deason at the Emporium on board. We'll take care of that tomorrow morning first thing."

"You think Deason will cooperate?"

"Lucinda's positive he will."

"She'd know if anyone. She can take the measure of both a man and a situation in a crow's wing beat."

He started up the stairs but she wasn't quite ready to let him go. "And the doctors, Yoder, and the police, they're going to help?"

He grinned. "Everyone is enthusiastically on board except Deason. Let's hope Hemsley hasn't caught on and turns up tomorrow as scheduled."

As he climbed the stairs to his third-floor room he felt another stab of guilt. He realized that the total absence of playful censure in her words revealed just how much she'd worried these last few days.

THIRTY ONE

Eich exited the Emporium and paused for a moment, face upturned, seemingly savoring the unusually warm fall sunshine. He leveled a gaze at the café across the street and nodded before picking up the handles of his cart and trudging away down the sidewalk.

Sage, Lucinda, and Christina stood. Sage dropped money on the table and they crossed the street to enter the Emporium, the bell's cheery tinkle marking their entrance.

Inside, the air smelled of canvas, grains, spices, and the old wooden floor. Edgar Deason stood behind the counter and looked up eagerly at their entrance. His smile faded when he recognized them and fear took over. He sent a searching look at Christina. "Oh my, what's wrong, Christina, I mean Miss Randall? Why are you here so early and with your friends? Are you quitting? Did you bring them to make sure I pay what I owe you? Did I offend you? I never meant to. Why it's the last thing in the world I'd ever want to do. Christina, . . . I"

The object of his focus took advantage of his pause for breath to step forward. She touched his hand where it clenched the counter edge. "No, no, Edgar. I love working for you. You are such a kind man." Christina gestured at Sage and Lucinda. "The three of us are here to help you!"

"Hel . . . help me?" Deason stammered in confusion.

Sage cleared his throat and stepped forward. "Mr. Deason, you may remember me. I came here with Sergeant Hanke earlier—the day after your cousin Aldus was murdered.

Recognition widened Deason's eyes and his shoulders relaxed a bit. "Why sure. Now that you remind me, I recollect you being with the police sergeant. You also came in a few days after that. You're Mr. Blake."

Lucinda spoke for the first time. "Edgar, we three are here to talk to you about something quite serious. It's best if we aren't overheard. Christina needs to turn the sign to 'closed' while we explain."

Deason shot an inquiring look at Christina.

"Please?" she implored.

He nodded and she reversed the sign, locked the door, and pulled down the shade.

Sage cleared his throat, "I think it best we confer in your office." He sent a pointed look at the swinging doors into the creamery.

Deason caught on fast. "Right." He turned and led the way. Once the four of them stood inside the tiny office, with the door shut, Deason had recovered his equilibrium because he said with dignity, "Okay. If these two ladies agree with you, I guess I best listen to what you have to say." He glanced at Christina and Lucinda before fixing his eyes on Christina, expecting her to respond.

"Please believe me Edgar, this is important," she urged.

Lucinda added, "We better keep our voices low. We don't want Gribble to hear should he wander into the store."

Sage gestured the women toward the room's two chairs, saying to Deason, "I'm afraid you and I must stand." He nodded encouragingly at Christina. They'd agreed that she'd be the best one to explain since Deason trusted her the most.

Gentle regard softened her voice as she began, "Edgar, Mr. Blake has been searching for your cousin's killer. His investigation turned up some not-nice things about Aldus. Things that will be painful for you to hear."

Deason interrupted, "But, the police have arrested the murderer! It's that woman doing the books for him—Ruby somebody. That's what they told me. I don't understand."

Deason started wringing his hands, his eyes flicking between their faces.

Lucinda asked, "Edgar, did they tell you why they think she killed Aldus?"

Deason's forehead wrinkled once again as he answered, "Well, no, they didn't. I figured, what with them being here all alone maybe he tried something he shouldn't.""

He turned to address Christina, "I promise that I never approved of his ways with women and he knew it. I figured that was why he never brought them here until after I left for the day."

Christina's face softened and her voice matched his for earnestness. "I know that Edgar. You are a good man. You are nothing like your cousin."

Deason flushed, blinking away sudden tears.

Sage cleared his throat to grab everyone's attention. The time had come to tell Deason the truth about his cousin. "The police think Ruby Fowler killed Aldus because she blamed him for the death of her infant son."

"What? Why would she even think that?"

"Your cousin and that cretin, Gribble, have been adding formaldehyde, embalming fluid, to the Emporium's dairy products."

"For . . .formaldehyde! Why on earth would Aldus do that?" Deason's shock struck Sage as genuine. He'd not known of the scam.

Lucinda took over. "He added it because the milk doesn't sour as fast and looks thicker. When the baby took sick, his mother gave him Emporium milk. The doctor thinks that poison, on top of the diphtheria, became too much for the baby to handle. He was Mrs. Fowler's only child. She's unable to have anymore."

Words failed Deason and after a few tries, he raised his hands to rub his face as if wiping away horrific thoughts. Christina rose from her chair to lay an arm across his shoulders. Tenderly she asked, "You didn't know, did you, Edgar? You didn't know what Aldus was doing with the dairy? "

He raised a tearful face. "I promise you, on all that is holy, I didn't know, Christina. I swear I didn't." Sage saw the man's eyes widen with realization.

"That's why customers say our milk is better because it doesn't spoil. When I mentioned that to Aldus and asked why, he just laughed. Claimed he'd found some special cows. He lied to me, didn't he? No special cows exist."

"Yes, I'm afraid he lied, Edgar," Sage said.

"That poor woman. That poor little baby took sick and died because our milk poisoned him. If that was my child I'd want to kill someone too! Oh my God," He whirled to grab the doorknob. "I gotta go dump the milk, . . ."

Sage caught the man's arm. "You can't do that right now, Edgar. Our plan will soon make things right. But, we need your help."

Christina spoke again, entreaty in her voice, "Please Edgar, we're certain that poor woman didn't kill your cousin. We know that someone else did. Mr. Blake thinks he knows who. Unless you help us, we can't prove it and that poor woman will maybe hang."

"Who killed Aldus?" Deason demanded before lowering his voice and leaning toward Christina as he said, "Of course, I will help you, Christina. Why I'd do anything for . . . ," his voice trailed off as he blushed crimson once again.

Sage gave a mental headshake. The poor fellow was well and truly hooked. He hoped that Lucinda figured the situation right and that Christina felt something for this gentle, timid man. Deason's feelings resonated with Sage. He knew how it felt to be besotted. He glanced in Lucinda's direction and caught her smiling at him so lovingly that his heart stuttered.

She, however, switched to the business at hand. "Edgar, I saw when the food inspector came to see you." Her words sent Deason's eyes in an evasive skitter around the small office.

Christina jumped to rescue him yet again. "We figure the inspector threatened to close down the Emporium unless you paid him a bribe." She touched Deason's hand again, "Edgar, we believe that inspector is the one responsible for Aldus's death. He's also responsible for that baby's death because he's supposed to make sure our food is safe to eat and drink. Instead, he allowed Aldus to poison that milk in exchange for money."

Sage cleared his throat and continued the explanation. "We think Aldus got worried about the arrangement, and maybe said something that made the inspector nervous. Maybe he started thinking that, if the scheme became known, Aldus might not keep his mouth shut. So, the inspector killed him."

In the silence that followed, Deason struggled to grasp the meaning of Sage's words. At last, he took a deep breath, straightened his shoulders, and said, "Okay, I'll help. What do you need me to do?"

The three of them gave mental sighs of relief since their alternative was for Hanke to grab Deason and hold him while they set their trap.

Minutes later, Deason stood in the creamery with Sage at his side for support. He gestured for Gribble. When the man came up to him, Deason said, "Mr. Gribble I need you to head out to a farm near Helvetia."

The creamery manager's face twisted. "I can't leave now! I'm needed here to process today's milk and butter"

Deason flicked a glance at Sage and received a reassuring nod. His voice firm, he said, "Yes, you can, Mr. Gribble. Instruct your helpers to take over for you. Goodness knows they've been working here long enough to know what to do."

Gribble shook his head. "Sure they know the basic stuff. But, I've always been in charge of the finer points in the process."

Sage saw Deason's hands clench and silently willed the man to stay in control. As for Sage, he fought against his lips trying to twitch into a sardonic smile; his mind busy thinking, "I just bet you took care of the 'finer points.'" But he held his tongue. This was Deason's show. He was only there in case Gribble decided to physically resist Deason's instructions.

Deason had confessed that he was a bit afraid of his creamery manager who had, in the past, used his fists to run off more than one creamery worker. Comparing Deason's slight figure to Gribble's bulk, Sage thought that fear reasonable. Besides being well-muscled, Gribble exuded an air of suppressed rage.

Deason stayed firm. "I understand. Nevertheless, I need you to talk to the fellow who owns the Helvetia dairy. He's making a variety of cheeses there that I think might sell well. I can't go to my appointment with him because I have an unexpected meeting with the Emporium's lawyer today."

They hadn't discussed what Deason would say if challenged, leaving Sage impressed by Deason's logical explanation. For the first time, he felt admiration for the man. Maybe Deason was smarter than they'd figured.

Deason wasn't finished. "Mr. Gribble, this is an important assignment. You will be representing the Emporium. So, you best go don your Sunday suit and tie." Those words, indicating an elevation in status, seemed to mollify the creamery manager because he stood straighter, though he still sputtered a few more objections before grudgingly giving in.

Minutes later, under Deason's eye, Gribble issued brief instructions to his helpers and departed. As soon as he did, Deason gave the helpers some coins and told them to treat themselves at the nearby cafe. They left as instructed, clearly mystified by the morning's unusual turn of events.

At the workers' exit, Lucinda and Christina appeared and the four of them searched the creamery. Soon a row of canisters stood by the creamery's back door. Sage stepped into the alley and gave a shrill whistle. Immediately Eich's pushcart creaked into view. Soon, the canisters were being rolled away toward Dr. Hampton's laboratory.

When the two helpers returned, Deason issued a string of orders. The milk, butter, and cream already processed were to be thrown away. All of the equipment and the entire facility was to be scrubbed and sterilized. In the future, nothing was to be added to any product without Deason's express permission.

Deason seemed to grow in stature, as if he found bossing to be a heady experience—particularly given Christina's open admiration.

When he said, "Edgar, you've made a fine job of this," Sage meant it.

While Edgar and Christina finished up in the creamery, Lucinda opened the store and readied to take care of customers. Sage left them to it. He had more bases to cover and little time.

THIRTY TWO

The shop bell tinkled. "Right on time," Sage mouthed to Lucinda as he slipped his watch back into its pocket. The office door stood open just a crack. She peeked, gave a slow nod, and raised two fingers. Hemsley had arrived and brought a friend. Both of them held their breath, straining to hear.

The plan was simple. Deason and Christina would move from behind the counter where Hanke crouched. The creamery workers had been sent home for the day leaving two officers waiting behind the creamery doors, ready to rush in if the sergeant called. Another officer stood on the sidewalk to prevent an escape through the front door. Eich blocked the side door with his cart while Fong lurked nearby.

Christina insisted on staying with Edgar. So, she'd signal, by dropping a jar of pickles on the floor, the minute Hemsley made his bribery demand. Lucinda also insisted on staying. She said she wanted to be available. For what, she couldn't say though he didn't object.

"Good afternoon, Mr. Deason. I am here to conclude our business and set a schedule for the future." Sage recognized Hemsley's voice.

"Who's that fellow with you?" Deason's voice quavered even though his question was reasonable.

"This is Mr. Stibert, though I don't think it necessary that you know that. And, who might this lady be?"

"This is my clerk, Christina." Deason's voice lost its quaver as he ordered, "Christina, please go straighten the shelves over by the side door. Mr. Hemsley and I need to conduct business."

Lucinda and Sage exchanged a look. Evidently, Deason felt threatened and wanted Christina out of harm's way because his command to her wasn't in the plan.

"Perhaps it best if we confer in your office," Hemsley suggested.

"No. We need talk here. I've . . . There's paperwork all over the floor in there. My cousin left things in a right mess. We're still trying to sort them out." Deason sounded scared. Hemsley might wonder if something was amiss.

Sage decided he better go off script. He slowly pulled the door open, aware of Lucinda's worried glance. He sent her a reassuring smile and stepped onto the first of the two steps leading down from the office. "Greetings," he called, "Remember me?"

Hemsley reacted way faster than Sage expected, immediately snatching a small revolver from an inside coat pocket. "Stibert, grab the girl!" he shouted.

Stibert started to push past Deason who jumped to block him. Hemsley pulled the trigger, Deason crashed to the floor, and Christina screamed.

Chaos ensued.

Hanke jumped up from behind the counter, brass buttons and gun both catching the sunlight coming through the door window. He shouted, "Hands up! Police!"

By that time, Stibert also held a gun. He fired a shot at Hanke who dropped to the floor behind the counter. Stibert started toward Christina but stopped when she rushed forward to kneel beside Deason.

Hemsley pointed his weapon at Sage. "What the hell are you doing here?"

"It's over Hemsley. Give it up." Sage said.

"I don't think so, Miner!" Hemsley shot just as Sage dived for the floor and scrambled behind one of the shelves. A second shot and a pickle jar exploded overhead, brine drenching Sage where he crouched.

Sage couldn't return fire because he wasn't armed. Peering low around the edge of the shelf he saw Stibert yank Christina to her feet and jam the muzzle of his gun into the side of her head. He jerked her around until the two of them faced the counter where Hanke sheltered. Hemsley kept his gun pointed in Sage's direction, pinning him behind the shelving.

Hemsley chuckled and said, "Officer, you best stand up and drop your weapon or my friend here will kill this young woman. The same goes for you, Miner."

Sage slowly stood up, stepped into the aisle, and raised his hands, saying, "I don't carry a weapon. I'm a lousy shot."

Hanke rose and laid his gun on the counter.

Keeping one eye on Sage, Hemsley commanded, "Shove your gun off the counter, onto the floor." The Sergeant's gun landed with a thud.

Meanwhile, Christina yanked her arm away from Stibert as she tried to reach Deason at her feet. Stibert grabbed her arm again and twisted it until she cried out.

"Let me go to him," she demanded. She didn't look afraid. She looked furious.

Sage tried reason. "Unless you plan on killing four people, it's over, Hemsley. You and Stibert need to drop your weapons."

"I don't think so, Miner. Sidle over behind that counter, next to the officer. Move now!" Hemsley waggled the gun, "I surely wouldn't mind shooting you. They say the second try's the charm."

Sage crossed to the counter's end and moved behind it until he and Hanke stood side by side.

Sage tried again. "Hemsley, it's no good. The entire police force knows about your bribery and extortion racket." In for a penny, in for a pound, as Ma says, Sage thought once again. Aloud he said, "We know that you killed Aldus Block. Sergeant Hanke's been on the telegraph with the Salem police. Bardon is already in custody. He's going to give you and Stibert up. His brother Clem is next on the cops' capture list. He'll talk for sure."

Stibert shot an alarmed glance toward his boss, keeping his gun pressed against Christina, though he'd moved it to her ribs.

Hemsley sneered. "I don't believe you."

Sage took a chance. "He's already taken them to the grave site where you buried your former assistant. Samuel, wasn't he?" That was a lie though he saw it was a lucky guess.

Alarm flashed over Hemsley's face before his expression hardened. "I guess you can't trust anyone these days. Stibert, bring the girl over here."

Stibert forced a resisting Christina next to Hemsley, who said, "Stibert, hand her over to me. Keep your gun trained on the cop and Miner. "

Sage, meanwhile, saw Lucinda slowly easing down the office stairs in her stocking feet. Since Hemsley and Stibert stood with their backs to her, they didn't see her. Sage fought to keep alarm from showing on his face. He wondered how unarmed Lucinda hoped to help. He was relieved when she soundlessly disappeared behind the nearest shelves.

Hemsley clutched Christina's arm. "I am sure you gentlemen will excuse our abrupt departure." He spoke to Christina, "Too bad your boss is a dirty little snitch. That got him shot you know. I might shoot him again, just to teach him a lesson like the one I taught his cousin."

"You're a damn bastard!" she retorted and tried to twist from his grasp only to freeze when his gun jabbed painfully into her ribs.

Sage tensed readying to act whatever Lucinda's plan, even as he tried to keep his voice sounding relaxed as he taunted, "Well, Hemsley, you're not very smart are you? It happened the other way around. I'm the one who told Deason about you killing Block and about your extortion scheme. He didn't know about it until this morning."

Hemsley's face twisted and he snarled. "Who the hell are you?" He jerked Christina closer and snapped, "Never mind. There's no time to find out. We best be on our way—the three of us are leaving."

Before Hemsley moved, two things happened. Shouts and crashes sounded from beyond the creamery door. Simultaneously, two cans flew over the shelf, one after another. They hit Stibert's head and back hard. Shocked, he reached for his head and started to turn, gun in hand.

Sage vaulted onto the counter and launched into flying leap at the man, knocking him backward. As Stibert fell, his head hit the shelving with a crack. The shelf collapsed, sending cans and bottles on top of him. Stibert's gun flew out of sight under the shelf.

Hanke, following Sage, reached the countertop only to freeze when Hemsley roared, "Nobody move! You do, and she's dead." He backed toward the front door, shouting, "Stibert, on your feet!"

Stibert didn't move. Sage looked at the man lying beside him on the floor and said, "He's out cold. Feel free to wait around until he wakes up."

"I ought to shoot whoever is hiding behind that shelf."

"You try it and you're a dead man. I promise you," Sage said as he saw Hanke reaching for the knife he kept strapped to his leg. Sage gave a small headshake. Christina's situation was dire because Hemsley's finger was curled around the trigger. If he jerked in surprise, she'd die.

"Ha. I'd like to test you but can't spare the time. I best make my departure. This little lady will keep me company."

Damned if Christina didn't spit in the man's face. Talk about pluck. She rivaled Lucinda in that regard. Through gritted teeth, she said, "If you killed Edgar, I'll make sure you end up dead."

As if hearing her words, Deason stirred on the floor, drawing everyone's eyes in his direction. Groaning he sat up, his hand clutching his bloody shoulder. "Christina, look. I'm okay. Please do as the man says."

To Hemsley Deason said, "If she does what you say, you'll let her go unharmed, right? There's no reason to harm her. She's not involved with this. Take me. I'm the one who agreed to trap you." He struggled to his feet, swaying once he stood upright.

Hemsley laughed. "I think not little man. You're able to barely stand, let alone walk. She's a much better hostage." He edged toward the front door. Edgar started moving forward only to halt when Hemsley barked, "One more step and she dies."

Sage slowly rose to his feet, hoping to distract Hemsley from the idea of shooting Deason. Behind him, he heard the soft rustling of Lucinda moving away. Soon, there was a swishing sound as the creamery doors opened and closed.

Sage's movement and that sound distracted Hemsley's attention away from the storekeeper. That distraction proved unnecessary as Deason fell to his knees and toppled over in a faint.

Sage figured he knew where Lucinda was heading; out the creamery's back door, down the alley, and to the sidewalk where she'd alert Fong. If she was successful, Hemsley didn't stand a chance. He needed to keep him inside for just a few minutes more.

"I don't understand, Hemsley. You had a well-paying job, a respectable position. Why risk everything by extorting folks? Not to mention allowing your fellow citizens to be poisoned."

Hemsley shook his head. "You think I wanted to remain a low-level bureaucrat? I want more—maybe governor or senator or head of a big corporation. Those plans require money and the influence money buys. I was well on my way before you gummed up the works. Now I'll be starting over. But, at least I've stashed plenty of money. That'll make it easier. Different name, different place. Men vanish all the time under similar circumstances."

As Hemsley blathered, Sage heard the cart rattling away from the side door toward the street. Hemsley heard it too because he frowned and resumed stepping backward toward the front door, dragging Christina with him.

Sage didn't move. The cart's movement meant Fong was in position. Smart girl, Lucinda.

Hemsley reached the door. Still facing Hanke and Sage, he ordered Christina to open it with her free hand, while he kept a tight grip on her arm and his gun against her ribs.

Unseeing, she flailed behind her and found the knob. Her eyes stayed fixed on the unconscious Deason until she raised them to look at Sage.

"Promise me you'll find help for Edgar before you chase after us!" she pleaded, tears in her eyes.

Sage nodded. "He'll be our priority. Don't worry. Please comply as Hemsley says,"

Hemsley jerked her arm. "Open the damn door and step outside," he ordered.

She pulled the door open just as the ragpicker's cart slowly rolled forward and halted beside the door. Hemsley didn't see it because Sage drew his attention by stepping forward a few paces, his hands still raised.

"Leave the girl," Sage said. "People are going to notice you walking down the sidewalk holding a gun against her ribs."

"Nah, I don't think so. She'll behave. We'll just walk real close together. Like lovers." Hemsley shoved Christina toward the open door. She stumbled across the threshold. For the briefest of moments, the gun fell away from her side.

Suddenly, she was jerked from his grasp and sent flying sideways between the storefront and the cart. Shocked, Hemsley turned, leading with his gun. In that moment Sage leapt forward and swung his right foot up toward the man's head. Though not a solid connection, it still landed hard enough to send Hemsley stumbling outside.

Sage rushed forward to follow, halting once he realized he was unnecessary. It had been a while since he'd watched Fong in action. Most times, Fong dispassionately played with his targets, hurting them just enough to make them give up, seldom more. Not this time. This time, Fong was not in a playful mood.

A roundhouse foot sent the gun flying across the street and made Hemsley grab his elbow. Fong snatched that gun arm and jerked Hemsley forward, ramming his belly into the same foot. As Hemsley bent over, gasping, and clutching his gut, Fong said, "That kick for Noah." Next, he delivered a paralyzing chop to the side of Hemsley's neck that drove the man down onto the sidewalk. "That for dead baby."

Fong crouched, the knife edge of his palm, raised to deliver a deadly blow. In unison, Sage and Hanke shouted, "No! Mr. Fong!"

Their shouts worked. Fong froze, rose, and stepped back with raised hands. His face was blank but rage glittered in his eyes.

Hanke stepped from the doorway, yanked a groaning Hemsley to his feet, and snapped on the handcuffs.

Meanwhile, Christina pushed Sage aside after running from where she'd been crouching behind the cart, beside Lucinda and Eich. Rushing into the store, she dropped down beside Deason. She was followed by Victoria Hampton who ran across the street from the cafe, doctor satchel in hand.

A policeman, who'd seen everything but left the capturing to Fong, stepped forward to accept custody. "Officer Ford, wait here until I retrieve more officers from the creamery to help you. Then, I'll have you and the other officers take him and his friends to the lock-up," Hanke instructed.

Only when Hanke followed the women inside did Sage recall the tussle he'd heard happening in the creamery. A glance told him Fong had vanished. After flashing a grateful grin at Eich and Lucinda, he followed the Sergeant inside.

THIRTY THREE

Unlike the first half, the second half of the drama spun out like clockwork. Inside the store, Sage saw that Deason was conscious. His head lying in Christina's lap, he gazed adoringly up at her while Dr. Hampton efficiently cut away clothes and pulled out bandages.

"How is he?" Sage asked.

"With good nursing and no infection, he'll be fine. Somehow, I think he'll be getting that good nursing," she smiled at Christina who started tenderly stroking Edgar's cheek.

Just then, the creamery doors flew open and an officer hurried out on a beeline for the front door. Behind him came Hanke and another officer. A protesting and handcuffed Gribble stumbled sandwiched between them. The disarray of his suit explained the noise they'd heard coming from the creamery. He'd fought capture.

Stibert still lay unconscious on the floor. Hanke wasn't taking a chance. He knelt, rolled the man onto his stomach, and handcuffed him as well. Stibert groaned when Hanke flipped him onto his back again. Good. He wasn't dead.

Turning to Sage, Hanke said, "Do you mind fetching Eli and Noah? It's a good time since both men are here." Sage nodded and exited out the side door.

In the cellar, he found Eli and Noah near the door, a piece of lumber in Eli's hand. He dropped it and grinned upon seeing Sage. "Boy howdy, you had quite a party going on up there!"

"Yeah, things didn't go exactly as planned. Still, the bad guys are subdued and handcuffed. They'll soon be in jail. In the meantime, we are ready for Noah. So, how about you two come up and join the party?"

Noah hesitated when they reached the store's side door. Sage didn't blame him for having a spasm of momentary fear. Confronting the man responsible for the terror he'd experienced would be scary.

Once inside, they crossed the store to where Stibert lay on the floor. Noah looked at his face and shook his head. "That's not him," he said, clearly disappointed.

Hanke was standing back and to one side, gripping Gribble's arm. He stepped forward, tugging an unwilling Gribble with him "How about this fellow, Noah? Have you ever seen him before?"

When Noah looked, his eyes widened and he took an involuntary step backward. "That's him. That's the man who shoved me in the barrel!" he exclaimed, pointing an accusatory finger at Gribble.

Gribble snarled in response, "Shut your damn mouth, kid!"

That earned him a hard clout on the side of his head.

Looking toward Eli, Hanke said, "I hit him so you don't need to, my friend."

This evening, they totaled over twenty in number in Mozart's dining room. The most to ever attend what Sage thought of as their mission wrap-up supper and celebration. Sage, Mae, Eich, Fong, and Lucinda decided they'd invite everyone provided they all agreed to secrecy, each promising never to talk about the involvement of Mozart's people or Lucinda.

Noah and Eli came. They'd stay the night in Fong's upstairs room before heading home at the crack of dawn to milk their cows.

All four doctors also came to sit at the long table—Lane with his wife, Pohl, Hampton, and Hutchinson. Hanke and Sarah Evans also sat at the table. The other couples present included Millie Trumbull with her husband, Laidlaw with his wife, as well as the besotted Deason with his Christina.

Even Ruby Fowler showed up, full of gratitude and with her husband at her side. He acted both affectionate and attentive. Perhaps he'd experienced a change of heart. More likely, Victoria Hampton had given him a piece of her mind. Whatever the reason, the man seemed to adore his wife. Ruby, for her part, was engaged in an earnest conversation with

Trumbull. Sage thought he knew the topic. Hampton told him the couple decided they'd adopt children—the decision sending Ruby "riding over the moon with joy."

Mae, Sage, Fong, and his wife, attended solely as guests. Ida had insisted. So, Mozart's cook, her husband Knute, and her nephew, Matthew, served the bowls of food, their ears fanned out to catch the story. Sage didn't mind. They'd proven themselves trustworthy. Once serving bowls covered the table, he asked them to join the party.

This gathering was their tradition. After the frustration, fear, and danger of a mission, they wanted to gather and share the victory story with all those who made that victory possible.

Night fell beyond the windows and people were done eating when the time came for the telling. At Sage's suggestion, Deason and Christina began. With great enthusiasm they described the confrontation in the Emporium, stepping over and correcting each other's rendition. The flying cans triggered laughter all around.

Sage reached beside him to hug Lucinda as he said, "That was brilliant. Those cans distracted Stibert perfectly. Things might have turned out badly had he stayed in play."

She waved a hand at Eich who sat next to her. "I can't claim credit for that idea. When I first entered the Emporium, Herman told me he'd throw canned goods if I needed rescuing."

Eich chuckled. "And, what did those cans contain, Lucinda?"

"Peas, just like you said," she said, laughing as she affectionately laid her head on his shoulder.

Hanke's explanation came next. "We've charged Hemsley and Stibert with Block's murder. Hemsley's also been charged with murdering his assistant, Samuel. Stibert said Hemsley was the one who pulled the trigger. Bardy eventually led the police to the poor man's grave. Seems like they'd dug a second hole as well. Luckily it stood empty."

Mae, Fong, Eich, Laidlaw, Lane, and Sage exchanged looks. Hanke continued, "Stibert also claims that Hemsley forced Block to drink the embalming fluid. He claims he just chloroformed and tied the man up beforehand, all at Hemsley's orders. Hemsley was there supervising.

"Stibert and Bardon are charged with Samuel's kidnapping and as accessories to murder after the fact. As expected, the Bardon brothers are spilling all the beans in the hope they'll escape the noose. According to Bardy, they kept Samuel briefly at the asylum thanks to Clem's cooperation. So he too is charged with Samuel's kidnapping.

Bardy says that Samuel was alive when Stibert took him away. The next Bardy knew, they were forcing him to dig a grave for the body. He claims by that time, he was terrified Stibert and Hemsley would kill him if he refused."

Sage snorted in disbelief. Bardy wasn't as bad a man as Stibert and Hemsley. He didn't take pleasure in his actions. But, Bardy hadn't tried to stop Hemsley's plan to kill Sage. Still, he remained silent. Those in the know agreed not to mention Sage's kidnapping. It wasn't necessary. Execution lay ahead for Hemsley and Stibert. So, the other lesser crimes they committed seemed superfluous when it came to meting out their punishment.

Despite hating bad guys, Sage wasn't sure he believed in hanging. Trials weren't always fair. And, too often only poor men climbed onto the gallows, while those responsible for more heinous crimes used their wealth to escape the noose.

Hanke finished up his report. "Hemsley's a broken man. He's confessed all. I suspect he plans to throw himself on the mercy of the court."

Lane asked, "Who is the sentencing judge?"

Hanke shook his head. "Judge Bergquist."

"Oh boy," commented Lane. "Bergquist is no respecter of class. Two cold-blooded murders are difficult to overlook, particularly by Judge Bergquist. Almost makes me feel sorry for Hemsley. But, not quite."

"Don't forget, Noah came close to being another victim of Hemsley's schemes," Hanke said. This cued Noah, Eli, Fong, and Laidlaw to take turns relating their parts in resolving the shanghaiing saga. The particulars of that story were new to most of them.

"Goodness, gracious! That sounds like an adventure story in one of those penny-dreadfuls," declared Laidlaw's wife, even as she grabbed her husband's arm to prevent him from snagging a second helping of mashed potatoes.

Once the laughter died down, Mae, Lucinda, and Millie told how Noah's kidnapping resulted in the closure of yet another despicable house. Raucous laughter filled Mozart's as the three related the final act—giving vivid descriptions of three men running down the street wearing only flowered curtains.

But the mood sobered and tears filled Millie's big brown eyes as she said, "Their parents sold those poor children to that place. No way we'll return them to their families. So we need to find them homes, ones that will treat them with lots of patience." Sage noticed Ruby and her husband exchange a look. The husband nodded. Ruby's eyes filled with tears.

"Will anything happen to the owner of that house?" Solomon wondered aloud.

Millie sighed. "Thanks to Lucinda, we learned his name. But, all of this took place without involving the police. We felt we couldn't wait. Maybe we should have. Anyway, the owner hasn't escaped unscathed. He's fled Portland. His house is for sale. I've heard that he and his wife separated. Why I'm not sure. I hope it's because what he'd been doing horrified her and not because he lost his job with little hope of finding another."

"Somehow, I don't find that reassuring. Can't he just move somewhere else?" asked Laidlaw's wife.

Millie shook her head and answered,. "We've done our best to warn people. There are over half a million women in thousands of women's clubs across the country. I've sent the man's particulars and a drawing of his face to the National Federation of Women's Clubs. They've promised to circulate the information."

Lucinda jumped in to declare, "Grab your hats men, here comes Millie!" triggering another hearty laugh all around.

Esther Pohl took up the tale next. "Thanks to a source, who'll remain nameless, and Mr. Solomon's porters, we're compiling a list of businesses that receive formaldehyde shipments. Whenever a barrel arrives for a business other than a funeral home, we are sent its name and address. The porters are helping us conserve our limited resources. I hope you tell them of our deep gratitude, Mr. Solomon."

Angus Solomon nodded gravely and said, "Once they knew storekeepers put embalming fluid in their food, they proved more than eager to help."

Dr. Hutchinson, who'd seemed bemused the entire evening, spoke up, "When a new address comes in, I visit that business and take samples. Dr. Hampton does her test lickety-split. So, far, every test has been positive for embalming fluid. I immediately return to the business where I offer the owner a deal: Surrender all the stored formaldehyde and promise never to use it again or, be arrested for fraud. We've confiscated several barrels."

"My lord, what are you doing with all that extra embalming fluid?" asked Mae.

Hutchinson chuckled, "Mr. Adair solved that problem for us," he said, nodding at Sage.

"Coroner Hadley is dispersing the windfall to all his undertaker brethren, free of charge. He's feeling quite popular these days," Sage said.

He leaned forward and caught Lane's eye. "So, Harry, we expect you to hire a proper coroner once you're elected mayor. Undertakers don't want the job. Hadley finally volunteered because no one else would. The position is tearing him apart. It is not what he is meant to do."

Harry cleared his throat to promise, "I'll add that to my growing list." He grinned and looked down the long table, his gaze encompassing everyone. "I am delighted to tell you that the State Board has decided to take itself seriously. We've demanded a say in the selection of the interim commissioner. And, we authorized Dr. Hutchinson to continue his inspections here in the city on a part-time basis until there's a city market inspector.

"That possibility is closer now because the State Board has joined with the City's Board of Health in requesting Judge Bergquist to order confiscation of Hemsley's extortion account. He's agreed. That money will be used to hire Portland's first market inspector." Clapping hands and hurrahs from everyone, especially from the doctors, followed that news.

In the aftermath of that mirth, Sage cleared his throat to draw everyone's attention. Turning to Lane, he said, "By the by, Harry. How about you tell us what happened to those night soil jars up in the Chinese garden?"

Harry's response was teasingly evasive until his wife mock-slapped his shoulder. "Time to own up, Harry Lane. After all, every person here has been sworn to secrecy. What is said at this table, stays in Mozart's," she declared, looking at everyone and receiving nods of assent.

Harry nodded and his trademark grin stretched from ear to ear as he began, "Well, you see, I'd been telling people for months that using night soil for fertilizer spreads diphtheria, typhoid, and other infectious diseases. The problem was, nobody wanted to listen . . . "

The End

HISTORICAL NOTES

HISTORICAL RESEARCH ALWAYS YIELDS SURPRISES. One of the biggest ones for me was to discover that many, if not most, of the social justice advances in Oregon were spearheaded by women progressives. It seems like every time I begin researching a progressive advancement, I find a woman or women at the forefront. Remember, this was the time period before the women's suffrage amendment passed. The pure food fight was no exception. Another surprise in researching this topic was how progressive the farmers' Granges were in the early 1900s. Those discoveries and more are discussed below. I do apologize for the length of these "Notes." Believe me; they could have been twice as long!

Pure Food Legislation

1. The following pure food advocates in this story are based on actual historical progressives: Dr. Harry Lane, Dr. Esther Pohl (later Lovejoy); Dr. Victoria Hampton; Dr. Woods Hutchinson; Millie Trumbull, Sarah Evans, and James Laidlaw. Lane and all of the named women were also major players in the women's suffrage movement. Their lives and specific contributions are discussed in greater detail below.

2. Every claim in the story regarding the additives and impure food was taken from numerous books and articles written about food quality in the United States during the early 1900s. The show and tell offered by the character, Dr. Woods Hutchinson, is an accurate depiction of some of what was being found in non-dairy foods. The statements made by the speakers at the woman's club lecture concerning dairy products were based on their actual words, taken directly from contemporaneous writings.

3. We all know the unregulated industrialization of the late 1800s and early 1900s was deadly due to dangerous working conditions—Andrew Carnegie being one of the greatest offenders. There were also deaths due to rampant, unvaccinated diseases like smallpox, scarlet fever, and diphtheria. This story adds another dimension to the reason why the average life expectancy in the 1900s was a low of 48 years. It is reasonable to believe that people died, or were made vulnerable to disease, because of the poisoned, unhealthy food they ate.

4. The key reason for the increase in impure, unhealthy food was the industrial revolution and its attendant urbanization. The character of Eli Yoder discusses those reasons as well as the powerlessness expressed by well-meaning farmers of the time who wanted their products to reach consumer tables in a pure, healthy, and unadulterated state.

5. The glucose of the day, a substance that was often substituted for pure products in syrup, honey, jams, jellies, candy, and other food, was made from a variety of substances, including rags, paper, sawdust, and woody fiber. The process to create glucose required the addition of sulphuric acid which is a poison.

6. The complaints made by the characters in the story about inadequate enforcement were complaints taken from contemporaneous news articles and writings. Drs. Pohl, Hampton, and Hutchinson all lobbied the Portland City Council for better regulations as well as asking for funds to conduct inspections, testing, and enforcement. The Food and Dairy Commissioner

of that time, on the other hand, lobbied the legislature to enact laws prohibiting local governments from passing such regulations or conducting independent inspections. [Interestingly, today, Governors Abbott and De Santis, of Texas and Florida, are using the same tactic. They have pushed through legislation that prevents local governments from enacting regulations that would benefit their citizen's health—like limiting exposure to heat and dehydration.]

7. The first national pure food legislation was enacted in 1906. It prohibited mislabeled and adulterated foods. Prior to that, some states enacted legislation that minimally addressed food quality. The history of Oregon's pure food legislation efforts is murky at best. Certainly it was enacted in a piecemeal fashion. For example, it appears its first effort was legislation pertaining to fat content in milk. Laws governing additives and purity came years later—often in the guise of preventing fraudulent labeling. Even as late as 1909, Esther Pohl was still lobbying Portland's governing body for more inspectors, meaningful enforcement, and enhanced penalties for repeat offenders.

8. State Commissioner Abner Hemsley is a fictional character. I found no evidence that the Food and Dairy Commissioner of the time solicited or accepted bribes. That said, the Commissioner of that time did attempt to obstruct the enacting of local pure food legislation and irrefutably misrepresented the quality and purity of dairy products as well as other products sold to consumers. The public statements made by the Hemsley character are taken from news reports and attributed to the actual Commissioner of that time. Logic and reason dictate that the actual Commissioner's cozy relationship with business resulted in Oregon citizens having higher rates of morbidity and mortality than they would have otherwise experienced. That "unholy alliance" dynamic is still true today.

The Real Life Progressives

Harry Lane

9. Harry Lane grew up in Lane County which was named after his grandfather, the first territorial governor and senator of Oregon. Despite being educated in elite Eastern schools, Lane chose to forego the privilege his family's wealth and history offered. Instead, he became a rabble-rouser and doctor to Portland's poor. He was, in fact, known as Portland's "Poor People's Doctor."

10. Considered "witty, unafraid, and pugnacious" Lane fought unsuccessfully for a meat inspection code for local packing houses. He also fought to prevent the use of "night soil" as fertilizer on Portland's commercial truck farms.

11. The Lane character's statements against consuming milk in the story are taken directly from newspaper articles of the day. They were made by the historic Lane to those attending a public health conference in 1904.

12. Lane was appointed director of Oregon's hospital for the insane but he only held the position for four years. He immediately took on the rampant corruption and graft at the hospital which earned him the strident and effective opposition of contractors, government administrators, and politicians. He lost the position because of it.

13. During his brief tenure at the hospital, he oversaw the construction of new hospital wings, electrified the facility, and enthusiastically promoted the idea of the Cottage Farm. The Farm was created as he envisioned and successfully served as a half-way-out facility that transitioned folks back into the outside world.

14. Disgusted with the City's lack of response to his very accurate and forceful demands for certain social hygiene practices, Lane successfully ran for Portland Mayor in 1905. While in office, he stayed loyal to middle and lower-class Portlanders and

attempted improvements—all of which were in the vanguard of the progressive changes being sought nationwide. Of course, his entire tenure was bedeviled with unrelenting opposition from the business and developer classes which had the majority representation on the city council. Even today, the charter language governing Portland's water bureau prioritizes the interests of developers over that of the citizens. That fact explains a heck of a lot about the actions of that particular bureaucracy.

15. Lane was the first mayor to value the inclusion of women in traditionally male roles. He appointed Dr. Esther Pohl Lovejoy as City Health Officer; Victoria Hampton as City Chemist, Sarah Evans as City Market Inspector; and Lola Baldwin as the nation's second policewoman.

16. Also as mayor, Lane took on the major corporations by demanding better regulation, especially of the railroads and utilities. He promoted public ownership of utilities, started the Portland Rose Festival [though I suspect its origins lay in the Woman's Club's annual fundraising flower show], and spent his two terms as mayor battling special interests, fraudulent contractors, prostitution, and gambling.

17. Newspapers of the time report an incident where Mayor Lane learned that the new sidewalk curbs were hollow—evidently, it was a way for the contractor to use less concrete than required. Lane took a hammer out to the sites of the new sidewalk construction and began hitting the curbs to see if they were hollow. They were. Young boys were watching him so he enlisted them to throw stones at the curbs and put a chalk "X" on all those that rang hollow. Most of the new curbs did. Lane saw to it that the contractor wasn't paid.

18. Lane's consistent advocacy of progressive change stood him in good stead when he ran for the U.S. Senate because he handily won the office. He continued to have great support from his constituency until he was confronted by the World War I vote. He was one of only six senators who opposed the war. In Oregon, the response to his vote was a campaign to impeach

him. He died on May 23, 1917, while riding the train back to Oregon to face his critics.

19. Lane is also noteworthy for his advocacy in the U.S. Senate on behalf of Native Americans. As a youngster, he spent a considerable time with a local Native American Kalapuya tribe in Lane County. In the Senate, he honored that experience by proposing numerous pieces of legislation that would have benefitted the people he argued had been cruelly and unjustly treated during the Euro-American invasion of the New World. He had little success however.

20. As you can tell, I am a huge fan of Harry Lane. He deserves a City monument. Even by today's standards, he took the right-side-of-history position on practically every issue. He always advocated for the "little guy." We need more Harry Lanes!

Millie Trumbull

21. When I started writing this series, I'd never heard of Millie Trumbull. Now, I feel something akin to outrage that there is no civic recognition of her contributions—no statue of her, no street named after her. Instead, most of Portland's streets are named after rich white men whose greedy self-interest shaped the city . . . as it still tends to do today. At last count, Trumbull was a board member of at least fifteen organizations dedicated to social improvement and justice. Not only did she sit on those boards, but she usually acted as the organization's secretary. In that position, she performed the yeoman's work of the organization—report writing, correspondence, public speaking, etc.

22. Among Trumbull's other efforts, she advocated before the legislature for minimum-age laws and compulsory education. She served as the Oregon Child Labor Commission's first staff person and inspector. She arm-twisted Portland's Common Council into outlawing underage messengers in saloons, brothels, gambling dens, and other disreputable places. I don't know if she ever raided a pedophilia house, but I wouldn't be surprised if she did.

Esther Pohl [later Lovejoy]

23. Dr. Pohl served as a member of the Portland Board of Health. She was the first woman appointed to that board. Later, as the city's health officer, she was credited with proactively preventing the bubonic plague in Portland even as other west coast cities were struck. She successfully advocated for the creation of the public school nurse program and became a significant proponent of public health on the national and international level with a focus on health issues related to war, famine, revolution, and poverty. She was also an active member of the Portland Woman's Club science committee.

24. Pohl was a tireless advocate for pure foods. She was a plain-speaking, forceful, and sought-after lecturer. The story relies upon her written words regarding the false labeling of sanitary bottles and other assertions she made regarding impure food. She was particularly skilled at building coalitions among progressive organizations to achieve pure-food-related funding and legislation. The Oregon Health Sciences University library maintains a collection of her writings and speeches.

25. Pohl did not come from a privileged background. She was raised on Hood Canal until her mother abandoned her father and took the children with her to Portland. To afford medical school, Pohl worked as a department store clerk at Lipmann & Wolfes and Olds & Kings. She graduated in the top of her medical school class. She was married twice, widowed once, and divorced once. Her only child, a seven year old son died of tainted milk in 1907, three years after the setting of this story.

Victoria Hampton

26. Victoria Hampton was a doctor, chemist, and forensic scientist (at the time, called a microscopist). She testified as a chemist and microscopist at a murder trial. Her hair and blood analysis testimony was considered the key evidence that convicted the defendant. She frequently testified as a forensic expert throughout her career. Her description to Sage regarding her heavy workload is accurate.

27. Hampton was initially appointed physician to the Portland Board of Health. In that capacity, she was involved in the effort to obtain legislation addressing the problem of adulterated food. Her statements regarding the adding of embalming fluid, coal tar, and other additives is taken directly from statements she made at a public health conference as reported in newspapers of the day. At that conference, a person objected to Hampton's assertions by claiming the person's dairy products were good because they were thicker and didn't spoil. Hampton countered by saying that those two characteristics were evidence of embalming fluid and coal tar dye adulteration. She further said that, out of all the Portland milk she tested, not a single one was free of formaldehyde. As in the story, she also reported that she had a pound of adulterated butter that was still unspoiled after over a year.

28. In 1908, Mayor Lane appointed Victoria Hampton the official chemist to the Portland Board of Health.

29. Hampton's life story was unique and suggests why she never married. Her Australian mother married a Mormon polygamist. The church records indicate that there was much discord and violence within that household. Her mother fled the marriage, taking Victoria with her. Eventually, her mother remarried a mining engineer.

Woods Hutchinson

30. Dr. Woods Hutchinson was secretary to the State Board of Health. He didn't hesitate to publically counter the misstatements made by the State Dairy and Food Commissioner of the time whenever the Commission made claims like "Portland milk is above reproach."

31. Hutchinson's statements in the story concerning dairy purity are taken from his statements in public meetings. His show and tell to Sage, regarding other foodstuffs, is a compilation of other reports of the misrepresentations, adulterations and filth in America's food.

Sarah Evans

32. Sarah Evans was the president of the Portland Woman's club. In that capacity, she led the Club's pure food efforts, including its demand for additional inspectors

33. Evans has been called the Mother of Oregon's Public Libraries because she led the successful fight to obtain public funding of Oregon's municipal free libraries. She also led the effort to erect Portland's first statue honoring a woman, Sacajawea.

34. Raised as a Quaker and trained as a social worker, Evans was widowed early in her marriage and left with children to support. In 1905, Mayor Harry Lane appointed her to the City's first market inspector post. She was the first woman in the country to hold that post.

James Laidlaw

35. For many years, as British Consul, Laidlaw tirelessly worked to prohibit shanghaiing and increase British trade with Oregon merchants.

36. He also collaborated with the Norwegian, Swedish, and other foreign consuls to put Portland's shanghai crimps out of business. The powerful businessmen of Portland opposed these efforts for the reasons stated in the story. In the end, it was steamships with their need for fewer but more highly skilled men, along with the unionization of the sailors, that finally halted the practice.

Progressive Organizations

Grange [aka National Patrons of Husbandry]

37. The Grange was first organized in 1867. It was modeled after the Freemason's organization which explains the Grange's officer titles. By 1874, the Grange was raising the alarm about

impure food. In 1879 the organization adopted a national resolution calling for pure food legislation and thereafter tirelessly lobbied legislators on the issue. Their effective opponents were the industrialized food manufactures. In 1890, the Grange adopted a resolution supporting women's suffrage.

38. History indicates that the most serious negative impacts on farmers were the civil war and the industrial revolution. The decades after the civil war expanded agriculture because of technological advancement and financial speculation. To compete, farmers had to invest in new techniques and equipment at the same time they faced falling prices due to surplus. Railroads were rapacious in raising transport costs and the increased debt load drove many farmers into bankruptcy. These factors caused farmers to unite in various organizations, including the Grange, to advocate for their interests.

39. In November 1904, over 3000 Grange members descended on Portland for their national convention. It was held in the Armory Annex in NW Portland. That building still stands and is now a theatrical and entertainment venue.

40. The Grange was serious about supporting women's suffrage. Sarah Gates Baird was a featured speaker at the Portland convention. She was first woman in the country elected to be a State Grange Master (Minnesota) and she held that elected office for 18 years. In Oregon, a woman was elected master of a local Grange around the time of this story. Women tended to be the mainstay officers of the local granges and had full voting rights in the locals and on convention business.

41. What was particularly admirable about the Grange was its dedication to educating its members. Every Grange had an officer charged with finding monthly speakers on current events and a myriad of other topics. Grangers attended discussions about the latest political and social matters as well as ones on literature and science. The Grange's striving to educate its members might explain why, in the last half of the 1900s, the Grange

was considered the most "liberal" organization functioning in Oregon's rural farming communities.

Oregon's Grange

42. The issues that gave rise to the National Grange also made life hard for Oregon farmers in the Willamette Valley. Oregon's Grange movement began with farmers angry about how monopolies were controlling shipping on the Columbia and Willamette rivers. The cost of freighting wheat was so high the farmers had no opportunity for profit.

43. In 1873, members of 37 Oregon granges and 4 Washington Territory granges met in Salem and organized the Oregon State Grange. Aims were: lower excessive prices for farm machinery and supplies, cooperative buying and selling, removal of obstructions in the Willamette river, and freeing the Willamette and Columbia rivers from shipping monopolies. Annually, they also adopted all of the National Grange's resolutions. By 1904 there were over five thousand Oregon Grange members. By 1931, the membership stood at around 22,000.

44. Twenty-nine local men and women established the Leedy Grange in Cedar Mill in 1906, a few years after the time of this story. They met in each other's homes, then in the current hall until purchasing it from The Modern Woodmen in 1913. The Leedy Grange is still operational in the Cedar Mill area and is rented out as a venue for community events. It is one of the few remaining Grange halls in the Portland metropolitan area.

45. Axes created many fields in the Cedar Mill area but, initially fire was used to down the old growth trees. In addition to agriculture, the area's saw mills later supplied lumber to the region's builders and railroad ties to the railway companies. A local lumber mill laid a plank road so that its steam engine could haul its products to the Beaverton rail yard and to the canyon road that descended into town. If anyone gave that steam engine a name, it is lost to history.

Portland Woman's Club

46. The Woman's Club was instrumental in pushing a number of progressive changes in the city. It supported and advocated for the free medical clinic, visiting nurses association, TB sanatorium, child welfare, juvenile delinquency services, libraries, school lunches, and a host of other civic and social improvements.

47. The Club had at least 12 standing committees including ones related to public health, science, education, libraries, history, and legislation.

48. Esther Pohl's inside joke, made during the lecture in the story, was in reference to Sarah Evan's own words in her weekly Oregon Daily Journal column in which she wrote about women's activities in Oregon and nationally.

49. The Portland Woman's Club undertook the task of entertaining the non-member wives of Grange members attending the 1904 convention. One of their offerings was an excursion train to the town of Hood River.

50. Like the Grange, the Portland Woman's Club also endeavored to educate its members and frequently held lectures on current event topics. As with women's clubs across the country, they became deeply involved in the pure food fight. Their lectures were held in the meeting hall on the third floor of the lovely 1895, Selling-Hirsch Building. Like many of early Portland's architectural wonders, that building no longer exists.

51. It is worth noting that, in 1888 Portland's first night school for adults was started by the Portland Women's Union in their boarding house for women. It was managed by Miss Mary Cook. Men were eventually admitted to the night school. Following its acknowledged success, the Portland Public Schools (PPS) took it over and it became Portland's first public night school. Eventually it transformed into the Portland Community College which continues offer night school classes.

National Women's Clubs

52. Many, many of the progressive improvements in American culture and economic life were carried to fruition by women's labor. Often, men were the public relations make-it-so figureheads while women carried out the mission on a daily basis.

53. Women's clubs were at the forefront of positive social change. By 1904, there were women's clubs in nearly every town and city in the country. The membership totaled over five hundred thousand. Many, if not most, of their progressive successes were obtained before women were accorded the right to vote.

54. Nationally, women's clubs were highly active and forceful in pushing for the pure food legislation. One author, Gail Jarrow, estimates that more than one million women joined the pure food movement. They held meetings and lectures, passed out pamphlets, and wrote news articles. In 1906, Theodore Roosevelt signed the first federal pure food legislation into law.

Returning Series Characters

Herman Eich

55. The character of Herman Eich is based on the real Herman Eich who was lovingly called the "Ragpicker Poet of Portland." He was an anarchist, ragpicker-recycler, and poet who died in 1896 at a young age while riding the rails as a hobo. His admiring words to Lucinda Collins were the words of the real Herman Eich in his poem, *Freedom*.

Angus Solomon

56. When the exclusive Portland Hotel opened for business, one of its drawing cards was that its dining room service was supplied by exceptionally well-trained African Americans imported from the Carolinas. One of these men did, in fact, establish a hotel for black railroad porters.

57. Many of the Portland Hotel's skilled, hardworking men started other side businesses. In time, their families became the nucleus of Portland's black middle class. Particularly prominent were the Rutherford brothers who started a barber shop and a haberdashery. Their descendants have contributed much to Portland's development and culture.

Lucinda Collins

58. Despite the outward appearance of staid propriety, Portland had over 400 houses of ill repute operating during the early 1900s. Many of these establishments were owned by the "respectable" wealthy men of the city. Some historians also report that children were removed from a Christian helping agency to work in pedophile brothels. And, unfortunately, some parents sold their children to those brothels.

59. Not all brothel owners were venal. Some were kind to their employees and supported those women who wanted to leave the business—even holding parties to celebrate their transitions to respectable lives. The Lucinda Collins character was inspired by one such Spokane parlor house madam known for her kindness to those who worked in her house. Many of those working in such houses were first the victims of childhood sexual abuse as is the case today.

Vincent St. Alban

60. The story's mythical behind-the-scenes character, Vincent St. Alban, is modeled after Vincent St. John whom many workers called "the Saint" because of his kindliness and bravery. He became a hero when he entered a mine to rescue trapped miners, when no one else would. He lost an arm in that effort. He eventually became one of the founders of the one-big-union, the Industrial Workers of the World (IWW) organization. Its members were known as the "Wobblies."

Treatment of the Chinese

61. The federal Chinese Exclusion Act of 1882 made immigration to the United States very onerous. Those who managed to sneak in often came through Mexico.

62. The US wasn't alone in trying to suppress Chinese immigration. The Canadians levied an entry fee of $500 on Chinese, which would be over $18,000 in 2023 dollars. It was effective. Less than 50 Chinese a year were able to enter Canada following its enactment.

63. Canneries in San Juan Islands relied on cheap Chinese labor for catching and canning fish. In the Pacific NW, the Chinese tongs generally controlled which Chinese could work in a cannery.

64. Salem's Chinatown was an area roughly bounded by the Northeast Ferry, Liberty, State. and High streets. The first Chinese arrived in Salem mostly from California. Around 1904, the Salem city council condemned a vibrant block of Chinatown that contained a number of stores.

65. In 1890 there were nearly 400 Chinese living in Salem. By 1920 their numbers had dwindled to 72.The federal Chinese Exclusion Act of 1882 made life harder for those residents already here. Chinese residents were not able to own property which allowed developers to push out Chinese residents using ever increasing rents.

66. The characters of Dr. Wo and Mr. Sun are very loosely based on real people, Dr. Kum Bow Wo and George Lai Sun respectively. Wo was a druggist and doctor who practiced out of his drug store. Sun was called the mayor of Salem's Chinatown. In 1927, an alley in Salem was named after him. That same year, when Sun was asked to speak at the anniversary of a prominent white businessman in Salem, he said the following:

> *I have been here so long, for fifty-four years next June, I ought to be a citizen. I ought to be voting too. I see some*

country-man come over to this country; he stay not very long, three or four years; he can vote. Why I be here fifty-four years altogether, why I cannot vote? I ought to be citizen too. They must make mistake, something wrong.

Oregon Asylum for the Insane

67. The Asylum, now the Oregon State Hospital, is home to a wonderful museum staffed by volunteers. It is interesting and very well done. It neither sugarcoats nor depresses. There were tunnels beneath the buildings. The descriptions in the story are taken from contemporaneous pictures—including pictures of both the laundry carts and the tunnels with their tracks.

68. Dr. Calbreath was the superintendent at the time of this story. He had a positive reputation among the inmates. The 1900 patient census showed 24 Chinese men and 2 Chinese women as living in the insane asylum. The number of inmates grew in subsequent years

Miscellaneous Bits

69. The story's $50 per month bribe to the dastardly Hemsley would be worth $1,705 per month today.

70. The erroneous assertions made by the real Commissioner at the public health conference were addressed by Dr. Woods Hutchinson who immediately rose to rebut them using data obtained by scientific analysis performed by Emile Pernot, a biologist assigned to the State Board of Health and by Dr. Victoria Hampton, assigned to Portland's Board of Health.

71. Oregon has had an on-again-off-again relationship with capital punishment. Until 1904, hangings took place in the courtyard of Portland's courthouse. Thereafter, they were performed behind the walls of the Oregon State Penitentiary. In the 1970s, during an off-again period, the Superintendent of the Penitentiary,

Hoyt Cupp, told me that if capital punishment was reinstated he would resign as superintendent. He said he'd only seen poor men executed, never rich men who'd done much worse. He said he couldn't bear to watch another execution. Voters reinstated the death penalty in 1984, the same year Cupp left the superintendent job.

72. In recent years, at dusk, the city experienced a gathering of crows in its central business district with the birds converging from all corners of the city. It was awesome to see. However, it proved bothersome in terms of droppings and noise so, the city hired falconers to chase the crow gathering to a park along the Willamette river.

73. Another progressive improvement was public and compulsory education. In 1900s, only 21 % of adults were literate, which means only 2 out of every 10 people could read.

74. Sometimes, when researching, something will be interesting but I have no thought of using it in the future. Then, lo and behold, it is needed but the source can't be found again. Two of those mystery bits turn up in this story. The first was that of Harry Lane shooting the night soil jars. I definitely read that because I considered it yet another reason to venerate the man. I did find a news article that reported his objecting, as a member of the State Health Board, to the Chinese gardeners using human feces for fertilizer. But I was unable to locate that source.

75. The second bit for which the source citation has been lost, comes from my reading about a group of drunks who broke into a store's cellar. There they drank from barrels they thought contained alcohol. Instead it was formaldehyde. It killed them. The peculiar nature of that bit lodged in my mind but I considered it suspect because, why would there be barrels of embalming fluid beneath a store? Thanks to the research for *Preservation*, I now know it was a commonly-used food preservation additive. That gives the-drunks-drinking-formaldehyde story more veracity. Unfortunately, I could not find the original source of

that story.

76. The pure food fight of the late 1800s, early 1900s, is well-documented. Unfortunately, like the other issues of concern raised in the Sage Adair series, the problem is not solved. The historical gains made by progressives continue to be eroded or the same problems resurface. Thus, the battles progressives fought over one hundred years ago are still being fought today—including the problem of unhealthy products in our food supply chain. That is particularly true now that the food supply is international.

77. The battlefields may have changed but progressive, well-meaning folks today are doing their darnest to ensure that our food is safe and healthy. The following are just a few of the food-related concerns they are addressing: local sourcing for freshness; fertilizer, herbicides, pesticides contamination; irradiated and genetically modified food; use of antibiotics and hormones to increase production; animal abuse and sanitation; animal feed contents; mercury and bacterial contamination, and nutrition deficits among others. Marion Nestle is a well-respected nutritionist who publishes a blog at *https://www.foodpolitics.com/*. Her work allows readers to keep up with the latest in food science and advocacy.

78. Prior to the 2016, Toxic Substances Control Act (TSCA) as amended by the Obama administration, the EPA tested only 20% of the 400 new chemicals entering the marketplace each year. The Obama amendment now requires the EPA to test 100% of all new chemicals, domestic and imported. Once again, the tireless work of citizen advocates deserves the credit for the Obama amendment. We, and people of the future, owe these citizens a debt of gratitude. They too, like the advocates of the early 1900s, will be adjudged to have been on the right side of history—where progressives have always stood.

ACKNOWLEDGMENTS

Every book in the Sage Adair mysteries has benefitted from the assistance of librarians and archivists. This is particularly true of *Preservation.* I have yet to encounter a disinterested or unhelpful librarian or archivist. All are passionate about their work and their mission preserve history and to help those searching for accurate historical truths.

For this book, I want to especially acknowledge some of these helpful folks by name. As always, Scott Daniels of the Oregon Historical Society's Research Library was particularly helpful. He and the library remain true treasures of Portland's historical research community.

Liz Paulus of the Cedar Mill-Bethany Library went above and beyond when it came to being helpful. She found and forwarded a wealth of information about Cedar Mill's early years. Another very helpful librarian, Meg Langford, was discovered at the Oregon Health Sciences Library. She also provided wonderful assistance and access to the Dr. Esther Pohl Lovejoy collection.

And lastly among those who guard our historical treasures, is always, the staff at the City of Portland Archives, in particular, Madeline Moya. She and the Archive's staff continue to provide a great service to our community, one that will forever educate future historians.

Also helpful, though not a librarian, was freelance food writer, Hannah Wallace. She gives readers accurate and current information about what we eat, serves our neighborhood's houseless people as a volunteer, and carries on doing good works just like the progressive women of yesteryear.

I am also very grateful for having found my book creator, Slaven Kovačević. He is fast, he is accurate, and he is a great pleasure to work with. I highly recommend his services.

Those acknowledgments aside, any errors or inaccuracies remain solely my own.

Readers remain the most important contributors to the Sage Adair saga. It is cheering to see that these mystery stories are steadily building an audience. The readership increase is heartening. Bottom-line, it is the readers who are responsible for Sage continuing to adventure. Thank you one, and all, so very much!

Lastly, words cannot begin to describe the gratitude I feel for having George Slanina as my life partner. Through thick and thin and, in all ways, he is lovingly present. He deserves much credit for whatever good I have been able to accomplish with the Sage Adair series and with life in general.

Thank you for reading **Preservation**

*We invite you to share your thoughts and reactions with
your library and on
Goodreads as well as on your favorite social media and
retail platforms. Your comments help and encourage
authors whose work you like and support.*

Request for Pre-Publication Notice

If you would like to receive notice of the publication
dates of the next Sage Adair historical mystery novel,
please contact Yamhill Press at

www.yamhillpress.net.

**Other Mystery Novels in the
Sage Adair Historical Mystery Series**
by S. L. Stoner

Timber Beasts

A secret operative in America's 1902 labor movement, leading a double life that balances precariously on the knife-edge of discovery, finds his mission entangled with the fate of a young man accused of murder.

Land Sharks

Two men have disappeared, sending Sage Adair on a desperate search that leads him into the Stygian blackness of Portland's underground to confront murderous shanghaiers, a lost friendship and his own dark fears.

Dry Rot

A losing labor strike, a dead construction boss, a union leader framed for murder, a rag-picker poet, and collapsing bridges, all compete for Sage Adair's attention as he slogs through the Pacific Northwest's rain and mud to find answers before someone else dies.

Black Drop

In this ripping yarn, President Theodore Roosevelt has left Washington D.C., embarking on his historic train trip through the American West. Little does he know that assassination awaits him in Portland, Oregon. The words of a dying prostitute warn Sage Adair and his allies that they will be blamed for Roosevelt's murder. Since life is never simple, Sage also learns of young boys who need rescuing from a fate worse than death. As the presidential train and the boys' doom rush ever closer, every crucial answer remains elusive. Who is enslaving the boys? Who plans to kill the president? Can either tragedy be stopped?

Dead Line

Sage Adair encounters murder and mayhem midst the sagebrush and pine trees of Central Oregon's high desert. This captivating land of big skies, golden light and deadly secrets is the home of hardy and hard people–some of whom intend to kill him.

The Mangle

During a blistering 1903 summer, Portland's steam laundry women are working ten hellish hours a day. Exhausted and ill, they demand a nine-hour workday. Sage Adair, and his mother, Mae, join their fight until women begin disappearing. Desperately searching for the missing women, Sage and Mae face grave danger midst suffragettes, prostitutes, social workers, white slavers, arsonists and heartless bosses. Inspired by actual historical events, this is the sixth book in the award-winning Sage Adair mystery series.

Slow Burn

Arson, murder, kidnapping and false accusations abound in this seventh book of the Sage Adair Series. What begins as a simple assignment—helping the city's firefighters unionize, catapults Sage onto firefighting's front lines and into solving the deeper mystery of who is burning down the city and why.

Bitter Cry

Night fog drives a young newsboy into a seedy saloon where his appearance catapults Sage Adair into a world of painful memories, child exploitation and frantic searches for missing loved ones. In the series' eighth mystery, Sage and his colorful allies find collaboration to be the path to survival.

Unseen

Sage Adair is working on mundane business accounts when an urgent message arrives. Within hours, he and his friends are struggling to comprehend the harsh reality of Indian reservation life. They journey into that strange and dire world to fight greed. Soon things turn ominous when an Indian Service inspector is murdered and time starts running out for a prominent tribal leader. As they and their tribal allies begin uncovering the reservation's secrets, a small boy disappears, taking the biggest secret with him. This ninth Sage Adair story inserts historical facts into a fast-paced adventure mystery unfolding within the deadly confines of an Indian boarding school and reservation.

NOTES